LUKE'S COVENANT

Alma Chronicles IV

Toby Fesler Heathcotte

Mardel Books

Luke's Covenant is a work of fiction. Names, places, and incidents either are products of the author's imagination or are used fictitiously.

Luke's Covenant ©2009 by Toby Fesler Heathcotte

First edition released in 2009 by

Mardel Books
6145 West Echo Lane
Glendale, Arizona 85302
mardelbooks.com

Cover design by Zanne Kennedy
Author photo by Dennis Habbershaw

ISBN: 978-0-9819961-3-4

Willing to sacrifice his life on Nine Eleven, Luke instead finds himself required to live. He must protect himself and his family from an ancient vendetta at the hands of a man compelled to murder them all. Although failing before, Kegan has been reborn with paranormal skills that give him the advantage this time. He'll finally get the revenge he deserves.

"A deliciously evil villain stalks the hero throughout time in a thought-provoking and mystical excursion into the realm of reincarnation. The novel explores the impact of psychic experiences and past lives on present lives and relationships."
Michael J. Murphy, Suspense Novelist

"*Luke's Covenant* gives meaning to the tragedy of September Eleven. In this time of reckoning, the message shines as one of hope for a kinder, more spiritual society."
Vijaya Schartz
Science Fiction and Romance Author

"*Luke's Covenant* captivated me. It weaves haunting memories and incarnations from earlier centuries with the currents and stresses of modern life. Luke is a courageous, empathetic character who struggles with fleeting images from his past while he seeks protection for his son and fulfillment of his own needs in the present."
Greta Manville
Mystery Novelist and Steinbeck Fellow

"Our culture needs to find a new story . . . the story of the recycling of consciousness across multiple incarnations, of carrying forward everything we learn, of extending the human story into the story of the soul ... of learning to 'see into' and commune with the previously invisible world of spirit."

Chris Bache, Institute of Noetic Sciences

Suddenly I realize

That if I stepped out of my body I would break

Into blossom.

James Wright

The Alma Chronicles

Incarnations of the Souls

50-10 BCE England	1700s CE England, Scotland, & Maryland Colony	1900s CE Arizona, California, & Afghanistan	2000s CE Arizona and California of Greater Hispania
Alma	Alison	Angie	Angela
Taliesin	Thomas	Ty	Todd
Lugh	Lainn	Luke	Luke (living)
Morfran	Mac & Megan	Melinda	Melanie
Caitlin	Catherine		
Kegan	Colin	Karim	Kendall & Kegan
	Henry	Hank	
	Emily		Euphoria
	Judith & Jeannie	Jillian	Janice
	Aaron & Donnie	Aaron	Aaron (living)
Emmons (in Afterlife)	Emmons	Emmons (in Afterlife)	Emmons (in Afterlife)

One

The School of Life

Afghanistan, 1986

More than anything, Karim Hijazi al-Kabul wanted to run away, but if he did Father would catch him and carry him back. He knelt on the dirt floor in the tent and held tightly to the stack of pillows, lumpy against his hands.

His mother's body shook beneath the brown *burkha* that covered all except her scared eyes. "Please don't take my baby away."

Father picked up his *kufi* hat from a metal trunk and stretched it over his head. He spoke in Farsi. "In the name of Allah, woman, leave off."

"He is my life." Mother sounded sad.

"He is not yours. He belongs to Allah." Father set his hands on his big hips and looked mean. "The Imam will make a man of him."

When Mother bent down, Karim reached up to be taken into her arms. She said to Father, "Wait until next year when he turns six, please."

Father snatched Karim from her. "Let's go, son."

"I can't let you do this," Mother whispered.

"You what?" Father set Karim down and spoke in that quiet way he always talked when he got very mad. "You can't let me? You insult me once too many times. I call on the grace of Allah. He requires that I tap you."

Karim screamed even though he knew it would not help. Other times when Father tapped her, she always fell down and cried.

As Mother backed away, Father yelled, "Karim, go get in the cart."

This was no time to disobey. Karim scurried through the tent flap. He climbed into the wooden cart and buried his face in his hands. He could not hear anything except his own sobs. He must have been a very bad boy to cause Father to need to tap Mother.

Father came outside, a duffel bag in his hand, and patted Karim's back. "Quiet, boy."

Two neighbor men, dressed like Father in tunic, pleated hat, and vest, passed and nodded without speaking. Father took up the shafts and pulled the cart down the paved road. On both sides, eyes peered through slits in tents.

"Karim, Karim," came the beloved voice. Mother staggered down the road toward them.

Perhaps Father had not heard her because he kept on going. His baggy pants flapped around his sandals in the hot wind.

"Mother is coming. Please, wait for her. Mother is coming."

"No, she's not. It's all right, boy. We're going to a very good place where she is not allowed to follow."

Mother lagged farther and farther behind. She sagged down in the dirt beside the road, and Karim watched her until she faded out of sight. The cart bumped along on ruts. Karim's heart hurt because he wanted Mother to come with them. He missed her and was afraid without her. His tears flowed over his face and down his soiled tunic, but he did not sob anymore.

They went a long, long way, past stone houses and gray hills. An occasional shrub dotted the rocky landscape. Carts, camels, and cars filled with people passed, going the other direction.

2

The sun rose high and made Karim's cheeks feel hot. The tears all went away. Karim's bottom hurt from bouncing, and his stomach ached. Glad to stop, he bowed happily in the dirt beside the road for prayers. All praise be to Allah for His food.

When Father took out two *pita* breads, Karim noticed that his other tunic and pants lay folded inside the duffel bag. He did not understand why they were taking his clothes. The bread tasted good with buttermilk from a jug.

Late in the afternoon Karim and Father reached a place with many stone buildings. Roadways ran through it. Men in *dishadashas* sat about, talking, the lengths of their gowns held up to keep them out of the dirt. Some stood in booths with chickens and potatoes for sale.

An airplane flying over made Karim wish he could ride in one. Someday he would. That would make him happy and proud.

At the end of a street, they stopped and entered a low building made of round bricks the same gray as the rocks. Inside, the walls gave off coolness.

An Imam with a beautiful beard met them. He wore a white *dishadasha* with fancy sewing on it, and his eyes looked as if they sank into his face. "In the name of Allah, welcome to my school." He spoke Farsi with a scratchy voice. The ends of his headdress fell across his face when he shook Father's hand.

Father looked down at the marble floor even though he spoke to the Imam. "I wish to place my son in your care. He is an ignorant boy and needs to learn the ways of Allah."

"We can save him from absolute desolation and the pain of unending need." The Imam clasped his hands. "Can you pay the tuition?"

Shaking his head, Father shifted his eyes to another part of the floor.

"Praise be to Allah, one of our brothers, a true benefactor who believes in holy *jihad*, has reserved scholarship funds for such youths as yours. They are our most important resource."

"Thank you, brother. I would pay if I could." Father bowed and turned toward the door. He glanced back toward Karim and shook one finger. "You be a good boy, Karim. Mind the Imam and grow up to be worthy." He scuttled out the door.

"Father, take me, please." Karim tried to run after his father, but the Imam grabbed Karim's shoulders and held him back. His head barely came to the Imam's waist. Why did Father not want him anymore? Karim needed Mother. Tears fell down his face onto his bare feet.

"Tears are for women, Karim." The Imam guided him toward a doorway. "You will not show your weakness. You will stop crying and turn your heart toward Allah. Beg him for mercy for your unworthy soul. Praise be to Allah for all His mercies."

Karim choked back a sob.

The Imam thumped the top of Karim's head and spoke in a voice like Allah's. "Say it!"

"Praise be to Allah for all His mercies." Karim wiped away the tears.

They walked into a room where boys of different ages sat in rows. All bent over books and none appeared to notice Karim. The Imam pointed to an empty seat in the back. After Karim sat, the Imam opened the book before him and said, "Someday you will memorize every word. Then you will know worthiness. Praise be to Allah."

Imitating the other boys, Karim gazed down at the book. It looked like a chicken had walked across the page with mud on its feet. He wanted to cry but did not dare. Allah could never love such a weak boy, one whose father did not want him, one whose mother let him go. She probably did not love him anymore.

Karim vowed to make Allah proud of him. And the Imam. And the benefactor brother who paid money for him.

Karim did not know what benefactor meant, but it must be good.

Then Father and Mother would come and bring him back home. Karim mumbled, "All praise be to Allah for His mercies."

Two

Starting Over

Phoenix, Arizona, 1990

God, how he wished he could pray. Or even believed prayers would help.

Luke Brock tipped back on the dining room chair and cracked his neck, unable to relax muscles that had been tight for months. He rubbed throbbing eyes and left off staring at the screen of the laptop set among stacks of bills and folders. He downed the last swallow of tepid beer.

As darkness crept into the room, the computer monitor gave scant illumination.

Bending down to the playpen beside him, Luke laid his hand on the toddler's back. Just feeling Aaron's shallow breaths going in and out relieved Luke's mind more than prayers or consoling words, no matter how well intentioned.

Baskets and vases of wilted cut flowers and drooping green plants sat around the floor, flooding the whole downstairs with a funereal stink. He should have taken the mortician's advice and donated them to Good Samaritan Hospital right away, but at the time Luke had the idea that getting rid of the flowers would upset his mother.

How insane a thought was that? Like he had not known for months that the cancer would kill her. Like he had not watched her shrink to a tiny shell of herself. Like she could come back from the dead and haunt him the way she'd teased that she would.

If only!

How she had fooled herself with that psychic baloney.

Angie Brock had not ventured back to Earth in spirit form since the day of her death. How long had that been? Hours or weeks? She felt as insubstantial as a moonbeam when she floated into her dining room. She had eaten most of her meals in this room for over twenty years, but it looked oddly milky, blue and indistinct, like an underdeveloped photo proof. Her earthly life in Phoenix, Arizona seemed a distant memory.

There sat Luke scowling at the computer, as he had done so often during her illness. She owed him a great debt of gratitude for his care.

Hello, honey. It's me. Can you see me? Angie wanted to speak, but her thoughts didn't quite make it into words.

Moving to him, Angie tried to lay her hand on his cheek. Her hand appeared like a shadow to her, and she failed to feel the warmth of his skin beneath her touch. She felt joyous at being able to see the two of them, the beloved son and grandson, again.

Luke, Aaron, I'm here. I'm alive.

Aaron stirred in the playpen. Perhaps he had heard her. Little ones were often more sensitive. Angie would love to hold him and kiss his chubby cheeks. She floated to the playpen and tried to wrap her arms around the baby, but again she failed, her movements wispy and insubstantial. He settled back into sound breathing.

How brash she had been while still living, actually crossing into the astral plane to meet her lover. She had considered it her right. Now, from the other side, she had much to learn about trafficking between the worlds.

She gazed at her loved ones. How wonderful it would be just to touch them again.

My sweet ones, I will content myself with seeing you, for now.

Luke obviously hadn't heard her because he typed a few words then leaned back in his chair. "Damn, damn, damn."

Uncertain about why he seemed so agitated, Angie hovered behind her son and read the words as he typed them.

Pissed at himself all over again, Luke returned his fingers to the computer and scrolled though the letter to his mother, the one that the know-it-all grief counselor had told him to write. So far Luke did not feel one damned bit better, and some vague feeling of disloyalty lurked inside him, into the bargain. Ignoring it, he keyed in words in a furious push to try once again to release his pent-up hostility.

You picked a fine time to die, Mom, just when my wife left me. Who'll help me raise Aaron? I know I should feel some sadness or heartache because you're dead, but all I feel is abandoned. My predominant feeling, like ninety-nine percent of me, is angry. Rage is a better word, rage that Melinda is gone, rage that you're gone.

Until you got sick, I had enthusiam for life. Not that everything went well, but I could always find moments that rated a headline. No matter how hard I try, no headline comes to me now. Where in hell will I get the motivation to continue?

What is there to show for your life? Or that your death had meaning? My birth was a cosmic accident. Just like my death will be. Just like yours. A hundred years from now, what difference will it make anyway?

Maybe I'm just a cold-hearted asshole—

The doorbell rang. Luke rose and kicked back his chair. He leaned down and squinted at the words on the monitor. "This is stupid."

Luke deleted the file without saving it and strode down the hall to the front room.

Oh no, honey. Don't do that. Angie hadn't even finished reading. She ached for him and wished she could make him feel better.

Somehow she had to get him to realize that she still lived, that he would live again. Then he could go on with his life with more energy. If he knew she was alive, would he be okay? How could she make her thoughts known in her son's mind?

If anyone had asked her to describe the spirit world before she died, Angie would have guessed it was a quiet place of refuge, rest, and reflection with fountains and music and soothing architecture. A more or less biblical heaven with modern angels playing trumpets and wafting around elegant buildings studded with inlaid gold and jewels.

Well, at least she got the fountains and architecture right.

Angie still had a lot of questions unanswered about the spirit world. On her return other members of her soul group had mentioned The Plan, something that had transpired in the Afterlife during her lifetime on Earth. She didn't know much about its details, but she did know that Luke and Melinda had volunteered.

More importantly, Luke's grief was pulling Angie back into his life. Emmons, like a good guide, cautioned her to be careful until she became more adept and not to upset any forces already set in motion. She always tried to follow his instructions, at least those she could understand.

Because of the warmth of the February evening, the plank door stood open to catch the breeze. As Luke went to answer the doorbell, he could discern through the screen that a woman was on the porch.

He flipped the switch and beneath the porch light's yellow glow stood Melinda resplendent in her workday finery, royal blue satin blouse, gray pin-striped suit, and a Gucci bag hanging from her shoulder. He used to think her glamorous with her long black hair and sultry black eyes. Now he thought her about as vacuous as a circus clown. All glitz and no guts.

Melinda inspected the bare *palo verde* tree and some bedraggled rose bushes beside the porch. "These could use some water."

That was so typical of Melinda, to show more nurturance for plants than for her own child, whom she freely abandoned for a fucking job opportunity.

"What are you doing here?" Luke didn't try to conceal his antagonism.

"I thought I'd take Aaron for a few days." Her brows arched in that way Melinda had of making her beautiful face look cocky, but her voice betrayed her by faltering. "You know, parental visitation?"

"That's supposed to be tomorrow."

They had agreed she would pick up the baby from daycare, so they would not have to see each other. Melinda scheduled everything with great efficiency. No, she had another reason for showing up here tonight.

"May I come in?"

Grudgingly, Luke opened the screen. "You sure you can spare the time?"

Melinda passed by him and rubbed her hand across his unshaven cheek. "You could use a haircut and a pluck."

Repulsed by her touch, Luke strode toward the playpen. Her heels clicked on the parquet as she followed him.

"Stay there. I'll bring him." Luke refused to even give her civility tonight. She did not deserve it. He wished he could keep her from taking Aaron.

Luke picked up the toddler, trying not to awaken him. When he returned to the living room, she had perched on the arm of the sofa with its worn blue floral pattern. Melinda always looked out of place in his mother's home with its cozy décor. One thing his wife had never been was cozy. He hated releasing Aaron, the one bright spot in this dismal life.

As he held out the baby, Luke said, "It would be a lot less upsetting if you'd pick him up from daycare like we agreed, instead of whisking him away in the night. He has little enough to depend on, as it is."

With a smile so warm it would almost pass for motherly, Melinda rose and took Aaron. "I hadn't thought about that."

"So what else is new? You never think about anything except yourself." Her presence worked a lot better as a catalyst for releasing anger than some damned letter. Luke enjoyed venting on her. No one deserved it more.

"I'm sorry about your mother. I had a lot of respect for Angie, especially at the end."

"Oh, and so you showed it by avoiding her sickroom completely until the night before she died?" Cowardice, there was nothing else to call her behavior. Melinda should have helped him care for his mother.

Blushing, Melinda gazed down at her feet. "I wish I could have been here for the funeral, but it was just one thing after another with getting the loan and finding the location to set up the office in L. A."

Maybe she'd slept with the investor to get him to fund her accounting business, but the thought seemed so repugnant that Luke put it out of his mind. Even though he didn't voice his suspicions, they fueled him and gave him energy enough to cope with her. "What makes you think we need you? We're just fine without you."

11

"I sent flowers. Did you get them?"

With a shrug, Luke gestured toward the dining room. "Check it out and see if yours are there. I brought all the flowers home."

"That's not necessary." Melinda moved Aaron back and forth with a rocking motion. "My parents said the funeral was very nice."

"Oh, they're speaking to you?"

"Just barely." Melinda looked sheepish.

Mother and Father Chacon had acted appalled that Melinda had walked out on her family. The fact that Angie had lain near death made the abandonment far more despicable in their eyes. They had told Luke so and apologized over and over. With those traditional Catholic values of theirs, they could not begin to understand their sophisticated, worldly daughter. Neither could Luke.

Melinda's brow knit in what for her might be a sincere expression of concern. "Please, let me do something."

"Be good to the kid."

"I will."

"Don't leave him with the babysitter the entire time he's with you."

"Okay." Melinda shot a surprised glance that showed he'd guessed her intentions. In the awkward silence that followed, she looked at the floor. "Are you going on a business trip?"

Luke didn't answer. It was none of her business where he went. If she'd thought about it, she'd realize he'd not gone on a business trip for months. The partners at his law firm had acted far more understanding than she about his obligations to his mother. They'd never put any pressure on him, and he took off as much time as he needed near the end.

"What's that for?" Melinda pointed to his open suitcase on the floor with jeans and a sport shirt folded inside along with that hateful metal urn.

Luke stared at the suitcase, and dread at his errand overcame his hostility. "I promised Mom I'd bury her in Indiana. It would have been a nightmare to get her body there, so I'm taking her ashes back to scatter them over her father's grave. I hope that will be sufficient."

"By yourself?"

"Are you completely clueless? Of course, I'm going alone." All of a sudden weary of his own anger, Luke trudged through the archway into the small kitchen and took a beer out of the fridge. The trash was heaped with beer cans and pizza boxes.

Melinda adjusted the child on her hip and followed him. "I'll go with you, if you want. Aaron and I, I mean."

For a moment, Luke questioned whether he'd heard correctly. Of course, he wanted her with him. The separation had been her idea, not his. No one should have to go through this grief alone. He wished she could just once make things better instead of worse.

"What are you doing, Melinda? You said you wanted a divorce. You said I could have Aaron. You said your business was the only important thing. Well, go do it and leave us alone."

"I was wrong to say those things, especially at a time like this. I didn't mean them anyway. I wish you would come with me. You can take the California Bar and handle all the tax-related cases in my firm. Or start your own firm." Melinda spoke quickly, as if she'd practiced a speech and feared she'd forget it if she did not get it all out fast. Whatever you want to do." She fell silent with an embarrassed expression.

What in hell was she doing? When Aaron whimpered, Luke patted him. "It's okay, big guy." Luke needed comfort, too. This woman, his wife, had just offered it to him, the last thing he'd have predicted she would say. "Did your parents shame you into making this offer?"

"No. I...we...talked it over. It's the right thing to do." Frowning, Melinda reached out and laid a hand on his shoulder. Her touch was warm, and for a moment the woman he had fallen in love with swam before his gaze. She murmured, "You don't have to decide right now. Just think about it, please. Do it for Aaron, not for me."

The familiar pine scent of her hair mingled with the sweet smell of Aaron's skin. Together they overpowered Luke. This going it alone sucked.

With a shudder, Luke enfolded his family in his arms. He needed to love and feel loved. Melinda's back stiffened and she let out a little cry. Maybe that meant she needed the same thing.

Aaron awoke and wiggled between them. "Mama." He laughed. The poor little kid didn't have any notion that his mother had walked out on him.

One of the last things Angie had said before she died was that Luke would have to forgive Melinda to save his own soul. He chalked up another bull's eye for his mother's predictions.

He had an overwhelming feeling that he had to do something, that life had some great significance that eluded him. For the life of him, he couldn't figure out what. He sure as hell needed Melinda now. Would that be enough to let him forgive her?

Three

A Flurry of Ashes

The wipers slogged through sticky snow on the windshield of the rental Luke had picked up at the airport in Indianapolis. He'd not seen another car since turning off the interstate onto this two-lane road. Occasional houses set far back among bare-limbed trees made the area difficult to categorize as town or countryside, but he should reach the cemetery before he hit the town limits.

Luke pointed to an arched entry ahead. "Is that it?"

"I hope so." Melinda perused the map open in her lap. When Aaron bellowed in the back seat, she said, "He's tired of riding."

"Aren't we all? Got any more Trix?"

"Sorry, all gone." Melinda held the cereal box upside down and shook it in front of the baby, who grabbed the box and banged it against his car seat.

At least he stopped crying, Luke thought, grateful for the momentary silence. He could barely make out the words Medfield Cemetery in relief on the stone archway.

"That's it. Turn here." Melinda's shrill tone grated on his ears.

When Luke entered the grounds, he saw avenues marked east wing and west wing. As far as he could see in the late afternoon gloom, tombstones large and small sat as stark silhouettes that faded into the snowy distance. Down the west avenue, a station wagon idled with its lights on and frosty exhaust coming from its tailpipe. He pulled his car alongside.

In the other car, Tearlee Beckman rolled down her window and waved to him. A pretty woman of forty or so, she gave them a friendly smile. "I was afraid you wouldn't make it. The weather's been so bad." Her words carried the mellow, flattened vowels of the Midwest.

"Thank you for meeting us." Damp snow fell on Luke's face. "Damn, it's cold."

"Just follow me around," Tearlee called.

As they drove along the gravel road behind the station wagon, Melinda pulled Aaron into her lap. "I should've brought our ski coats." She bundled him into his windbreaker and tied the drawstring. "Now tell me who this woman is again."

"She's the sister of Ty Beckman, the guy my mom was supposed to marry."

"Oh, yes the one who died in the plane crash."

"Yes, Melinda." Luke didn't even try to keep the sarcasm out of his voice. She knew Ty's identity but got a kick out of acting obtuse.

Luke followed Tearlee's car to a set of graves far back on the west side, and they piled out of the cars. Melinda drew her London Fog around her and carried Aaron. Luke took the miserable urn out of his suitcase. The metal felt cold as he tucked it under his arm. He shivered both from wearing a light wool blazer and the melancholy nature of his errand.

With an alpaca coat and toboggan hat, Tearlee looked much better equipped. She pulled an umbrella out of the station wagon and opened it, offering them shelter. After the introductions she said, "I'm sorry my husband and children couldn't be here. They're at work and school."

"Oh, I didn't expect them to. They hadn't even met my mother."

Luke knew no one in Medfield any more except the Beckmans, even though he'd been born here. Angie and he had returned only once. He believed he might have some great aunts and uncles on his father's side but didn't know their names. There would have been no point in notifying them anyway. No one had stayed in touch since his mother and father divorced. As far as this town was concerned, Luke might as well have been born on Mars.

"I was always fond of Angie." Tearlee spoke in a respectful, low tone as they walked along. "When I was a kid I assumed she would marry my brother, but then they broke up. Strange how things worked. As if they were doomed. Just when they finally found each other again, he died. And now Angie's gone, too. I can't believe it."

Luke remembered Ty's funeral, the only time he had ever met Ty's father or sister. "How's your father doing?"

"He's not well." Tearlee's face went slack. "Not well at all. He never recovered psychologically from Ty's death."

"Sorry to hear that." Luke had liked the old man.

They trudged past tombstones, huddling beneath Tearlee's umbrella. She brought them to a red marbleized stone, commemorating a single grave.

Luke dusted the snow off and read the insignia. Capt. Wiley Brandon, USAF, born December 14, 1907, died December 20, 1948. "My grandfather." Luke knew little about him except that Angie had loved him a great deal. Seeing the birth and death dates made Luke realize why his mother had always disliked Christmas.

"I didn't know your grandfather was in the military," Melinda whispered in an awed way. The desolation of this place probably got to her too.

"A test pilot after World War II."

"How did he die?"

"Plane crash."

"You're kidding." Melinda looked shocked into some kind of sympathy. She huddled against Luke's side. He could feel Aaron wiggling in her arms, but not crying, a brave little trooper, that boy. They must look like dumb Arizona people, not dressed for winter in March. He wanted

17

to make this visit short for their comfort's sake. Still, he wanted to honor his mother in an appropriate way.

"Well, we might as well..." Luke set the urn down beside the tombstone and opened the lid. He glanced up at Melinda and Tearlee, who both wore sad expressions. He expected them to cry. A good cry might make Luke feel better although he doubted tears would ever come. His chest hurt from the thumping of his heart.

Luke composed himself. "My mother always said her father was a hero and to be proud of that because not every family had a hero. I think we may have had more than our share. My mother, Angela Brandon Brock, was a true hero. She lived her life as selflessly and honorably as she could. There were times when I questioned her way of relating to the world, but she always remained true to herself. When it came time to die, she faced her death with great courage. She went off morphine, controlled her pain, and said the things she needed to say, words that gave meaning to all of our lives. She deserved a monument. I wish I could write a headline across the sky: WELL DONE, MOM!"

Glad that he wore his driving gloves so he wouldn't have to touch it, Luke picked up the urn and overturned it.

A flurry of ashes fell into the damp snow flakes. Tiny pieces of bone clattered against the tombstone. The sound sickened him. He could hear the two women sniffling, and Aaron began to wail.

Grabbing the baby out of Melinda's arms, Luke turned his back on his mother's ashes. "Let's get out of here."

As they all hurried back to the cars, the snow turned to drizzle and the wind began to blow. Tearlee pulled Luke and Aaron against her. The damp alpaca smelled like a barnyard.

"That was beautiful," Tearlee said. "Angie would have loved it. Maybe she'll appear to you to tell you so herself."

Her teeth chattering, Melinda glanced at Luke with alarm. "She couldn't do that, could she?"

"Well," Tearlee said, "she was psychic. At least that's what the newspapers reported after Ty died."

"Making predictions about the future is what she did," Luke said. "And not all the time, just once in a while when something special happened."

His mother had seen the crash of Ty's plane in a vision but couldn't keep Ty off the plane. The grief almost destroyed her. She'd seen Melinda running away with a baby. That had happened too. He remembered his mother's tease that she would haunt him. That had just been wishful thinking on her part. Dead meant gone forever.

"Mom isn't going to come back from the dead. That's impossible."

"Absolutely not possible." Melinda headed to the rental car. "Let's get going."

"Oh, you're probably right." Tearlee opened the door of her station wagon and slid into the driver's seat. "Why don't you all come back to the house and get warmed up. I've got something I need to tell you."

Luke shook his head. "That's all right. We've got a plane to catch. Thanks again for coming."

"Don't mention it." Tearlee drummed on the steering wheel. She didn't appear willing to say good-bye. "Luke, I really hate to tell you this, especially at a time like this...your father, Russell Brock. He died. In Chicago...of an overdose. He's been an addict ever since Nam. He didn't live here and I didn't know him, but news gets around in a small town. I just thought somebody should tell you."

"Good God, what else?" Melinda cried.

Luke stared at Tearlee, then Melinda. Abandoned first by his father, then by Melinda, then by his mother's death. Now his father's death? Luke's life had turned into something. Whether tragedy or high comedy he didn't know.

Angie sat on her father's tombstone and listened to her son's benediction to her life. She'd been reminded of Mark Twain's comment that the reports of his death had been greatly exaggerated. Angie wasn't quite dead either.

It touched her that Luke had made the effort to bring her remains back home. She'd thought her bones would be burned to dust though. She wished to let him know she appreciated him, but trying to make contact right now was out of the question. He had such a tight clamp on his emotions, nothing could get through to him. She didn't blame him for being self-protective. She understood.

That Luke and Melinda reconciled amazed Angie. The girl had such brittle ways she could manipulate Luke and he didn't even know what happened to him. Karmic issues held them together, at least for a while. They'd been married in a previous lifetime, and Luke had cheated on her. He would more than pay off that karma in this lifetime if Emmons's predictions came to pass, and they usually did.

Melinda had feared Angie in life and still seemed to think of her as a witch. Well, come to think of it, her current situation sort of had a magical element to it. Even though Angie had not practiced witchcraft, her psychic abilities had scared the liver out of Melinda, a humorous outcome in itself since she was such an annoying soul.

Tearlee's little bombshell had been news to Angie too. Her ex-husband, Russell, had died, obviously, but she had not seen him in the spirit world. She hadn't seen her father, her brother, or her grandparents. The only spirits she had actually made contact with were Ty and Emmons. She assumed all the other members of her soul group were incarnated right now.

Those matters concerned her far less than her connection to Luke and his little family. Was it his grief for her that held her? Or hers for him?

The news of his birth father's death caused barely a blip on Luke's grief radar. Another non-memory. The only feelings he had echoed his mother's resentment. His birth father had done them wrong and thus become a highly forgettable person. Ty, Angie's fiancé, had been the love of her life and Luke's only hope for a father. Now all three were dead.

Those relationship holes nagged at Luke.

Most importantly, why had his father not cared enough to stay in touch? During his childhood, Luke had tortured himself with the belief that there was something wrong with him, something that had caused his father to leave them. Luke could remember many sleepless nights of self-examination. What had he done that caused his father to dislike him? He'd figured out that his father had left at least in part because of Luke's epilepsy although his mother never said so specifically.

Luke knew as an adult that he had no responsibility in the matter. He could feel fatherly love toward his own son and question the character of any man who abandoned one. It did not feel good to conclude that his father had been a second-rate person.

From Indiana, Luke, Melinda, and Aaron flew on to visit Luke's maternal grandmother. Although she had lived in Florida all through his growing up, she was his only remaining relative, and Luke wanted to see her. Maybe they could build a better relationship. After all, they had both lost Angie.

Grandma had always said she did not do funerals. Luke had not expected to see her at Angie's, and he had been right, but he had not anticipated the changes in her. The most recent husband said that, hours after Luke had called with news of Angie's death, Grandma had suffered a stroke.

The doctors cautioned against any optimism that she would recover her faculties. The husband took care of her, but very little remained of her mind. She did not recognize Melinda or Luke, let alone acknowledge her great grandson.

She looked past them with watery, dull eyes. Luke felt a forlorn sense of loss. He wished to hell he could at least cry over his grandmother, but he couldn't.

Late that night they caught a flight back to Phoenix. Heavy cloud cover delayed takeoff. Luke settled into his seat with Aaron asleep in his lap. Melinda sat in the window seat and flipped through the airline's magazine.

Luke hadn't slept through a night for months, anticipating his mother might call out in need of him. He wished he could nap, but noises intruded—the voices of other passengers, the swishing of the drink cart going by, the rumbling of the jet's engines. They sounded wrong to him, like one was cutting in and out.

"So," Melinda stuffed the magazine in the pocket. "So, have you decided about California?"

"To tell you the truth, I haven't. I've had other things on my mind." Luke got a kick out of keeping his wife guessing. She deserved that little revenge. Why had she even come on the trip with him? He might never understand her motives.

"You've probably noticed that I've been a very supportive wife on this trip." Melinda had no trouble at all bragging on herself.

"How about you? And your family? With your CPA, you'll always have a good job." Luke knew how lame that sounded. Why did he want to stay in Arizona anyway, with all his family gone? He thought it ironic that Melinda had a huge family. She was way down in a pack of ten kids. She had nieces, nephews, cousins all over the Valley, yet she couldn't wait to get away.

Melinda screwed up her face in disgust. "One of the real perks of going to California is getting away from them." She gave him one of those innocent, seductive smiles that had caused him to fall in love with her. "I think you're missing a bet if you don't go with me, but I'll not offer again." For Melinda, that comment was tantamount to saying please.

Luke wondered whether to trust her. Would he ever be able to forgive her for abandoning him? He could if she turned out to be a good mother. He didn't want Aaron to grow up with a parent either physically absent or psychologically absent.

A clap of thunder rattled through the cabin. The seatbelt and no smoking lights flashed overheard. The stewardess's voice came through the PA system. "The pilot requests that you fasten your seatbelts." Her voice sounded artificially calm. "There are several storms ahead. We'll veer north to avoid as many as possible."

"That doesn't sound good." Scowling, Melinda looked out the window. A baby started crying somewhere behind them.

"Are you afraid?" Luke asked. Aaron moved restlessly.

"No, I'm fine." Melinda leaned toward the pane. She seemed engrossed in the storm. Lightning silhouetted her face that betrayed a lot more fear than her gutsy voice.

Luke hugged Aaron to his chest. If this plane went down, his baby would die. His wife would die. Luke would die. The whole family wiped out with no one on his side to care, but for Melinda's family a calamity.

The worst possible thing that could happen would be the death of his family. It was Luke's destiny to keep them alive so they could fulfill their destinies. He knew that truth in his bones.

The plane jumped as if it were driving over boulders. Cries and frantic conversations sprang up all over the cabin.

A clap of thunder followed. Aaron cried out, and Luke clutched him close.

"Hush, baby." Melinda rubbed Aaron's back and gave Luke a worried smile.

After what seemed like hours, the stewardess came on once again to report the end of bad weather. She offered free drinks. Luke and Melinda took some wine.

Luke held up a wine glass? He wanted to be able to trust Melinda. She had almost done the same thing to Aaron that Luke's father had done. At least, she had come to her senses. Luke would forgive much in her to keep Aaron from ever experiencing the loss of identity that came from being abandoned by a parent.

"To the future" Melinda said.

"To our future!" Luke clinked her glass, and her face broke into a glorious smile. He hoped he'd not regret his choice and returned the smile.

Finally, safely on the ground, they returned to his mother's home and performed the melancholy task of emptying all the dead flowers into the dumpster. They shut down their past.

At thirty, Luke was too old to be an orphan but sometimes he felt like one. He put his mother's house on the market, quit his job, and, with his beautiful accountant wife and perfect little boy, moved to an upscale Los Angeles suburb

They drove their cars to California. No airplane ride this time.

Luke kept busy as the only lawyer in the employ of Melinda's firm,. She devoted herself to making it the biggest and best and most lucrative. To Luke's great surprise, they pulled together reasonably well and found that they made a great money-making team. They even had a passable sex life. Aaron had a full-time nanny.

The hollowness in Luke's heart eased but never quite went away. He did not sleep well. Many nights, when he did nod off, he'd startle awake, imagining someone had called him, then walk the floor till daybreak. Life should get better soon.

Four

Angels on High

Afghanistan, 1990

Karim sat in the middle row, surrounded by other whispering nine-year-olds. The ignorant babies were in the rear, the older boys in front. All wore short, neatly trimmed hair and white tunics. He skimmed the day's lesson and assured himself he had memorized each sentence perfectly.

Certain it was his turn, he longed to be called on today. Surely the Imam would remember and not skip over him, so he could show his progress and hear praise.

Without looking up, Karim knew from the sudden silence that the Imam had entered. All the boys knelt and pressed their foreheads to the floor. Then they sat back on their heels and intoned the prayer the Imam spoke.

Once the boys had climbed back into their seats, the Imam called out in Farsi, "Karim, recite 5:36 of the most holy Koran as received from Allah by His most holy prophet Mohammed. Peace be upon Him."

Leaping to his bare feet, Karim said in Farsi, his native tongue, "Praise be to Allah for this opportunity to serve." He began to recite in Arabic, even though he did not understand the meanings of the words he repeated by rote: "5:36: The punishment of those who wage war against Allah and His Apostle, and strive with might and main for mischief through the land is execution, or crucifixion, or the cutting off of hands and feet from opposite sides, or exile from the land: that is their disgrace in this world, and a heavy punishment is theirs in the Hereafter."

"Perfect. Thank you, my son."

Karim pretended not to notice the Imam's wonderful comment and gazed down at the text, certain of the jealousy in the heart of his friend Ibrihim in the next seat. The rest of the day flew by because Karim knew he had earned honor in the eyes of the Imam and of his classmates.

After the Imam dismissed class, the hour before sunset, Karim and Ibrihim dashed outside the enclave. In crisp, autumn air, they sprinted past open-air shops filled with plucked chickens, potatoes, and holy books. This was his favorite time of day, before dinner and evening prayers, a time to test his skills against Ibrihim.

Once outside the village, Karim gave himself to the race. Taller and thinner, Ibrihim won more often but not all the time. Today Karim felt strong.

They ran along the paved highway, past rocky hills and the tents of the local residents. He fell behind but Ibrihim taunted him. A solitary ficus tree stood as the Imam's outer boundary beyond which they dared not venture. Karim made one long push and lunged for the gnarled roots. He touched them first.

Panting, Ibrihim fell beside him. They laughed as they eyed each other in the pretense of belligerence.

"All right," Ibrihim gasped. "You beat me today. Enjoy it because it won't happen again."

"Allah be praised. I expect to win every time from now on."

"Oho, you wish. Just because you earned the Imam's praise today, you think you're better than I am."

"Well, that's pretty obvious. Get used to second place."

"Perhaps you're right." Ibrihim sat up and brushed dirt off his skinny feet. "I'll never get the hang of recitation in Arabic. Don't you ever wonder what you're saying?"

Whatever the passage he recited meant, Karim did not have to know. It was enough to hear that he had done well. "Praise be to Allah for this opportunity to serve."

"It's hard saying words that have no meaning," Ibrihim whined.

Karim feared for his friend. "Allah will send you to hell for such talk. Never say that again."

"Don't you ever wonder why we're here? In school? Why we were even born?"

The memory of his mother weeping beside the road crossed Karim's mind. He wondered if she had forgotten him but pushed the thought aside. Women were too weak to understand. "We have a divine purpose, Ibrihim, never doubt this. We must carry the name of Allah forever and bring *jihad* to the world of devils and demons across the great ocean."

"How can you be so certain? Do you believe the Imam is always right?"

"The Imam speaks the truth. I know because my angels tell me so."

"You talk to your angels? I know I'm supposed to have two of my own. We all are, but I've never seen mine or had a feeling that they were present."

Recalling his recurring dream, Karim visualized the angel in glorious blue light as clearly as if he were standing in the road right now. "Oh, they're around all right. Listen carefully in your dreams. They will speak to you as they do to me, I'm certain of it. I'm nothing special." He was not positive he believed that last part, but the Imam had taught him to always express humility and he did not wish to disobey.

"What do they tell you?"

"That the Plan is in motion, that I was born for great work, and I must always trust Allah."

Ibrihim cast a suspicious glance at Karim.

"I would never lie to you. You know that."

Folding his arms, Ibrihim cast a look of challenge. "But how do you know you are not being deceived by the jinn? They can take the form of a space alien or a ghost and lead ignorant boys astray with just the least effort. You should pray to Mohammed for protection. Upon him be peace."

Karim watched the lights of a jet streak across the sky. Secure in his belief, he felt a burden to watch out for Ibrihim, who did not seem to have so much heavenly support.

"My angel is not a jinn," Karim said gently. "He is not Mohammed, upon him be peace. He is an angel, sent by Allah to guide me. His name is Emmons. Upon him be peace."

Five

The Business of Life

Los Angeles, June, 2001

In his private office, Luke poured over a brief he had prepared for a potential partnership. He wanted to make certain Melinda encountered no legal problems in the event she found a willing backer. Feminine laughter came from the cubicles outside his closed door. While he wondered what his co-workers found so humorous, a knock came on the door.

"What you want?" Luke grumbled in a good-natured way and rose from the overstuffed swivel chair he'd fought with Melinda to keep when she redecorated the offices. He'd won and everyone else had to sit on those uncomfortable ergonomic contrivances.

He opened the door and looked up at a six-foot tall gal in a bikini that fit her voluptuous figure well indeed, right down to the stilettos. She had a cowboy hat on her head and a big grin on her face. "Are you Luke Brock?" When he nodded, she stuffed the strings of a handful of baby blue balloons into his hand. "Happy birthday!"

"Uh, thanks." Luke felt surprised and silly.

The cowgirl belted out an off-key rendition of *Happy Birthday to You*. She sang in a sultry, Cher sort of way and rubbed her hands on Luke's cheeks then clung to his hands. She smelled of Juicy Fruit gum.

Behind her, Melinda and four female accountants, three Hispanic and one Anglo, all giggled too hard to join in the singing.

There was nothing to do except laugh too, so Luke did. He applauded the performance. The cowgirl turned, gave him an exaggerated twist of her butt, and flounced across the geometric pattern of the tile floor. She waved to the line of accountants standing outside the row of maroon cubicles. The automatic doors of the entry slid open, she passed through, and they rolled shut.

"Come back, please," Luke called after her in fake agony. "I think I love you." He and Melinda tried to outdo each other with birthday surprises. Embarrassing the other person into the bargain always made it better. He headed toward Melinda with an accusing tone. "I'll get even with you for this."

Melinda wiped a tear away from her still beautiful face. Amazing what creams and lotions would do despite the fact that she kept threatening next year she would have a total facelift. It was doubtful a surgeon could find anything to pull up.

"I just had to do something," Melinda said. "A fortieth birthday is too special." She gave him a quick hug, something in itself because she never displayed affection in front of the employees. "Happy birthday."

"Hey, Dad, wasn't that cool?" Aaron jumped off the bench beside the young girl computer tech where he'd evidently seen and heard the whole thing.

"Melinda," Luke said, "you're corrupting our twelve-year-old. Why aren't you in school, young man?"

"It's five o'clock. School's out." Aaron pouted, looking just like his mother with his perfect brow and cheekbones, black hair and black eyes. A skinny kid, he displayed hardly any resemblance to Luke's stocky build or facial features.

The new secretary, also a girl of course, Luke being the token male in the firm, came into the room carrying a small package tied with a green ribbon. When she smiled, her heavy reddish brows never moved. It was hard for Luke to trust her even though he hadn't caught her in a lie so far. "Here's a present from the boss."

"What's this?" Luke eyed Melinda and Aaron, who exchanged excited glances. Luke handed the balloons to Aaron, tore off the wrapping paper, and held up a car key. A Jaguar dangled on the chain. He showed the key around the room. "Does this fit anything?"

Melinda nodded. "It's in the parking garage."

"I can't wait to see it." Luke certainly told the truth there.

"It's silver," Aaron said. "Just what you wanted."

How extravagant a present! So like Melinda. Luke knew they could afford it with business going so well. He'd always wanted a Jaguar but thought it more prudent to drive a Buick. Melinda, on the other hand, loved the excess. She always bought top of the line. She wanted the best of everything, and to her credit she enjoyed sharing her wealth, one of the best things about her.

Luke used to think having a big family was the life he wanted. Now, with so much financial abundance in their lives, he had to admit she had probably been right to limit children to just one. Feeling fortunate, he gave Melinda a squeeze big enough to make her wiggle with awkwardness and kissed her cheek. "Thanks, hon. This is perfect."

One of the Hispanic accountants carried in a sheet cake, and they all stood around the receptionist's desk and ate. Devil's food, Luke's favorite, with caramel icing.

The secretary of the eyebrows called out, "Birth story. Birth story." When everyone appeared confused, she added, "In my family, the person whose birthday it is must describe his birth in as much horrific detail as possible. Or if the mother is present she can usually do a better job of it."

"Sorry," Luke said. "My mother would probably have enjoyed the tradition, but she has been dead for eleven years." The image of Angie's lifeless body, wasted from cancer, gave him a rush of grief. He pushed it down. No reason to revisit the past that can't be undone. He wished he could visualize her healthy and vibrant as she had been before the illness. He hoped that his voice carried a lightness he didn't feel. "My birth must have been awful because Mom never gave me a single detail. Sorry."

"Well, can't you remember it yourself?" the secretary asked. "Gracious, you've lived in California all these years and you've never had a rebirthing experience?"

With an indulgent smile, Luke scanned his memory for anything relevant. "No, I know nothing about it. Tell me more about this rebirthing." He didn't really want to know about it, but he wanted to shift the subject of discussion away from himself. While the secretary plunged into a recital of her own rebirthing session, he glanced at Melinda, who bore a peculiar expression he couldn't read.

After they finished the cake, Luke begged off because he really had to go see his new toy. He rode down in the elevator to the parking garage level with Melinda and Aaron.

The car was a knockout, just as he knew it would be. A brand new 2001 model, silver and gray inside and out. They all climbed in, with Luke in the driver's seat, Melinda on the passenger side, and Aaron in the back seat. Luke took a moment to enjoy the luxury of the contour of the bucket seat. It fit him perfectly. The new-car interior smelled intoxicating. He leaned toward Melinda in the passenger's seat, whispered that she couldn't have chosen a better present, and gave her a passionate kiss.

"Yuck, Dad. Quit slobbering around on Mom. Let's go."

The sound of Melinda hearty laugh delighted Luke. He adjusted the radio to a rock station for his son and set the back seat speakers. "Let's see how this baby runs."

The Jaguar inched through rush-hour traffic. When they arrived at the nearest mesa overlooking the ocean, Luke pulled off the road and parked. He rolled down the electric windows. The ocean's waves covered the traffic sounds, giving an illusion of quiet in the city. Twilight dulled the cloudless blue of the sky. Pelicans searched and dived out of view beneath them.

Melinda gazed through the windshield for a long while. "I do love the ocean far better than the desert. I've never been sorry I moved here." She sounded more reflective than businesslike, for a change, unusually preoccupied. "Your mother said she worried that I might drown."

"Yes, I remember." Luke recalled that his mother had also known that Aaron would be a boy. She'd predicted that her fiancé's plane would crash and that Melinda would leave Luke. His mother had been a force to reckon with. "She made some predictions that came true so you need to keep on heeding her warning."

"There's no problem about that." Melinda shuddered. "I'm terrified of going in the water. It's been a long time since I've heard you speak of her. Are you okay with it now? I mean have you forgotten?"

Aaron stuck his head between them and gave Luke a dispassionate glance.

"I'll never forget her," Luke said. "How could I do that?" Just when he thought Melinda began to understand things a bit better, she said something insensitive like this.

Aaron turned his head toward Melinda like he was watching a tennis match. Luke turned off the music since his son seemed more interested in this family tiff, if it developed into one. Luke and Melinda took a lot of potshots at each other, and Aaron seemed to consider them almost as interesting as Cartoon Network.

"Oh, right, I just meant, well..." Melinda fell silent.

"I'm over the pain of it." Luke did not believe his own words, but he did believe that he *should* be over his mother's death. He admonished himself with the phrase time heals all wounds, and such other clichés.

"I just don't believe in that psychic stuff," Melinda said. "Never did even when she was alive. It gets in the way of things. Mostly coincidences, anyway."

"I don't think about it now that Mom is gone. It's not a part of our lives anymore. Why are you bringing it up?"

Melinda's face had the same odd look he'd noticed earlier back at the office. "I don't know."

"Hey," Luke held her chin between his fingers. "What's going on in that pretty head of yours?" When she tried to turn away, he prevented her. "Come on, out with it. There's something you haven't told me, and we'll keep after you till you do. Won't we, Aaron?"

"Right, no secrets allowed, Mom. That's what you always tell me."

Melinda furrowed her brow. "I'm not sure this is a good subject for the child to hear discussed."

"I'm big now. Almost a teenager!"

"Let's hear it, Melinda. I'm fascinated."

"Well, all right. Just to shut you two up. This is definitely not a psychic experience. It's more like an odd memory. Probably a dream. But I...oh well...It seemed like I was tossed around and I can remember moaning. I felt all out of control. When I was, you know, being born. I saw this light that was entirely too bright to bear. I felt very cold and terrified that I wouldn't remember my goals and plans. You know, what I'd come to do. And here's the really odd part, I remember my mother saying she wanted to go back to Mexico, and I knew if I had to go there with the family, I might not be able to find you, Luke. I know that doesn't make sense. Father asked my name, and Mother said Melinda, and I thought that wasn't the right name."

Luke was startled. He'd never heard her talk in such a way. "And what was your right name?"

"I don't know. It's all insane, anyway."

"Geez," Aaron said, "I don't remember anything like that. What happened when I was born?"

Melinda looked relieved to change the subject and teased, "You were just as much the rascal then as you are now. You tried to be born too early. We barely got to the hospital in time, and your father was driving through town so fast I thought he'd kill us in a car wreck before you were even born."

"Is that all?" Aaron sounded disgusted.

"No, that's not all," Luke almost shouted. Her words had revived one of his most precious memories. He had felt a timeless bond with his child. That sense of recognition defined his fatherly love. "I got to cut the cord."

"The what?" Aaron yelled.

"Don't tell him that, Luke. For heaven's sake, he's too young. We shouldn't even be talking about this. Now let's go home."

"Okay." Luke winked at Aaron to try to satisfy him that he would get the rest of the story later. They talked about guy things when Melinda wasn't around. Aaron would probably find the cord cutting a grossly fascinating detail. He was already a big fan of bugs, spiders, and caterpillars.

Aaron winked back. "Can we go to MacDonald's? I'm starving."

"MacDonald's in a Jaguar?" Luke felt happy with his little family at this moment. His fortieth year had turned out better than expected. He might like becoming mature. Distinguished even.

"Let's go to P. F. Chang's." Melinda said.

"Naw, Mom."

Melinda won as she always did. After P. F. Chang's they went home. With his studious nature, Aaron had asked permission to attend summer school. He headed straight to bed so he could get up early and do homework.

As soon as he'd said good night, Melinda took Luke by the hand. With a wicked grin, she said, "Tell you a secret. I've always had a thing for older men." She led him up the white stucco staircase of their ultra-modern home.

Maybe it was the wine at dinner. Or maybe the delight of the Jaguar. Or maybe the true confession of her birth memory. Luke didn't know which, but he appreciated Melinda's enthusiasm, especially for oral sex, something she'd not volunteered to do since the early days of their marriage.

Because she had once abandoned him and Aaron and because of the possibility of a repeat performance, Luke didn't love Melinda like he once had. He felt comfortable with her in a shallow sort of way, and she looked drop-dead gorgeous. Any man in his right mind would want to have sex with her. Luke was definitely in his right mind. They had a very pleasing romp.

After they finished, Luke dropped off to sleep immediately and rested unusually well.

The next morning at breakfast, he asked her why she seemed to know about him at the moment of her birth. Melinda wouldn't even address the question, calling herself foolish, saying she wished she'd never brought the subject up, and vowing never to speak of it again.

Luke thought the idea that she'd had mature thoughts at birth might indicate she was remembering some kind of disembodied existence, an interesting idea. Or, perhaps she had a greater fear of losing him than she'd ever owned up to. Even that didn't fit. He just didn't understand her well at all.

Angie sat in the bay window in Luke and Melinda's over-trendy kitchen nook and listened to them talk around the subject of consciousness, as they talked around most subjects. She felt impatient with Luke's progress, particularly. He closed his mind to so many possibilities. If he were open to the notion of immortality, he would realize that of course Melinda had been conscious at her birth. Luke had also.

All humans carried consciousness with them from the spirit world to Earth. The challenges required to learn to manipulate a physical body and deal with family and culture forced forgetfulness. Why didn't Luke understand?

Many times over the years she had come to whisper to him. In dreams sometimes he acknowledged her, but she found the quality of communications in dreams inferior compared to what they could achieve if he were awake and aware. Perhaps time would improve their connection. At present he remained a very difficult human to haunt.

Regardless of whether she lived on Earth or in the spirit world, Luke provided her with a vehicle for learning patience. Emmons reminded her whenever she forgot. She had gained in understanding and abilities during the eleven years since her last incarnation ended. She would continue to take classes on building the psychic energy necessary for bridging the levels of reality.

The next big challenge would probably be the manifestation of the Plan. Souls everywhere worried about it, and some doubted it would actually transpire. The Plan had originated in the spirit world as an extreme alternative, an effort to intercept humankind's selfish focus and turn it toward love.

Now the forces set in motion were happening quickly and would soon become irrevocable. Humans appeared to have little interest in loving each other. The negative aspects of the Plan troubled Angie, particularly with so many of her soul group involved.

Ty had returned to Alpha Centauri to remain until the time scheduled for their next incarnation. While she waited, Emmons had assigned Angie the task of intake counselor, a role she looked forward to and dreaded at the same time. At least she got to work in a dazzling garden.

One night a few weeks later, Luke awoke in the middle of the night, filled with fury. He bolted out of bed and ran out of his dark bedroom, wearing only briefs. His bare feet slapped on the carpeted stairs as he hurtled down as fast as he could go.

The pool lights cast an eerie blue tinge to the leather furniture as he dashed through the living room and into the hall. Passing through the dark kitchen and utility room he grabbed the knob to the garage door, held his ear to the door, and recognized a sound he shouldn't be able to hear...whispers.

What the hell?

With one hand, Luke opened the door and with the other flipped the switch for the overhead florescent lights in the garage. Under flickering yellowish illumination, Luke glared across the empty concrete stall where Melinda normally parked her Porsche. What he saw made him livid.

The silver door of the Jaguar hung wide open. An intruder in the driver's seat gaped at Luke, eyes wild with fright above a scraggy beard.

"*Que pasa?*" a voice whispered from beneath the car.

"Get away from my car, you sons a bitches!"

The intruder scrambled out of the car, dashed to the rolling door, and forced it up with his arms, spread-eagling himself. He looked to be the same height as Luke, about five eight, maybe ten years younger, definitely strong.

Luke would have no trouble at all taking this scum out. In fact he looked forward to the exercise.

With a ferocious whoop, Luke lunged for the intruder, grabbed him around the waist, and slammed him down on his back on the concrete. The door clanked and shuddered.

From under the engine, another man scrambled through the opening on all fours and disappeared into the darkness.

It enraged Luke that he couldn't fight both at the same time. He straddled the grunting scum beneath him and pounded his face.

The intruder tried to fight back. Even though off balance, he punched Luke in the jaw.

"You asshole." Luke landed solid blows one after the other.

Blood spewed out of the intruder's nose. *"Por favor, por favor,"* he cried and tried to turn his face away.

Luke cracked him across the head with a solid fist, and the intruder's head bounced. He lay still. Both men panted.

Bruising swelled his dark eyes, and the intruder tried to cover his face with his hands. *"No, senor, no—"*

"Never steal my stuff." Luke grabbed the scum's neck to emphasize his outrage. "You hear me? Never. I'm gonna call the police and turn you in."

If he wasn't such a civilized person, Luke would cut the bastard's hand off to keep him from stealing again.

"No policia." The scum looked as if he were about to cry. *"Por favor."*

Projecting what might happen, Luke visualized the police arriving, the questions, the explanations, the paperwork, the request for the rationale for his use of force. It had been exceptional, and Luke knew he couldn't explain why.

The police would say Luke should have called them when he heard the whispers. Not likely when he could beat the shit out of scum like that. He wished to hell the other one hadn't gotten away.

Luke released the intruder's head and thumped him back to the concrete. "Get out of here and don't ever come back."

"Si, senor." The intruder rose and ducked his head, hopefully in shame. He limped onto the driveway and down the sidewalk then slunk away.

Luke crossed to the electronic button and depressed it to roll down the garage door. He wondered if any of his neighbors witnessed the fight. If so, they got a good glimpse of him in his skivvies, a surprising picture on this quiet suburban street.

He gave the Jaguar a once over. A wire lay on the carpeted floorboard, but nothing seemed to be disturbed. The two clowns evidently intended to hotwire his car, but they hadn't made much progress. Guess they'd learned the error of their ways by now.

Assholes.

After closing the Jaguar's door, Luke walked around it once to check for damage. It looked perfect, unmarred. Good thing Melinda had driven to San Diego on her business trip or those scoundrels might have managed to steal her car.

Back in the house, he went into the hall bathroom and flipped on the light. His hands were banged up, but they didn't hurt much. It had been very satisfying to smash that lowlife in the face.

Luke washed the blood and snot off his hands and spat a wad of bloody saliva into the bowl. He glanced up to inspect his jaw, some edema but it would heal fast.

A pajama-clad Aaron reflected in the mirror. "Dad, what's going on?" He stared in horror at the sink lined with blood and dirt and then back at Luke. "You're hurt."

"No, I'm fine."

"What happened?"

Anxious to calm down, Luke dried his hands with a towel. "Nothing for you to worry about, son. Now get on back to bed."

"Dad! Tell me!"

"All right. I suppose you have to know. Some...guys were trying to steal my Jaguar."

"No shit?"

"Watch your mouth."

"So how did you know? You must have heard them."

"Yeah, I must've." That sounded logical even though Luke didn't remember hearing any noise from the garage.

"And you went after them? Without your robe?"

"Guess I surprised them. Now get on back to bed. You've got school in the morning."

Aaron headed back through the house. "Hey, Dad, that's awesome."

Following, Luke turned out lights his son must have lit all along the way. "I don't know about awesome. I think I overreacted. I should've called the police."

At their bedroom doors, they exchanged goodnight hugs. Aaron still wore a look of admiration when he closed his door.

Luke went into his room and dropped on the bed in the dark. What in hell had gotten into him? He couldn't remember a time in his life when he settled a problem with his fists. He'd always been the puniest kid in his class and smart enough not to start fights he'd lose.

Winning felt terrific. This fighting could be addictive. He liked the finality of it. What's more, in the midst of it, he had felt completely justified in taking out his anger on the stupid asshole, a criminal really. Now Luke regretted that he'd busted up the guy so badly. The police might have taken Luke to jail too, had they seen the intruder's condition.

Once in a while Luke had wondered how he'd react under this kind of stress, whether fight or flight. Guys who went to war probably had a lot clearer concept of their mettle, what they'd stand for and what they wouldn't.

Luke knew he'd never choose flight, whatever that said about his character. He had never known he could feel such wrath. Now that he understood, he'd better keep it in tight check.

How in hell did he come to realize there were intruders in the garage? It seemed illogical that he heard them so far away. He had bought the quietest garage door opener possible so he wouldn't hear it go up and down when Melinda came home late from business trips.

Thinking back to the minutes before the fight, Luke realized the sound of the garage door opening had not awakened him. As a matter of fact, a dream had awakened him. He had dreamed two Mexicans were in his garage, hovering around his Jaguar. When he got downstairs—

Oh shit, that was way too spooky. Sounded like something his mother would do. Ridiculous. He must have remembered the dream wrong.

Six

The Business of Death

New York City, July, 2001

After thirteen hours in the air, the plane on which Karim and Ibrihim traveled circled above John F. Kennedy Airport. Just seeing the Saudi Arabian countryside and a big city like Jeddah from the Imam's car had fascinated Karim, but those sights could not compare to the towers of decadence in the skyline of New York, the most evil city in the entire world.

So charged up was he that Karim ignored the restrictive feeling of the American style wash-and-wear trousers between his legs and the scratchy texture of the polo shirt he wore. He experienced no weariness from the trip, rather excitement to experience this terrible place he had only seen in pictures and heard lectures about since his childhood. The other passengers, most Saudi nationals in traditional garb, murmured all over the plane. They sounded impressed too.

Karim loved to look at the beautiful American flight attendant. He couldn't tell whether he enjoyed more seeing the shape of her bosoms under her Navy blue uniform or her bare, white, shapely legs sticking out beneath her short dress. He'd never seen a girl's legs before, but he felt certain hers were far lovelier than the average. As she passed down the aisle, she spoke with her strange speech, so unlike the British English he had studied and in which he had made poor grades. Distracted by her odd scent, a combination of

43

coffee and flowers, Karim failed to understand her. Fortunately Ibrihim in the seat beside him gestured for Karim to fasten his seat belt.

The plane landed, and they grabbed their duffle bags packed with all that they owned—Koran, prayer rug, shaving gear, toothbrush, comb, and a change of American clothing exactly like the ones they wore. It was easy to see how American people fell into sin when their clothes revealed the lewdness of their body contours to everyone who wished to look. They deserved their fate.

On deplaning Karim and Ibrihim walked through the carpeted tunnel with the other passengers. People of many different skin colors, in all kinds of dress, bustled about.

Ibrihim said in Farsi, "Stay behind me." He looked up at a huge computer monitor then pointed toward a sign that said Immigration. "Keep your mouth shut. I'll do the talking for us."

Karim lacked any confidence in his ability to communicate in this country and felt glad to let his taller, skinnier, unquestionably uglier, but better-spoken friend take the lead.

In the immigration area with empty tables and bare walls, they stood in a queue with many of their Arab neighbors. Karim doubted there were any other Afghans among them because the Imam and Brother Bin Laden had made special arrangements to get Karim and Ibrihim out of the country without notifying the Taliban. Such consideration only came to them because of the value of their mission, and Karim felt honored to be so trusted in the service of Allah. The task ahead had too high a priority for the ears of the Taliban foot soldiers, who everybody knew weren't the cleverest brigade around.

A large man, dark skinned like an African, wore a brown uniform and stood at a turnstile. When Karim and Ibrihim came forward, the officer said something in an unintelligible accent. Ibrihim frowned and handed over his passport and a forged letter.

Ibrihim turned away from the officer and whispered to Karim, "Show him your papers."

The officer looked at the papers, peered into Ibrihim's face, and pointed to the table. "Open yo suitcases, please."

Karim followed Ibrihim to the table where they unzipped their bags. The officer rifled through their things, rumpling the clothing. Such disregard bothered Karim because he hated his attire to appear anything less than perfect, even if it was devil American clothing, but he remained quiet.

The officer said to Karim, "You goin' to college?"

Ibrihim said in English, "Yes, we both are. The American Graduate School in Arizona."

A challenging look crossed the officer's face. "You don't look old enough to go to college. Spacially a graduate school."

"We are honor students and got scholarships," Ibrihim said as he had been tutored to explain.

Nervous, Karim feared his own silence might draw unwarranted attention to him. "Yes, scholarships," he said in English.

Ibrihim pointed to the forged letter from the college. "See, here is our admission papers."

Karim was certain that should have been *are*, a dangerous mistake. They had come too far to end in failure. He held his breath.

With a nod, the officer shoved the duffle bags toward Karim and Ibrihim and handed their papers back. He glanced beyond Karim. "Next?"

Looking as relieved as Karim felt, Ibrihim, said, "Let's go." They grabbed their bags and hurried toward the sign that said Concourses and followed it to the American Airlines counter. They bought tickets to Phoenix on a flight leaving that night. Using their credit cards proved to be no problem at all. Praise be to Allah.

Karim found much to look at in the airport, with the moving sidewalk, the restaurants, and especially the women. They shamelessly showed their faces, arms, and legs. Some even had their underclothing showing at their shoulders. He wished he might spend the rest of his allotted time on earth, sitting in the airport and admiring these women. He noticed Ibrihim also gave a good deal of notice to the women passing by.

To Karim's great delight, they found a little storefront Greek restaurant that served hummus, pita, saffron rice, and lamb wrapped in grape leaves. It wasn't exactly home cooking but close enough to appease the appetites of two ferociously hungry Afghans. He and Ibrihim had to remain standing at a table while they ate, one of the most remarkable of American customs he had noticed so far.

Ibrihim swallowed a bite of rice. "I finally decided I believe in your angels."

"You do?" Such an admission surprised Karim since his friend persisted in believing that evil jinns were out to get Karim.

"You said your angel Emmons, peace be upon him, told you that we would have trouble in the American airport but everything would turn out all right."

"Yes, that was my dream last night. I guess he meant the officer who questioned our papers." Karim chewed on a grape leaf thoughtfully. He loved its chewy bitterness. "Even though my angel doesn't come to you, we are both protected and loved by those in heaven, just as our prophet Mohammed promised. Peace be unto him. It has all been planned out in advance, and we are Allah's agents."

"Praise be to Allah for all his mercies."

"Wonderful as it is to serve Allah in all we do," Karim said, "I'm very excited because I'll get to do the one thing

I've wanted for as long as I can remember—to fly an airplane."

"I, too. We both have always had that desire. It's probably why we were chosen."

"And you know what I think will happen when we get to flight school in Phoenix?" Karim laid down his napkin and folded it slowly, enjoying the tension he caused in his friend. "I will beat you out for the number one slot."

Ibrihim rained blows on Karim's shoulders in fake anger. "Never, never. You'll only qualify to be my co-pilot, if you're lucky, on that great day."

Seven

The Plan

Los Angeles, September 10, 2001

Late in the afternoon, Luke dropped Aaron off at the sitter's then drove the Jaguar down the freeway toward home. The gear shift and dashboard reminded him of an airplane cockpit. He wondered if he'd ever become a pilot. With the epilepsy under control, he could probably get a license. One of these days he might try although the prospect made him nervous. He flew when he had to but didn't enjoy it.

When his cell phone rang, he recognized Melinda's number on the screen. "Hey, Melinda, you got there all right!"

"Sure, no problems with the flight. Sorry I didn't call last night, but there was a mix-up at the hotel. For some reason they messed up the reservation. Yours is fine for tonight, but I'm at the Holiday Inn across from the Hilton. I stayed here last night too and got a lot of shopping done today. I needed a break from work." Her voice didn't sound like she'd had a break. She sounded very professional.

"Will you be back at the Hilton tonight?"

Melinda paused, odd considering she only need answer yes or no. "No...uh...I'll just stay here. You won't be in until late anyway, so I just wanted to tell you I'd see you at the meeting."

Luke wondered if she were still miffed at him. Probably. He cleared his throat. "Melinda, I apologize again for the inconvenience of changing our flights. I just didn't feel comfortable."

"I understand perfectly. I agree. We should always take different flights. It's a small risk, but we wouldn't ever want to leave Aaron with no parents. You were right." She didn't sound angry at all, on the contrary, obliging.

"Glad you think so. Well, I'm packed, and Aaron is already at Billy Winston's house. I gave Mrs. Winston all our phone numbers. I've drawn up the contracts, too, and they look pretty slick."

"Good old Luke. You always handle everything." Melinda sounded less self-consumed than usual, almost warm. "Oh, I had a preliminary meeting with Bolton today. He's definitely interested in buying into our partnership. I think the conference tomorrow will just be a formality. No need for negotiations, but I want you there anyway, just in case."

"I will be. This is going to double our income without a doubt."

"The whole deal just has a perfect feel about it. Destiny, I guess. We're where we're supposed to be, and I've got you to thank for getting us this far." She had definitely warmed up to him now.

"You can thank me in person tonight." Luke laughed at the prospect of getting to do it in another place. Maybe that would perk things up for both of them. This keeping a sex life interesting took a lot of work.

Melinda's voice hit a high pitch, as if she had become suddenly angry. "No, don't forget. You're staying at the Hilton, and I'll see you in the morning. Oh, and the meeting has been changed. It's going to be at Bolton's office in the South Tower. Floor Sixty-Two. Nine in the morning. See you then. Gotta go. I've got some paperwork to do." She hung up before he had time to respond.

Luke thought it odd indeed that she had arranged for them to sleep in separate bedrooms, or maybe that was the hotel's fault. With so many conventions in town, the hotels around the towers probably had a tough job to do.

Maybe she had a lover in New York. She certainly had opportunity enough with three trips during the summer. Luke felt a surge of jealousy. On the other hand, he doubted she had a lover, no better than she liked sex. Once a month seemed to pretty well satisfy her.

Phoenix

Atop a braided prayer cloth, Karim sat on his heels, facing the closet on the east wall of the hotel room. His co-pilot, Ibrihim, stood by the window, looking out at the city lights.

"O God, you are my Lord," Karim prayed, "There is none worthy of worship except You. I rely upon You, and You are the Great Lord of the Throne. Whatever God wills happens, and whatever He does not will does not happen. There is no power or strength except by God. I seek refuge from the evil in myself and beseech You to protect me." He touched his forehead to the carpet, folded the prayer cloth, then removed his cap and tunic.

Lying down in one of the two double beds, he pulled the sheet up to his chin. A tight ball of fiery fear lodged in his chest.

Ibrihim closed the curtains then came to stand between the two beds. "Are you all right?" Bushy black brows turned down on his narrow face. He looked more worried every minute.

Karim covered his eyes with one arm and nodded, less convinced than he had felt all through their training. "Allah forgive me, I wish I had a drink."

"You've never consumed alcohol? Or is there something I missed?"

"No, but, if there ever was a time for a drink, it's now."

"I know what you mean." Ibrihim raised the sheet. "May I?"

Despite the unusual request Karim could not deny to himself that he longed for some human contact. Just a touch would do. Ibrihim must certainly feel the same. This was a dark hour in their lives. When Ibrihim slid under the sheet, the touch of his leg sent a charge through Karim's body. The skin of another being felt surprisingly cool.

"Is there anything you regret?" Ibrihim whispered.

Sighing, Karim thought of the women he'd seen on the streets since he'd come to America. Their clothes barely concealed their luscious feminine forms. They were shameless, he knew, but he had sinned in longing for them. Now, he would never know their touch. He would die, only twenty, without ever knowing a woman. So would Ibrihim. It hurt too much to even say the loss in words. He hoped the promise of as many virgins as he wanted in heaven would come true. Better than no promise.

Even more troublesome to admit to himself, Karim was afraid to die. What if he died, and there was no Allah? "I'm not sure I have the courage."

"You do. We both do." Ibrihim put an arm around Karim. "The prophet Mohammed, peace be upon Him, will guide us. The Imam and Brother Osama will be proud of us tomorrow."

Karim hoped it was not a sin to take comfort from his co-pilot's strong arms. No one had held him since his mother so long ago. He closed his eyes and tried to recall her face, but he could visualize nothing. Although he felt ashamed, he could not stop tears from wetting his face. Ibrihim trembled as he pulled Karim close against him, and they sobbed together.

Once they calmed down, Karim fell into exhausted sleep.

In a dream, Karim spread his arms and flew into the night sky. Bright stars appeared all around him as he soared through space. Beneath him he saw a white building that looked like a mosque or temple of some kind. When he flew down, he saw an angel, a male being of bright blue light. The angel, Emmons, sat on the railing of a fountain where water gushed. Karim sat on jade grass at the feet of the angel.

Emmons exuded great love and said, "All is going according to the Plan. You have accomplished what you came into this life to do, to end overindulgence. You volunteered for the sacrifice you are about to make even though you don't remember. You will be rewarded for your sacrifice. Keep your mind on the reward."

New York City

At the bureau in the single room at the Hilton, Luke emptied his pockets of keys, billfold, cell phone, Palm Pilot, and epilepsy pills. He would never go anywhere without his medication. It worked so well he had no symptoms left. It amused him to wonder if that qualified him as normal.

The plane had been late and the taxi ride circuitous. Exhausted, he disrobed down to briefs, hung his clothes over a chair, and cracked his back both ways. He called Melinda's cell phone and got no answer then tried her room at the Holiday Inn. No answer. Where had that girl gone? Out for a late drink? More probably asleep. She was a very sound sleeper and might not hear the phone.

Luke rang the desk for a wake-up call at seven then set his travel alarm. He didn't want to take a chance on oversleeping and missing the meeting. With a sigh, he turned out the lights and settled in bed. After a few minutes, he must have gone to sleep because his arms and legs became heavy, immovable, in fact. But his mind remained alert. A most unusual kind of sleep.

While he wondered whether or not he could have a dream in such a state of mind, his mother walked in. She didn't look sick and frail like she had before she died. Rather she looked as young and pretty as in the days when Luke had gone to elementary school. She wore a lavender robe, belted like in pictures of angels. Her black hair glistened, and her skin glowed. She sat down beside him on the bed

"Mom, is it really you?" Luke managed to whisper.

"Yes." Her pale blue eyes seemed warm. "I came to tell you the Plan has changed."

"What plan? I don't understand."

Her voice sounded just like it always had but emphatic. "Emmons wants you to know that the Plan has changed. You must live for your son's sake. And develop your power the slow, tedious way on earth."

"My power?" Luke wanted to sit up and touch her, but he could not. His body felt completely numb. He must be dreaming, but at least he could speak. "What are you talking about?"

"Later, you will understand, I promise. Remember the Plan has changed, but you will still receive your reward. It will just take longer." His mother rose and walked toward the door like an ordinary person. She turned back and said, "I love you," then dissolved like water vapor.

Luke couldn't discern whether he slept or not, whether time passed or not. He felt as if he were floating on a great, glossy ocean of peace. At some indeterminate moment a phone rang, but he didn't have enough energy to answer it. He heard another sound, familiar but of what he didn't know.

The clatter of vibrating glass woke Luke. An earthquake? He looked at the clock. Nine. "Oh, my God." He jumped out of bed and threw on his trousers. Why in hell had he overslept? He never overslept!

The meeting had probably already started. He glanced out the window on his way to the bathroom then turned back because he didn't recognize the sight visible between the open curtains.

The North Tower of the World Trade Center billowed with smoke. He heard a roar as if the building itself cried out. Oh, God, had it been bombed? Sirens blared.

Out of the corner of his eye, he saw an airplane coming. He grabbed his head with both hands and held his breath. He knew what was going to happen.

In the cockpit of the 757, the windows and walls of the tower filled the frame of the windshield. No way to avoid it now.

Karim gripped the steering column so tightly his fingers bled. He screamed, Ibrihim screamed, the passengers in the cabin behind him screamed and banged on the door. The plane welled up on a flood of terror, but Karim's heart felt calm.

Allah would welcome him this day in paradise. Allah would provide bounteous food, a lovely woman, sumptuous gardens, a perfect life. Karim did the Prophet's work. Peace be unto Him.

As Luke watched, the plane slammed into the South Tower with a crunching roar. The window rattled, and the floor shook beneath Luke's bare feet.

A fire ball engulfed the building.

"Melinda!" Luke ran out the door. He took the stairs three at a time. He didn't want to think. He just ran. He had to get to Melinda.

Eight

Sacrificial Lambs

A wall of fire burst all around.

Karim's astral body popped out of his physical body and flew up on a wave of energy. He could not understand where he was or what propelled him, but he heard wailing and moaning. He knew somehow that many others floated up on the same current even though he saw no one.

From the distant darkness, a great force pulled him.

"No," Karim cried. "Something's gone wrong. Maybe I didn't hit the tower?" He felt sucked along a flamboyant column, unable to control his movements. Where was the angel of death? Why did no angel rescue him? Had Allah deserted him?

The sucking motion stopped, and Karim floated into a tunnel and along it for a long, long way. How could space be so empty? What had become of his airplane? And his co-pilot? Was Ibrihim floating somewhere, too, wondering what happened to Karim? Something had gone terribly, terribly wrong.

It must be the fucking Americans. They must have nuked the plane. Only the Americans could make such a diabolical move. Oh, no, he had failed. Karim had failed. Mohammed his prophet, peace be unto Him, would never want to set eyes on Karim. Neither would Ibrihim.

Poor Brother Bin Laden. He would be so sorrowful to know the mission had failed. Nuked out of the sky by the fucking Americans. Who would have thought it?

A light of enormous brightness began to glow at the end of the tunnel. Someone stood there waving. Karim should know that person. Maybe an angel had finally come for him.

It occurred to Karim that he might not be dead. He felt so disoriented he could not think. All went dark in the tunnel and in his mind.

By the time Luke reached the World Trade Center, the top of the South Tower had disintegrated in a fiery morass. People poured out of every exit—door, window, fractured wall. Firefighters hurried inside the building. So did Luke. Melinda needed him. He could think of nothing else. He had to get to Bolton's office, but Floor Sixty-Two had disappeared. Where to go? He started up the stairs anyway.

Hoards of people streamed down. In the packed stairwell, people cried, coughed, and yelled, "Get out, help me," and so many other things the voices all blended together in a horrendous confusion of sound. The building trembled. Smoke and dust clogged Luke's nostrils. The downward-sweeping human mass pushed him back three steps for every two he advanced.

Finally, Luke could make no upward progress. He turned with the exodus of people and ran back outside the collapsing building. He started looking for Melinda in the crowd growing outside. She had probably run down the stairs like everyone else.

Luke must have peered into a hundred faces. As his hope dwindled to despair that he could find her, he had a brainstorm. Call her on her cell phone. Why hadn't he thought of that before? He reached for his phone but hadn't clipped it onto his belt. In fact, he wasn't even wearing his belt. He realized he had run out with only his slacks—no shoes or socks, no shirt. He hadn't acted very logically. He felt like a fool.

Hurrying the several blocks to the Hilton, Luke distracted the clerk from watching the burning towers on

TV and got him to fork over another key. The man didn't even ask for Luke's identification. The clerk just mumbled, "This is it. Armageddon."

A large and loud group of people stood by the elevator. The lights weren't working above the door. Luke dashed up the stairs and into his room. He dialed Melinda's cell phone but received no answer, then her room at the Holiday Inn with no result.

Frustrated, he put on his shirt, tucked it in, and attached the phone to his belt. When he pulled on socks, he noticed dried blood on his feet. He must have stepped on some broken glass although he didn't remember doing so. No problem. His feet didn't hurt at all, so he put his socks and shoes on and headed back to the World Trade Center.

Police were trying to cordon the place off, but many ignored official directions. Debris and bitter-smelling smoke filled the air. When firefighters carried bodies out and laid them on the ground, Luke watched and prayed that Melinda's would not be among them. He didn't want to believe she had died. Many had survived, it seemed, otherwise why would they continue to mill around? People coughed and covered their eyes, but they didn't seem to be leaving. Many people asked if Luke had seen a certain person, describing specific attire or hair and eyes.

Luke did the same, telling them of his gorgeous Melinda with her black hair, black eyes, long legs, tawny skin, and silk business suit. He didn't know which color she had worn today. She owned so many. He remembered her saying she went shopping yesterday, so maybe she wore something he had never seen. It bugged him that he might not recognize her from a distance in new clothes and that he didn't know what to tell people in a description of her.

Every few minutes Luke tried the phone numbers again. Sometimes, the dial tone sounded odd, and he didn't feel certain he had connected to a roaming service provider. He called the babysitter, Mrs. Wilson, on the chance that

Melinda had phoned, but she hadn't. He did not ask to talk to Aaron because he feared alarming his son when so far Luke had nothing to tell him.

Mrs. Wilson, despite being far away in California, sounded terrified. She said she'd been watching the news. Her fear freaked Luke, and he strove to allay his panic. He had to stay calm and do what he could. It appalled him to realize that the whole nation, the whole world, in fact, might be seeing this dreadful event. What on earth had happened? Was this some terrible air traffic controller disaster? Were they at war?

Unable to avoid it any longer, Luke called Mama and Papa Chacon; they sounded frantic. They had been watching TV. They knew Melinda and Luke intended to go to New York and had prayed they weren't near the World Trade Center.

Mama broke down on the phone. In the most reassuring voice he could muster, Luke told her that he hadn't been hurt and that Melinda probably was all right too. He just hadn't found her yet. He described the congested mess around the towers.

Papa Chacon got on the line. "What's really going on there, Luke?"

"I can't find Melinda." Luke blurted out the wound in his heart. "I'm afraid she's dead."

"Have you checked the hospitals?"

"I didn't think of that. I will." Luke hung up, shocked at his own confusion.

Luke went to one of the hospitals that had ambulances standing by at the disaster scene. Considering the enormity of the damage to the towers and the number of people inside them, probably up in the thousands, the hospital emergency room stood eerily quiet and empty. He waited on a deserted bench for the attendant. When she arrived, Luke rose to talk with her, stumbled, and fell. His feet felt like they had caught fire.

The attendant hailed an intern who cut Luke's shoes and socks off then bandaged his feet. They wanted to admit Luke, but he refused, borrowed some crutches, and hobbled to a nearby Kinko's. He had his wallet photo of Melinda blown up and mounted on a placard.

Back at the ruins, lots of people looked at the placard, of course, because Melinda was so beautiful, but no one had seen her. When he tried to call her again, his cell phone went dead.

The police backed the onlookers onto the neighboring streets. Fire trucks and ambulances hauled people away, living and dead. Luke found a garden wall within sight of the crumbled buildings and sat down to wait. He feared leaving because he might miss Melinda if she showed up or, worse, if they found her. Imagining her mangled and dead beneath thousands of pounds of rubble sickened him beyond expression. He had to remain available.

Many hours must have gone by, but the time of day remained uncertain because smoke and debris had turned the air sooty brown. Luke coughed a lot, as did others. Emergency personnel worked diligently. An aura of sanctity pervaded the place.

A middle-aged woman in jeans and sweatshirt walked up to Luke. "Would you like something to eat?" She held up a sandwich and soft drink.

"No, thanks, I'm not hungry."

"It's pastrami. Really good stuff I make myself." She smiled compassionately.

Luke thought her very nice, but the idea of food made him want to throw up. He shook his head.

"Who are you waiting for?" She sounded a hundred years old.

As he started to tell her, his voice cracked. Luke had no interest in this conversation. The woman must have read his mind because she set the sandwich and soft drink on the wall then trudged away.

The woman's obvious pity for Luke mobilized him. He did not need pity. He needed action. Ignoring the food, he leapt off the wall and headed down the sidewalk away from the smoldering towers. His feet throbbed.

In an odd way, he welcomed the pain. It helped him participate in any pain Melinda might be experiencing. He remembered feeling the same way the day of Aaron's birth. She had dug her fingernails into Luke's palms so deeply they bled. Man, had she ever been pissed at him for getting her pregnant! But, of course, she forgot about it when she saw the baby. How happy they had been then, so far from now in time and place and circumstance.

Knowing how Melinda loved her possessions, Luke reasoned that, if she had survived, she would go to her hotel room to collect her stuff. He hobbled to the Hilton and checked out. Juggling his bag and the crutches, he journeyed the few blocks to the Holiday Inn. When night fell, to the east where the towers had been, no electrical power illuminated buildings. Ground light from searchlights and emergency power systems cast a surreal glow. To the west the city surged on, chastened and scared though its citizens might be.

Once Luke explained his situation to the desk clerk, she gave him a key with a tearful hope that his wife would be found. The simple trust the clerk exhibited seemed the order of the day, and Luke appreciated it. The disaster had created a small town atmosphere in a city of strangers.

Leaning against the elevator wall, he rode up with the realization that he felt faint. He wished he had taken the food offered earlier. He entered the hotel room. It had the beige walls, tweed carpet, and innocuous pictures of most any hotel room. Seeing Melinda's cosmetics, her hairbrush, curler, and even her white beauty mask strewn about, as if she'd just walked out, felt like a punch in the gut.

In the main room, her green lace bra and panties lay in a rumpled mess atop her empty suitcase, which stood open.

A green silk dress Luke had never seen before lay where she'd draped it over the arm of the easy chair. He picked up Melinda's dress, which exuded the piney fragrance of her perfume.

Melinda might be dead. Luke's throat constricted in horror at the abruptness with which life could end. He couldn't compute the idea. If he admitted that she had died, he would have to feel grief. As long as he held out hope, he could give in to exhaustion, a better choice.

Hanging the dress in the closet, Luke sat in the chair and called room service. He intended to order some food, eat, and then sleep. In the morning, he would deal with whatever morning brought. But room service did not answer, just as no maid had come to clean Melinda's room today, minor effects of the chaotic day.

A glance down to the floor at the base of the bedside table revealed an empty champagne bottle and two glasses. Melinda must have celebrated the merger early. Luke wondered who had celebrated with her. She'd mentioned having a meeting with Bolton. Perhaps it had been he.

The bed covers lay askew as if Melinda had just arisen and hurried out to the meeting. Now that he gave it some thought, the disarray itself surprised Luke because Melinda hardly even turned over during the night. Why would she have so churned up the bed clothes? Both pillows bore indentations from a head.

Hoping to belie the desolation spreading through him, Luke rose and jerked back the bedspread to reveal a dried stain that had discolored the sheet. Someone had had sex in this bed. Someone and Melinda!

Anger surged through Luke like an ugly flame. How could she do this to him? Why did she continually threaten the marriage with her selfishness? God, he felt sick of it. When he found her, he would kill her. He paced the narrow path from the bed to the bath and back again.

The truth that she might already be dead exhausted Luke anew. He dropped into the chair and closed his eyes, doubting sleep could overtake him. He ached all over, especially his heart.

The startlingly clear image of his mother's face seemed to appear in his field of vision, not as if he saw her in memory but as if she actually stood before him.

He jerked, awakening himself, and sighed with regret to see the empty room and the hatefully disheveled bed. He knew he had dreamed of Angie the night before but couldn't remember the dream's content although it had seemed important. He fell to sleep again.

In a dream, Luke saw Angie beckon to someone. Then, he saw Melinda. They both looked about thirty years old. Melinda seemed very sad and followed Angie into a valley filled with flowers.

They sat down beside an angel glowing in blue light.

Angie picked a flower, handed it to Melinda, and said, "In time you will understand. For now rest and renew."

An angry young Arabic-looking man joined them. He had a wide face with heavy brows. Melinda waved to him.

The young man said, "The Plan shouldn't have changed. I'm going back. I'll find Luke. I'll get him this time for sure."

Angie picked a flower, gave it to the young man, and said, "In time you will understand. For now rest and renew." She gave him a warm smile.

Luke struggled out of a great depth to awaken. He remembered a scrap of the dream and trusted that his mother's words had been intended for him: "In time you will understand. For now rest and renew." Luke would do that when he could. Right now he had to get up and get down to the ruins.

It took almost a week for Luke to admit to himself that Melinda had died and her body would not likely be recovered. When he phoned her parents to tell them he had given up, they'd already gone to Los Angeles. and brought Aaron back to Phoenix.

Luke couldn't help dwelling on the fact that his grandfather had died in a plane crash. Angie's fiancé had died in a plane crash. Melinda had died in a building crashed into by a plane.

There was not a chance in hell that Luke would ever get on an airplane again, so he rented a car. He had to wait three days for one to become available. Probably a good thing because his feet healed in the meantime. He drove to Arizona, stopping only for coffee and gas. Twenty-four hundred miles in thirty-seven hours and fifteen minutes. Not bad time. It deserved a headline, but he couldn't think of one.

Feeling neither sorrow nor anger, Luke did not cry. He experienced nothing except a longing to get back to his son.

When Luke arrived at the Chacon house, Aaron kept his eyes averted and acted as tight-lipped and distant as his father. They'd both turned out to be cold-hearted assholes.

Memories of Angie's death flooded Luke's mind. He knew without a doubt every emotion poor little Aaron was feeling. Luke wanted to take his son's grief away, an impossibility, but at least Luke would remain alert to the first clue that Aaron would accept support.

Melinda's parents arranged a ceremony for her. Luke argued against it because it seemed so final but bowed to their greater need to do something, for the sake of doing something.

The following Sunday Luke sat in the front row of wooden pews, with Aaron between him and Mama Chacon, in the rangy old Catholic church where he and Melinda had been married. The same wooden statues of Jesus and the saints adorned the niches. On the altar stood a placard bearing Melinda's picture, the one Luke had carried at the ruins on that terrible day. The baskets of flowers arrayed around the room he intended to donate to the hospital this time. Revolting repetition of this experience had taught Luke that much.

The employees from the accounting firm in Los Angeles and many of Melinda's brothers, sisters, nieces, nephews, cousins, and friends were scattered around the sanctuary. They acted more subdued than normal. Luke imagined many felt as confused as he did, no one knew what to call this event.

People needed names for things so they would know how to act. He imagined that everyone present wondered, as he did, whether to consider this a memorial, a celebration, a wake, or a prayer vigil. He hated to call it a funeral with no body, now and maybe never. People needed to see a body so they could say good-bye.

In lieu of music, the sounds of feet scraping, adults coughing, and babies crying echoed through the sanctuary. Father Garcia entered from behind the altar. The intervening fourteen years since the wedding had not been good to him. His eyes had sunk farther into his head and his surplice lay askew on his neck. He led the audience in a subdued recitation of the Lord's Prayer, first in Spanish, then in English. He looked at Mama Chacon with a sad expression and nodded for her to begin.

Rising, Mama Chacon plodded to the podium. Where Luke had once thought of her fifty extra pounds as happy fat caused by loving her own cooking too much, now she moved in a ponderous way as if she had no strength to drag herself through one more day. She had spent a lifetime bearing and raising children. Now she had lost one. Luke wondered whether she could take the pain of the loss.

Turning a tearful face toward the audience, Mama Chacon smoothed her gray hair with trembling hands. "I remember the day my Melinda was born as well as if it was yesterday. The room was cold, and the midwife had turned the overhead light on, causing a lot of glare. I felt very tired and weak."

Her voice came across so softly, people all over the room leaned forward, as did Luke, who anxiously awaited the birth story he didn't think he'd ever heard.

"The midwife laughed when she picked the baby up and washed her skin, then mercifully wrapped her in a pink blanket. The midwife says, '*Esta' su nina.*' That's when the baby got a first look at me, her mother, in my cotton gown, lying on drenched bedding in the tiny bedroom with photographs of Jesus and the saints taped on the walls. For a moment it seemed that she recognized me with those black eyes. She was such a smart girl, smarter than any of us."

Mama Chacon's voice grew stronger as she warmed to her story.

"The midwife laid the baby in the fold of my arm. I felt so cheerless when I looked down at her. "*Gracias*,' I says, 'Would you call my husband in?' The midwife went out the door. Then here came Papa with two days' stubble on his broad face. I heard the other children jabbering in the next room. He says to me, "*Como esta?* Are you all right?' Papa took off the blanket and examined the baby as if she were a species the world had never seen. His rough hands snagged the blanket, and I was afraid he would hurt her delicate skin. He says, '*Bien, bien.* She looks fine, plenty healthy. You do good work, Mama,' He called me Mama, still does."

With an expression only shared history could bring, Mama Chacon smiled at her husband where he sat in the pew with arms folded, a grim look on his beard-stubbled face.

"I should,' I says, 'I've had enough practice. Papa says, 'Solamente siete. Only seven. I will be happy to have seven more.'"

A smattering of laughter passed through the room, probably some of those others with their own memories of their sister. Luke had great fondness for all Melinda's siblings. Being an only child, he had loved becoming a part of such a big family.

Mama Chacon went on. "And I says, 'But I can't take care of the ones I've got. Papa, let's go back to Guadalajara. Please. My mother can help me take care of the children. We'll be so much happier there.' 'This is the land,' Papa says, 'where our children can have good lives. There is nothing in Guadalajara for them.'"

Something about this story started to seem familiar to Luke. Maybe Mama Chacon had told it before.

"Looking guilty, Papa chucked the baby under the chin and says, 'So what is your name, *mi hija?*' "Melinda,' I says, 'her name is Melinda" but I was sobbing so loud that the baby started crying too.' 'I tell you what,' Papa says, 'I'll go to Guadalajara and get your mother. I'll bring her back here to live. And your sister. And her worthless husband. Would you be happy then?' I'm sorry, Gilbert," Mama Chacon cast a glance at her brother-in-law in the back row. "That's what he called you. We stayed here and all you wonderful relatives came to live here with us."

Many of the family members sobbed along with Mama Chacon.

A pinched look on his face, Aaron jabbed Luke with an elbow. "Did you hear that, Dad? Mom got it right, even being afraid of having to go to Mexico."

"Well, I'll be damned." Surprise overwhelmed Luke. "She remembered her own birth."

"Well, I'll be damned." Aaron grimaced as if trying to push down tears.

"Aaron, watch your mouth. Not in church!"

Mama Chacon continued speaking from the podium. "And Papa says, 'This little one will grow up just fine. You'll see.' He took Melinda in his arms and held her up. He turned her like a jewel and looked at all sides of her. *"Mi Melinda,"* he says, 'What a beauty you will be someday. Men will beg to marry you. You will bear me many grandsons and make your father proud.' Melinda gave me the most wonderful gift. Her beautiful son, who looks just like her."

Now it was Aaron's turn to squirm under the loving gaze as his grandmother sought his eyes from the podium. She lumbered down to the pew, sat beside him, and hugged him tightly. He squeezed his eyes shut and didn't say a word.

Papa Chacon patted her hand and walked to the podium, favoring the gimpy leg that had required him to miss so much work over the years. He had rheumy eyes, and his stooped posture made him appear shorter. Luke couldn't remember the cause of the leg problem, not certain whether he'd ever been told.

Gripping the sides of the podium as if to keep from falling over, Papa Chacon said, "Ever since the days Mama spoke about, I knew Melinda was different from our other children. She was very special, and she grew up to prove my confidence in her." His voice grew rough and he worked his jaws, obviously holding back tears. "I remember the night she told us she wanted to go to college. Mama and I sacrificed whatever we had to, to make sure she got what she wanted. I have great pride in my American girl." He took a long look at the photograph. "I still am proud of her."

Many times Melinda had told Luke about that night. Her rendition had gone quite a bit differently. She always told it with the same fierce independence and determination that had so characterized her.

In Melinda's version, the big declaration had happened the night of her sister's wedding. A bit bored, Melinda had trailed through the carport behind her parents with Rosa and Priscilla, her two younger sisters in rumpled pink taffeta. They followed their mother into the laundry room where she kissed her lips then touched the crucifix on the wall.

Mama passed on into the kitchen, all her family members did also. "Thank you, Jesus, that Sylvia's wedding was so beautiful. And there were no problems." She picked up a plate of *galletos* and set it on the long table. The little sisters fell to eating and trailed sugary leavings on the oil cloth.

Unwilling to risk her 105-pound figure, Melinda grabbed a diet soda, sat beside them, and kicked off super ugly pink satin high heels. Never would she wear that grotesque color again. She'd been embarrassed to have some of her school friends see her in the froufrou dress. She'd not have worn it, but Sylvia had been so sweet and scared that Melinda didn't complain. Hopefully everyone would forget by Monday how awful they'd all looked.

After he locked the door, Papa limped in and sat beside his daughters.

A statue of St. Anthony hung over the dinged-up gas stove where Mama busied herself. "You want some hot cocoa?"

"No," Papa said, "but I'll take a beer."

Mama fetched it for him and popped the cap. "I think Sylvia looked happy, don't you?

"Two thousand dollars for a wedding." Papa took a long swig. "The cost goes up with every daughter, but at least we know that she married a smart young fella. He makes good money at the tire factory. He'll take care of her just fine."

"We're spending a lot of money." Mama sighed and stirred the cocoa. "If Ray doesn't get any scholarships, we'll have to pay all his tuition."

"Thank goodness, these three girls aren't old enough to get married. When they do, it will cost a bundle." Papa pulled up his trouser leg and rubbed his calf. "Melinda, you got your eye on some fellow or not? Just as well if you don't for a while. Give us a chance to get a little money ahead."

"No, I don't. You can forget that." Melinda loved her family, but when she thought about her future she despaired. She had no choice but to marry, Papa had said so many times. Mama always agreed with him.

Mama took liniment out of a metal cabinet. "Here, let me rub that for you." When Papa propped his foot upon the oil cloth, Mama sat at the table, scooped salve into the palm of her hand, and rubbed his leg. "You shouldn't have been dancing. What's the matter with you?"

"For my daughter's wedding? Of course, I danced. It's my duty to her." Papa winced but kept his leg still. "All my children are good children. They make me very proud."

Melinda had noticed what happened to her two oldest sisters in barely six years' time. They'd born five babies between them. Both were getting fat and Melinda dreaded seeing them on Sundays when they came to dinner. All they ever talked about was baby formula and buying television sets on time. Sylvia had become pregnant already, although Papa and Mama didn't know yet. Soon Sylvia would have nothing else to talk about either.

But the boys, now they had a different story. Her parents had helped the other ones go to technical school. Ray, a year older than Melinda, had grades so lousy he barely got promoted from year to year. Melinda helped him all she could with his math homework, but she had to face facts. Her incredibly handsome brother was incredibly dumb, too. He'd never make it through two years of junior college, and if he did he'd flunk out of the police academy.

Meanwhile he'd be eating up every dime their parents could cough up. Where would her money come from?

Melinda burst out, "I don't want to get married. Ever."

"Now, Melinda, dear," Mama said, "you'll find some nice young man. Don't worry about it."

"No, I won't. Give me my two thousand dollars. I'll spend it on college tuition."

"You? Go to college? Whatever for?" Mama looked astounded. How little she knew her own daughter.

"Now, Melinda," Papa said, voice firm, "just stop that talk. You're very pretty. Our prettiest, really. You're going to get lots of offers."

Melinda shouted, "I don't want any offers. I want to go to college. If you won't send me, I'll go on my own."

"What kind of talk is this? You're crazy!" Papa banged his fist on the table so hard the empty platter bounced.

"Girls, go to bed," Mama said to Rosa and Priscilla. They ignored her.

This was it. The moment Melinda had dreaded had finally come. She could keep her own needs to herself no longer. "I'm going, and that's final. I'm going to study math. Accounting."

"That's ridiculous," Papa shouted. "You're a girl."

"If you'd ever take the time to notice, I've gotten straight A's in math for as long as I've been in school."

"Is that right, Mother?" Papa looked puzzled.

"I think so."

Once committed, Melinda found the words easier to say. "I'm going to college, and you can't stop me. What's more, I'm going to make sure Rosa and Priscilla don't have to get married and get fat and sad, like our sisters."

"They aren't sad. Your sisters." Mama looked puzzled. "They'd have told me."

Melinda softened. "Oh, Mama, how sad are you?" She knew she made the right choice, the only possible one, for herself. "This is the Eighties, for goodness sake. Women don't have to settle anymore. All women, even Latinas. And I'm not going to."

And, Luke thought, Melinda had never settled. She had done everything her way. No wonder her father felt proud even though this one daughter had defied him. They should all be proud. Luke should, too. He would work on pride and try to make that his predominant emotion, instead of this hollowness, for everyone's sake.

"Dad," Aaron patted Luke on the knee. "It's your turn."

Luke glanced up to see that Papa Chacon had already taken his seat. Father Garcia signaled Luke to come up to the altar. He sighed, with little notion of what he would say, and trudged to the podium. "Melinda intended to devote her life to her career and to the careers of Hispanic women. She succeeded admirably. She never intended to marry anyone. I'm glad to say she failed in that goal. She was beautiful and smart. Everyone knew that. I did, too, the first day I met her. When we went to Sedona to the Jazz Festival that first summer, I knew that I would marry her someday. I felt destined for her without understanding why. It was as if only Melinda could satisfy some plan encoded in my genes." One look at Aaron showed Luke that tangible connection would never end. "She still is. I'll always remember her. And feel...proud."

After what seemed like endless hugging and handshaking, Luke and Aaron climbed into the rental car and left the church. On the radio, Celine Dion crooned *My Heart Will Go On*.

When they turned the last corner, Aaron's stony repression finally broke and he began to sob. Luke carried his son inside the Chacon house and laid him on the twin bed in the room that had once belonged to Melinda. A vase of paper flowers stood in the corner. Lacy curtains hung at the window. The walls showed old scuff marks and tack holes where succeeding Chacon children had stuck up pictures and posters.

Luke sat beside Aaron and smoothed the rumpled T-shirt over his shoulders. It broke his heart to see his son trying to suck up his anguish. "It's okay to be sad."

"I miss Mom." Big tears only kids can manufacture plopped from Aaron's drawn eyes. "Why did this have to happen?"

"I wish I knew. It seems like the most senseless event in the history of the world." Small comfort Luke could give. He'd felt the same way when his mother died, and now numb didn't even come close to describing his emotions.

"I loved her, but I didn't tell her," Aaron wailed. "I wish I'd told her."

"She knew." Luke held his son in his arms. Aaron's body felt very small and vulnerable. "No need to worry about that. And she loved you very much. Just like I do."

Besides inheriting her coloring and features, Aaron had his mother's earthy ability to face the facts. Luke let him cry it out and waited for that trait to kick in. Part of Luke wished he had tears instead of emptiness when he thought about Melinda. Another part didn't care, maybe his soul. Neither did it have any interest in grieving.

When Aaron's sobbing slowed, Luke said, "We need to make some decisions, son."

"About what?" Aaron sniffed and leaned back against the black velvet pillow.

"We can move back here so we can be close to Mama and Papa, or we can go back to our house in L.A. It will be lonely without your mom, there's no question about it, but your school friends are there."

"Which would you rather do?"

"If it was just me, I think I'd sell out and move to Sedona, but this is your life, too."

Eyes covered with slender fingers like his mother's, Aaron sat quietly for a long time. "Mama and Papa have so many grandkids. And besides, whenever they look at me, they'll be sad. Mama cries and says I look exactly like my mother." He knitted his dark brows as if struggling to think then sighed. "I barely remember Sedona. I think I was six or seven when we went there." He sat up, resolve on his rumpled face. "We better go on back to L.A., Dad."

"All right. I'm proud of you." Luke patted his son's leg and vowed never to mention that resemblance again. "It's not easy to think about things right now."

That had been their only real option. Any seventh grader would have made the same choice. It seemed like a fluke to mention Sedona as a possibility, more like a cop out. Even so, when Aaron chose L.A., Luke felt a tiny regret, a bit surprised at his nonchalance about the possibility of chucking a life he and Melinda had spent thirteen years building together.

Luke and Aaron went back to their rangy, modern house in the Los Angeles suburb and survived on Melinda's organizational skills at home. With housekeeper and gardener in place, all they had to do was feed themselves. Aaron displayed his mother's gift for hard work by going into the honors program at school and burying himself in schoolwork and soccer. Although Luke could not pretend to run the accounting firm as well as his wife had, he took over anyway.

The newspapers published photographs of all the terrorists. Luke poured over them, trying to comprehend from their visages what twisted mindset would cause them to commit such a horrific crime. One face stood out from the others, Karim Hijazi al-Kabul. Despite any logical reason for doing so, Luke thought he knew that man, or had met him somewhere, a disconcerting feeling.

Later a news story said that particular terrorist and one other had taken flying lessons near Phoenix, so Luke decided he must have seen Karim Hijazi al-Kabul on the street somewhere when back on a visit. Otherwise, how could he know such an evil man?

Angie looked down on Luke perusing his newspaper reports and realized things weren't much different there with him. As above, so below, or something like that.

Rumors spread throughout the spirit world, at least the part that Angie inhabited. The disaster, both there and on Earth, was worse than originally conceived.

Humans had not turned toward love. War festered in their hearts.

Although Angie had acted on Emmons's instructions in warning Luke, she had finally at least communicated with him. He saw her, talked to her, and did what she told him. Otherwise he would have died in the tower too. Now that she could influence his mind and action, should she? Dare she intervene in Luke's free will?

The most unsettling repercussion for her soul group was that Karim absolutely refused to be pacified. He insisted on reincarnating immediately. Emmons recommended counseling and meditation, but Karim ignored him. A guide can only do so much in advising, nurturing, and apprising of consequences. Thankfully, Melinda took their guide's advice.

In the last analysis every soul must decide its own path. And so, against the advice of Angie, Emmons, and the whole panel of elders who supervised earthly incarnation, Karim got his way. He would be born again right away.

Why did Karim persist in his vendetta? The seeds were too deep and too old. Angie had blood on her hands too.

No good would come of his return in Angie's view, but Emmons cautioned her to take heart. Good always came from bad. Angie redoubled her efforts in her energy classes because the time would come when her skills would be needed. She had so much to do, she wondered how she'd ever find the leisure to reincarnate. A physical body took much time and attention, but no other vehicle even came close to the possible pleasures and learnings.

Nine

A Date with Fate

Sedona, Arizona, 2006

In the five years after Melinda's death, her accounting business did passably well under Luke's tutelage. It continued to show a profit and employ a lot of Hispanic women, in memory of Melinda's passionate commitment to them. Luke hired an occasional person of another race or cultural group, even one guy, to prevent any discrimination lawsuits against the firm.

Watching Aaron grow was Luke's spectator sport. They could talk easily about work, school, sports, and anything else. Such a smart kid, Aaron read so much that Luke had little to give him in the way of guidance on how to get along with people or what to think about things.

Since his mother's death, Aaron had never mentioned the possibility of having a new mom. Luke didn't either. Sometimes in the line of work he met professional women who had casual ideas about relationships. They gave him interesting diversions but didn't touch his heart. Nor he theirs.

Whenever he thought of Melinda, he wished they'd been happier together. He felt sorry that he hadn't tried harder to make the marriage work, to make it less shallow. Dreading to ruminate on what he might have done differently, he gave up the thoughts and occupied his mind with work or soccer or going to the movies with Aaron.

Angie, Ty, Grandma Barbara, and his birth father all gone! Then his wife? Luke felt abandoned every day of his life. He nursed a brooding rage at all of them and didn't even care what that said about his character.

By the summer after his junior year, Aaron had grown to six feet. He stood four inches taller than Luke but was built just as stocky, a terrific looking young man. Girls started calling, but Aaron blushed and got off the line right away.

One day Luke found a *Playboy* magazine under Aaron's bed and figured that his avid interest in plants, geodes, and amoeba had expanded to include the female species. They needed to talk or Luke might lose any chance to impact his son's attitudes or behavior.

Because of that and general boredom, Luke suggested they rent a condo in Sedona for the summer. He wanted to take the Jaguar because of its comfortable ride and plenty of room for luggage, but Aaron wanted to drive his BMW instead. Cars represented opulence for both father and son. Neither could resist them.

With the top down, Aaron drove the white convertible into Sedona late on a perfect afternoon, temperature in the eighties, the sky wide blue paper. Ruddy mountains configured into shapes named by the locals, easy to see why. Coffee Pot Ridge, Castle Rock, Bell Rock, Cathedral Rock. The fantasy of red varied from coral to deep burgundy with dots of feathery green shrubs. On a cliff road, Oak Creek tumbled gaily along beneath tall pines. Luke had forgotten how much he loved the place.

Mountain shadows slanted off antique shops, art stores, restaurants, houses, and condos. In shorts, people of all ages thronged the sidewalks. They ate ice cream and climbed into jeeps for rides into the outback. Luke could hear their happy conversation, as if they and all the country had momentarily forgotten the wars in Afghanistan, Iraq, and half a dozen other spots. It made him feel good just to breathe the Sedona air, more alive.

"What a cool place!" Aaron pointed toward a gem shop. "I'd like to hang out there."

After parking the car, they first went inside an ice cream parlor. Luke ordered pistachio and Aaron double brownie fudge. No yogurt this trip. They slurped while they wandered through the gem shop. Aaron identified far more stones than Luke had any interest in knowing, but he felt glad for being there doing that, enjoying himself like he hadn't for a very long time.

Later they settled in a place called Enchantment that deserved its name, a complex of condos the same brick red as the mountains, set among undisturbed ancient pines. Luke looked forward to the next day even without a plan.

In the morning dressed in shorts and polo shirts, they hiked into Boynton Canyon. Aspen and firs in scarlet soil bordered the trail. Luke followed Aaron, who collected specimens of spiders, bugs, and butterflies, dropped them delicately into jars, and stashed them in his backpack. Luke breathed deeply and greedily. The scent of clean mountain air and trees nourished him. Birds sang a sweet tune, and the voices of other hikers carried on the pristine air. This place was too wonderful to be real.

Around a bend, they climbed over some rocks and dropped down into a small clearing. On one side a rosy cliff, on the other a gorge filled with evergreen shrubs went on for miles.

"Look at this." Aaron pointed toward a ring of stones set on the dry ground. Human hands must have set them in a circle about three feet in diameter. "Know what it is?"

Shaking his head, Luke shed his backpack, glad to have a break. The thin mountain air had him breathing a bit heavier than normal. He made a silent vow to work out more. Didn't want the kid to think his old man was out of shape. "Someone obviously placed these stones here. Wonder why?"

"I don't know. Maybe some kind of cult." Aaron bent down and looked closer at the circle. "There's a pattern. Every other stone is native to the area. The ones between are—"

"For divination," a bright female voice answered. "Indigenous rocks for grounding."

Luke and Aaron both turned as a lovely teenage girl strode toward them. Not very tall, she wore shorts and a tank top made of such soft cloth her firm nipples showed through. Long auburn hair flowed behind her. Luke doubted it had ever been cut.

If he felt surprised, she must have astounded Aaron. "Uh, hi," he said, cleverly.

The girl knelt beside the circle, picked up a deep blue geode with many facets, and offered it to Aaron. 'This is an azurite."

"Really?" Aaron had known that since third grade, but he grinned like an idiot. "You like gems?" Suddenly the handsome, solid student of a son turned to mush.

"They're very important to me. Are they to you?" Girls were born knowing when they'd made a conquest. This girl smiled at Aaron as if she owned him already.

"I study them in school." Aaron's gaze traveled back and forth between her tits and her cute face, as if under a spell. He looked like a boy who knew exactly what girls were for.

"I use them in my work." She stood and handed the stone to Aaron. "My name is Psyche. What's yours?"

"Aaron, and this is my dad."

"Hi, Dad." Psyche shook Luke's hand with a strong, enthusiastic grip.

"Hi." This whole scene was way too funny. What kind of a parent would name a child Psyche?

A female voice in the distance called, "Psyche, where are you?"

"I'm back at the circle," Psyche cried out. "Come meet my new friends."

All three of them looked toward the brush from whence the voice had emanated. Momentarily, an older version of Psyche appeared. Luke inhaled but forgot to exhale.

What a dazzling woman. She strode toward them as if she owned the world. All five feet of her. The woman's hair, a lighter auburn than Psyche's, floated around her shoulders. A smile filled her beautiful face, and her full boobs bounced along, happy to be with her. She wore a peach-colored gauzy thing, which seemed incidental to the huge leaf-shaped medallion around her neck. She gazed at Luke with an expression of wonder. Nothing, compared to his stare, he supposed.

"Mother," Psyche said and encircled Aaron's waist, "this is Aaron."

"Hello." The mother focused her smile on him.

"Ma'am," Aaron said, glibber today than at any time in his life.

Luke felt equally as overwhelmed. Being older he hoped he knew how not to show it.

"This is my mother, Euphoria."

Aaron shook her hand delicately while Luke mused about her name. Euphoria? Seriously? No parent in the history of the world had ever named a kid Euphoria or Psyche. Who were these people? Had he been taken up by a flying saucer?

Euphoria grabbed Luke's hand, and he felt like he'd experienced electric shock. His body came to alert, erection and all, ready for any advance. He and his penis were about as surprised as they'd ever been. She held his hand and stared at him with hazel eyes that glinted amber in the sunlight. Oh God, if he didn't have this woman, he'd get the DTs.

Like daughter, like mother, Euphoria knew she had unhinged Luke, and showed no compunctions about it. She said to him, "Don't tell me your name. I'll decide what I'll call you. I remember you."

"Remember me?"

"We've shared a past life together."

"We have?" Glibber Luke became every minute, just like his son.

"Shall we hike?" Euphoria asked.

Gladly, Luke used the opportunity to hitch up his shorts and relieve the initial reaction to Euphoria's sexy appearance. When he picked up the backpack, he noticed that Aaron and Psyche had already left the clearing. Their laughter echoed along the canyon wall.

Euphoria slipped her warm hand into the curve of Luke's arm. "I knew we'd run into you today." Her copper bracelets tinkled against his belt.

"How could that be?" He had a good deal of trouble focusing on her words and not her awesome presence.

"Let's just say I had a very strong feeling that I'd meet someone from my past life in Maryland. I didn't know it would be you, but now that I see you I'm certain you were with me there. You seem very familiar to me."

"Maryland, you say?"

"Stop, please. Let me find out what I can sense." Euphoria seemed very excited. So was Luke but for different reasons.

When they stopped walking, she nudged Luke and he backed up against an aspen tree. Its grayish skin prickled through the knit of his shirt. He felt certain he also wore a silly grin, but Euphoria appeared very serious.

"May I?" She raised her delicate hands and, when Luke nodded, laid them on his cheeks.

Her touch felt strong yet tender. She closed her eyes, which began to dart beneath the marble tissue of her lids. Pale blue spider veins ran back from the corners of her eyes across delicate white planes etched by life just enough to make her fascinating. She looked like a Highland girl whose skin had never had the chance to warm in the sun.

Just when Luke intended to say something clever, she moved her hands to the top of his head, barely touching, then down his shoulders, tracing their outline. She began to repeat the motion. Luke thought better of speaking. Hikers hailed each other in the distance, but Euphoria didn't seem to notice. Aaron and Psyche must have traveled far away by now. Maybe they would backtrack. Luke decided to worry about that later.

Finally Euphoria took his hands and began to speak, eyes still closed. "I see you standing at a table. You are working on something. Or someone. You are very intense, very kind. I think how much I love and admire you. I hand you implements. I am your nurse, I think." She paused for a long time, but Luke kept silent, not wanting to spoil whatever moment she was experiencing. He didn't have a sense of anything except her charm. She laid her hands on his forehead. "There's something behind you...shaped like latticework."

The word caused a picture to flash in Luke's memory, something very familiar, but he couldn't quite recognize what he saw.

"I'm sorry," Euphoria said, "I've lost it."

"That's all right. Maybe we can try later." This seemed a great entrée to see her again. Luke wondered if there might be more to what she said than he understood. Certainly, he was no guru. As they resumed walking, he said, "You know, my mother believed in reincarnation. She believed she lived in the eighteenth century, in England somewhere, I think."

"That's interesting." A bit distracted, Euphoria gave him a grand smile, but she didn't slide her hand through his arm again.

The hike became hillier and more demanding, the sun glinted through thin trees. The thought that he might have forgotten something nagged at Luke. He began to perspire.

Euphoria climbed over some rocks ahead of him, and he noticed that she wore flip flops. "Why didn't you wear tennis shoes?"

"Oh, I just came out to do the energy circle and my meditation. I didn't intend to hike."

"Well, then, let's go back."

"Shouldn't we find the kids first?

"Better yet, why don't we sit down here and wait for them. They have to pass this point to get back to the clearing." Luke shed the backpack, wiped rubble off a crimson rock the size of a big chair, then sat down. He patted the space next to him, hoping she would join him. "Tell me how you came to be named Euphoria. I've never heard that before."

Euphoria sat with her leg barely an inch away. The hairs on Luke's leg stood up, trying their damnedest to touch hers.

With an impish look, she said, "I named myself. My mother thought the name she gave me was beautiful, but I hated it, and for a long time I'd do anything to annoy her. Besides, I wanted a name that sounded more New Age and told people who I am, that said me in a sound."

"Happy, huh? That's cool." Luke sounded just as sophomoric as his son.

"Thanks."

"But...I think you're also saying you're not going to tell me your legal name?"

"Legal?"

"Guess I've not told you I'm a lawyer. I know about such stuff." When a look of alarm crossed her face, Luke said, "Just teasing, really. You can call yourself Tom Thumb or anything you want. As long as you've got a driver's license and an address, you're all right with the law."

"Really? Oh, I'm so glad. I'd never thought about legalities before."

"My legal name is—"

Pressing her palm across his mouth, Euphoria said, "Shhhh. Don't tell me. I'll guess it. If I don't, I'll name you myself."

The audacity of her spirit made Luke feel euphoric. She had the right idea. He couldn't remember a time when he'd had more fun being with someone. He didn't want their time together to end and promised himself it wouldn't. Euphoria had him spread-eagled in intrigue—what she could be to him and what she might lead him to. He felt like a prospector who had hit the mother lode.

As luck would have it, Psyche and Aaron came along the path. They held hands and he looked flushed. Luke would bet the Jaguar that Aaron had just had his first kiss but decided not to ask. He'd wait to let Aaron say so. Surely he would want to talk afterward, when they got back to the condo. Right now, he barely glanced Luke's way.

"Psyche, dear," Euphoria said, "we need to go right now. Otherwise, I'll be late for work."

Luke felt disappointed because he'd hoped to spend more time with her. Both kids looked as downcast as he felt. "Where do you work?"

"Crystal Cave in downtown Sedona. Know where it is?" When Luke shook his head, Euphoria said, "Can't miss it. The building that looks like a cave right by the creek. Want to meet us after?"

Luke could think of nothing better. Happy days were here again.

At the spot where Aaron had found the circle of stones, Psyche collected the agates and dropped them in a bag.

Euphoria scattered the red rocks and swiped the ground with a limb. "So no trace of the energy circle remained," she explained.

After arranging the time and place for the date, the two women disappeared among the shrubs. Luke turned to find Aaron adjusting his backpack.

"Come on." Aaron took off down the path. "We've got a long way to go to reach the top." Pebbles crunched beneath the red-stained soles of his hiking boots.

The trek ahead took a sharp turn upward. The fir trees seemed taller and thicker, the sky an indigo patchwork above them. Luke scrambled along behind with the knowledge that his son was full of business. He didn't look happy, maybe impatient. Luke on the other hand felt ecstatic, euphoric, he probably should say. He marveled at the lucky encounter and looked forward to seeing the women again, especially Euphoria.

A marker indicated a certain hiking club maintained the trail. It seemed odd that they would display the notice at this particular spot, but before long the mystery was dispelled.

A ledge of rocks about a foot wide formed an uneven bridge across a gorge. Once he had navigated that, he had to climb rock steps set uncomfortably far apart. This expedition had turned into work, not fun, more like mountain climbing. The hiking club probably had the foresight to turn back at this point.

"Hey, son, wait up."

Aaron waved, his body a scrap of a shape among trees and shrubs in the distance.

Encouraged, Luke tackled an incline, using sturdy shrubs for support. Despite the fact that the air had cooled this high up, his shirt filled with sweat that had not evaporated by the time he arrived. He breathed a lot harder than he preferred.

Aaron sat on a fallen tree, smirking. "What's the matter?"

What did he know? He was just a kid. Luke huffed, "Not used to the thin air up this high." He pulled off his backpack and sat down beside Aaron, ignoring his disgruntled stare. "All right, all right. I'll join a gym. I'll get back in shape while we're here."

"Sounds like a good idea." Aaron took out the sack lunches the resort had packed for them, handed Luke a ham and cheese on rye, and munched a potato chip. "I'll go with you. I can get in shape too."

"Not that you need it, but I'll be glad for the company." Luke bit into the delicious sandwich, with mayo oozing out. "Of course, now that you've got a girlfriend, you need to look good."

"Get out of here! I don't have a girlfriend."

"Oh, yea? I can see the headline now." With a sweep of his arm toward the sky, Luke said, "TWO UNCOMMON TEENAGERS FALL IN LOVE OVER COMMON GEODE." He was normally such a serious young man. Luke hoped Aaron could take the teasing because Luke couldn't help myself. "Well, did you like Psyche? She's very pretty."

With a shrug that supposedly meant he couldn't care less, Aaron popped the top on a cola can. He turned away to drink, probably to hide the flush rising along his throat. Just the way his mother always looked when something embarrassed her.

Luke felt a twinge of regret that she couldn't watch her son grow up and gratitude that he could. "Hey, I'm sorry, Aaron. I didn't really ask you if you wanted to go along tonight to dinner with Psyche."

A deeper flush suffused Aaron's throat. "Yeah, sure, it's okay. I'll go."

"And it doesn't bother you to have your dad going on a double date?"

"I'm okay with that." Aaron sounded nonchalant and opened the wrapping on a sandwich.

"Maybe we could bring our dates back to the resort. They've got a restaurant that looks nice. Of course, it's a little old-fashioned. Maybe you'd rather take Psyche somewhere more—"

"That's fine. Wherever."

While Aaron inhaled his sandwich, Luke tried to figure out some way to get his son to take Psyche out on a single date. With two kids present, Luke couldn't imagine how he would get to know Euphoria any better or get any closer to her. On the other hand, Aaron seemed so evasive about the whole thing, Luke thought better of asking if Aaron had kissed Psyche. Guess maybe he needed his dad to help him over this awkwardness.

"Hurry up, Dad. We've got a half mile to go."

At this point, Luke didn't feel certain he would make it till evening, but he crammed the rest of the sandwich in his mouth, swung the backpack up, and hurried on. After the tortuous half mile to the top, the downhill trek, if not easier, at least passed quicker. They returned to their condo at the resort.

After a shower and a nap, Luke felt great and eager for the evening. He and Aaron donned slacks and dress shirts. Aaron punked up his hair. Luke combed his away from the side part, as usual, and hoped the few gray hairs among the blond made him look distinguished.

Euphoria had another suggestion for dinner. They went to *L'Auberge*, a French restaurant at a resort. Luke thought the food would probably taste good because shorts-clad vacationers filled the large room decorated in country style.

Aaron and Luke sat on one side of a trestle table with a blue and white checkered tablecloth. Euphoria, still in her peach splendor, took a chair across from Luke and beside Psyche, who had changed into a tiny little black dress that covered less skin than her shorts outfit had. With her hair back in a roll of some kind, she looked far older than she had that morning.

Luke didn't want to come right out and ask her age. "Do you attend high school, Psyche?"

"Yes, I graduate in May." Psyche took a napkin out of a crystal water goblet and shook it free from its flower shape.

"Oh, then you're the same age as Aaron."

The two smiled at each other, and Psyche leaned across the table and whispered in his ear. Aaron looked baffled by his good fortune.

A thin young man in a tux paused by the table and set down menus with a plate of *pâté* and biscuits. "*Bonsoir, je m'appelle Henri, et j'ai le plaisir de vous servir ce soir.*" He spoke in a clipped, officious manner then moved on elegantly.

Euphoria nodded to the waiter pleasantly and said to Luke, "Psyche's seventeen. Same age I was when I bore her."

"So, you're thirty-four?" Luke had not wanted to ask her age either. "See how clever I am. I can add." He wondered if she had been married that young.

Euphoria gave him one of her dazzling grins. "I didn't get married, of course. I got pregnant by the first fellow who asked to sleep with me, but I never told him."

"Oh." Luke realized he hadn't had to ask. She must have read his mind. A date with a psychic definitely followed a separate set of rules. He determined to monitor his thoughts. Who knew when she might turn into them? He doubted he could prevent her from knowing he found her most unusual and stimulating.

With a wistful look, Euphoria nibbled a biscuit. "All I could think about was getting back at my mother for divorcing my dad."

"That's me, Psyche, a little bundle of revenge."

Aaron opened the menu in front of Psyche. "You've been here before? What's good?"

"It's all *très bon.*" Psyche included all of them with her instructions. "I'm taking French in school so you tell me what you want, and I'll tell the waiter. It will be good practice for me."

They all dutifully read the menus and gave their choices to Psyche. Luke noticed no one had tasted the *pâté*, so he did. Too rich.

"I had a hard time forgiving my mother." Euphoria spoke thoughtfully. "Probably the reason I'm so indulgent of my daughter. We moved out here from Minnesota and left Mother alone."

"That's something we have in common." It amazed Luke that she spoke of her past in such a straightforward way. Oh well, what the hell. "My parents divorced when I was three, then Mom and I moved to Arizona."

"I think your mother has passed on, hasn't she?"

"Over fifteen years ago." It seemed less plausible that so many years had gone by than that Euphoria could know.

The waiter slipped to the table, hands clasped behind his back, probably to show off his superior memory by taking the order without writing anything down. He raised an eyebrow to let them know he was ready for their orders.

Psyche spoke to him in exaggerated syllables. "*Garçon, nous desirons le petoncle au safran pour tout le monde. Encore, l'homme* wants...*uh...prend le filet au poivre—*"

"*Filet* and *oui*." The waiter repeated.

He got those, but everyone knew *filet* and *oui*, Luke thought. They hardly even counted as French words anymore.

"*Encore*." Psyche nodded toward her mother. "*Ma mère désire la salade Sainte Catherine et...* "

The waiter shifted his feet and gazed at Psyche. In a whisper, he said, "Could you give it to me in English?

"*Parlez-vous français?*" Psyche squealed.

"No, ma'am." The waiter dwindled before everyone's eyes.

Luke felt sorry for the guy. Everyone got a little cocky sometimes. The waiter probably thought every customer in the room had witnessed his humiliation. Actually, only thirty or forty had. The rest were busy talking. Luke recited the orders for those at his table in English. "Also, I'd like a bottle of your best Bordeaux. You like red or white, Euphoria?"

"Red."

Pleased that she liked the same kind he did, Luke asked the waiter, "What do you have?"

"What quality are you speaking of, sir?"

"Your best."

The waiter cleared his throat. "Well, we have an excellent 1974."

Luke winked at Euphoria. "You've all said your ages. It's time I admitted when I was born." He spoke to the waiter. "How about 1961?" That was a very good year."

"1961 is one of our most prestigious vintages." His officious tone had returned. "A Bordeaux, from *Chateau La Fleur*."

"How much is it?" Euphoria surprised Luke with her question.

"One thousand fifty dollars, madam, but it is the finest wine we carry. The World Series of Bordeaux, as the critics call 1961."

A tantalizing expression crossed Euphoria's face. "You're a champion then?" She was daring Luke.

He could rise to this challenge. Luke really didn't care about the cost. He had made so much money in the past few years and enjoyed spending it so little that he felt delighted. It would let the waiter off the hook, too, when management discovered he'd sold such a pricey bottle. "Indeed, we'll take that."

"Yes, sir, thank you, sir." The waiter scurried away.

Psyche gasped and Aaron looked amazed. Luke knew that his son had hardly ever seen frivolous behavior from his father. Euphoria chuckled, causing Luke to wonder if she'd been reading the poor waiter's mind or possibly his.

"So, Aaron," Euphoria said, "what is your interest in gems? Are you a sensitive?" She pronounced the word with a kind of reverence.

"No, Psyche told me that you use different geodes in your work. I actually study them."

"He's going to college next year, Mom. To study geology."

"Maybe," Aaron said. "I might decide on biology or chemistry. I haven't made up my mind yet." He bent toward Psyche, who whispered to him again.

It amazed Luke that she could tell his son so many things that pleased him and that her mother and Luke couldn't hear.

"That's great," Euphoria said to Aaron. "I sell gems in the store. Books too."

"You're a clerk?" Aaron looked confused.

"Sometimes I help the owner when I don't have appointments. My main work is to give readings. I generally hold a crystal or other stone in my hand to help focus energy, then I get impressions about people's lives and emotions."

"She's taught me a lot about doing it, too." Psyche looked approvingly at her mother. "Only she's a lot better at it than I am."

"Give yourself time, dear." Euphoria seemed to have great admiration for her daughter, and vice versa.

The waiter set soft drinks before Psyche and Aaron then showed the wine bottle to Luke flamboyantly. When he nodded, the waiter popped the cork and poured a thimbleful.

Luke raised the glass, and everyone looked at the ruby liquid, the color of Sedona at sunset. "To my birth!"

"Here, here." Euphoria clicked her water glass with a spoon.

The wine tasted terrific, light, dry, and crisp. "Excellent." Luke said, and it was enough to please the waiter, who poured the two wine glasses full and sidled off to another table. "I'm sorry you guys can't sample it," Luke toasted Aaron and Psyche. "The law, you know."

After taking a sip of the wine, Euphoria closed her eyes then sighed as she swallowed. "That was heavenly, so mellow."

"Let me," Psyche said and took the glass from her mother. In a heartbeat she and Aaron had tasted the wine, set the glass back on the table, and exchanged triumphant looks. Luke was glad they had defied the law.

Laughing in an approving way, Euphoria took a dark stone out of her purse and held it near the candle flame. "Look. I brought this from the store today."

Aaron leaned forward and inspected the shiny gem in her palm. "It's a moss agate."

Euphoria held the stone at a level beside Luke's eyes. "Usually it's used for healing or to obtain wealth, but today it spoke to me."

Her hand resting against Luke's temple felt good.

"Notice anything?" Euphoria asked.

"It's the same color as his eyes." Psyche gave a student-to-teacher response.

Her look of awe must have alluded to some special importance of stones to people with the same eye color. Luke took the mottled agate and rubbed its smooth surface. He had to admit, the yellow and green flecks within the shiny brown looked remarkably like his eyes, at least what he could remember from the mirror.

"She's right, Dad."

"This is the stone of Scotland," Euphoria told Luke, "and I feel it's very important to you, but I don't know why. That's the troubling part of my work. The images are sometimes incomplete, and at times I make mistakes."

"A busy restaurant seems hardly the place." Luke hoped he didn't sound too obvious. "Maybe we can try to learn more later, in a quiet place."

"Good idea." Maybe Euphoria liked Luke's interest in her. "Keep the stone in your pocket until then," she said.

Luke did as she told him. The waiter brought the dinners to the correct persons, having understood English exceedingly well. Luke hungrily cut into the steak, Euphoria into her salad, Aaron his goose, and Psyche her *poulet aux peches et brandy*, as she insisted on calling it.

They all had *crème brûlée* for dessert.

With the last bite still in her mouth, Psyche said, "Aaron, I'd love to ride in your convertible. Would you take me?"

"Of course, if you folks don't mind." Aaron grinned at Euphoria and Luke.

Luke had a feeling they'd planned the conversation in advance but agreed readily, glad to have time alone with Euphoria.

She also seemed delighted. "I'll show your father the creek while you're gone."

The words "your father" surprised Luke until he remembered her odd request not to tell her his name. She still didn't know it. At least he hadn't told her. Who knew what she knew?

They arranged to meet in the parking lot an hour later. After the kids hurried off, Luke paid the bill and strolled out to the creek with Euphoria, her arm laced through his. For the first time tonight, she moved close enough that he could smell her perfume, spicy and fresh like herbal tea. The scent suited her.

At the water's edge they sat on a wooden bench secluded beneath the overhanging branches of an enormous cottonwood tree. They listened to the creek bubble and the crickets chatter. Voices of others out this summer night carried on the water, but their words did not.

Elated from wine, from this charming woman, and from the sheer pleasure of the place, Luke wanted to relax with Euphoria and ignore the sexual tension for a while. "This is nice. I'm glad you suggested the place." He leaned back and closed his eyes.

"Would you answer a question for me?"

"Why don't you just consult your gemstones and find out all you want to know about me?"

"Some things are blocked." Her voice quavered. "Especially when emotion is involved." Euphoria's words made a serious counterpoint to his teasing.

Luke regretted flustering her. "Ask me anything." He wondered what emotion she was feeling.

"Are you married?"

Luke sat up and gazed at her, glad she cared. "I'm a widower. Aaron's mother died in the World Trade Center disaster."

Pausing for a moment, Euphoria cast her eyes down. "I'm sorry to hear you've suffered such sadness, but I'm glad you are single."

Her effortless transparency inspired Luke to the same. "Five years is a long time. We've healed. Aaron and I have a good life."

"Please give me the agate." When he did, Euphoria held it in the space between them and rubbed it in the palms of her hands.

Leaf shadows played across her face while she studied Luke. Euphoria looked at home beneath a tree like a fairy in a glen. He could see her frown then close her eyes. A sigh moved her boobs up and down. Luke wanted to kiss her, but she looked too defenseless, opening herself as she had to the vibrations of the cosmos.

The fact that she was psychic, a sensitive as she called herself, made her more desirable than Luke had ever imagined. He'd given his mother grief over her psychic abilities. Strange, how the world turned around.

Another exotic sigh escaped Euphoria's lips, and her features softened. She looked a bit tuned out. "Once again Maryland comes to me. This is the same lifetime I have seen before. You were kind to me. I worked for you. Dangerous work. You were brave, a revolutionary. I don't understand the meaning, but the words 'smallpox' and 'party' come to me. That sounds very bizarre so I'm not sure I can trust the words. Why would anyone celebrate that awful disease?"

"Is it all right if I talk?" Luke whispered, not wanting to break the mood.

Euphoria nodded. "You were definitely a doctor in this lifetime and I was your nurse. It was an important time. The Revolution maybe."

"Were we in love?" Luke could imagine having loved her if she'd been anything like this.

"I cared for you, but you did not return the feeling. You had a great love, a woman who brought about your doom."

"Doom?" Fascinated despite the melodrama of the word, Luke thought she probably should write novels. She raised her closed hands in front of her. He laid his hands over hers, closed his eyes, and let her words pour over him. "What else do you see?"

"I keep seeing the infirmary where we did our work. The high table where patients lay. The cupboards where we kept the medicines and potions."

Once again the image of an old lattice-work cupboard popped into Luke's mind. The same one he saw the day of Aaron's birth. Could two people share one memory, or had he allowed his rational mind to succumb to Euphoria's belief? Surely he'd not become that weak willed.

"Your name is Luh…La…your name starts with L."

"Luke. My name is Luke Brock." He felt awed that she had guessed so well. "Lucus Brandon Brock, actually."

Euphoria's pretty eyes flew open. "That's not the name I was going to say. I almost had it. Lance or Lake or some weird thing."

"My name is Luke, and I like a woman named Euphoria very much." Luke leaned toward her and brushed her lips with a kiss. They tasted like Bordeaux when she responded.

He breathed in her warmth, so gentle in an intense sort of way.

"I'm glad you did that. Are you convinced now that we lived together in the eighteenth century?"

"I don't know if I even believe in reincarnation, but I admit I'd like to." That way Luke could see his mother again.

"Then you'd get to see your mother again, huh?"

Euphoria's gift for mental telepathy would take some getting used to. Luke wondered why he had thought of seeing Angie but not his wife. Setting the thought aside, he concentrated on this precious moment with Euphoria. "I don't know much of anything about the Revolution, but I've always been fascinated by the Civil War. In fact, I've attended a couple of reenactments, just for the fun of it. It may not make much sense to say so, but I've always had a sense of pride when I think about the Civil War."

"Perhaps you lived in both of those times. That's not unheard of. And you were a real patriot during the Revolution."

"I'll do some reading about the Revolution. That should prove interesting."

"Possibly. We could try another day to uncover our past with hypnosis."

Luke grinned. "You're on." He leaned toward her, anticipating another kiss.

"It's time to go meet the kids." Euphoria sounded sweet but certain.

"Damn." Luke rose and offered her his hand. She smiled and took it with a squeeze that felt like a bond. He wondered if she had an intuition about their future. He hoped so. After only one day, he felt very much at home with her.

Ten

Time Travelers

On Sunday morning, Luke and Aaron made their regular call to Mama and Papa before the Chacons left for mass. This time, because of the close proximity, Mama insisted Luke and Aaron come to Phoenix for dinner, always a big event at their house.

Luke's hope had been that, on the two-hour drive down the mountain, Aaron would confide some of his feelings about the big date the night before, but he said not a word, even when Luke point blank asked him questions. Aaron shrugged a lot, made a few grunts, and that was about it. Luke said how much he liked both women and that he hoped to date Euphoria again. Aaron just nodded. He'd never been so close-mouthed on any topic in all his life.

They had a good time at the Chacons' house. Mama still cried when she kissed Aaron, but Luke supposed that was the way grandmothers acted, at least those who'd lost a daughter. Aaron appeared accepting of her display as if he'd become used to it. In fact, his demeanor through the entire visit seemed subdued. Luke chalked the change up to distraction about Psyche.

It was fun to see all the cousins crowded in and around the little bungalow. They ate off paper plates in the backyard, and one of the teenage grandsons played Latino pop tunes on a guitar. He had wired his speakers into a rangy mesquite tree for the whole neighborhood to enjoy. They ate shrimp *chimichangas*, Luke's particular favorite of Mama's wide repertoire.

Late in the afternoon, after taking their leave of Melinda's family, Luke and Aaron stopped by the glass tower of a library in downtown Phoenix. Luke checked out some books on the American Revolution. It pleased him to fill out the paperwork for a new library card and use an Arizona address. He'd not been aware of feeling homesick but felt fairly certain now that his time in California would end soon even though he didn't yet have a fix on a different direction for his life.

When Luke and Aaron headed out of town on the freeway, Luke asked, "What would you think about moving back to Arizona after you graduate? There are some good universities here."

Aaron shrugged and wrapped his arms over the top of the steering wheel. "It depends on where we lived. Not in Phoenix, for sure."

"Oh, why not?"

"I've got way too many relatives here that don't look like me or act like me."

"You don't have to hang around with them, if you don't want to."

"Yeah, I know. It's a lot easier to do in California, though."

Because Luke had no idea what Aaron meant, his face must have shown his dismay.

"You know..." Aaron's cheeks flushed. "With an Anglo surname, nobody expects me to fraternize."

"Fraternize? You're talking wild here, son. These are your cousins. You may look Anglo, but you're half Hispanic. I'd think you would be proud." Prejudiced thoughts in his son's mind worried Luke. "Your mother was a good woman."

"I know."

"Mama and Papa are good people."

"I know. I love them, but—"

"But what, Aaron?"

98

Aaron crossed into the carpool lane and pressed the accelerator down. Luke watched the BMW speed past other cars. "Slow down."

"I'm sorry." Aaron eased off the gas pedal and returned to the right lane. "I don't know what I meant. I won't mention it again." He looked contrite, flipped on the radio, and punched the search buttons, his way of ending an uncomfortable conversation.

Perhaps Aaron had had some trouble regarding race that he had not confided to Luke. Maybe Psyche had said something hostile to Hispanics, but she didn't seem like the type, too free spirited.

In the days of their courtship, Melinda had worried that race would hinder their relationship. Luke had never considered it a problem, and in fact it never became one. Of course, being the child of a mixed marriage, Aaron had had no choice, as Luke and Melinda had. In retrospect, Luke realized that Aaron hadn't had a Hispanic, Indian, or black friend in recent years. All his school chums were white.

Wondering how well he understood his son anymore, Luke gazed out to the west. The dark crags of the magnificent Bradshaw Mountains played tricks of light and shadow with the setting sun.

Once they returned to their condo at Enchantment— Luke loved that name—he got a beer, propped himself up in bed, and opened a history book. The condo, a glorified hotel room with two bedrooms, a living room, a fridge, stove, and two-foot counter, had the same teal and sand colors on an Indian theme everywhere. Teal appliances were a new one on Luke. Melinda would most certainly have wanted a set of them.

Aaron's animated voice from a phone conversation carried into Luke's bedroom. Luke smiled, guessing the person on the other end of the line to be Psyche.

Luke understood relatively little about the theory of reincarnation, having not given it a thought in all the years since Angie used to talk about it. Even so, it entertained him to think of himself in a different time. He felt curious to learn about the Revolution.

When he was back in Los Angeles, Luke seldom read late into the night because running the firm required a clear head for long work days. But, what the hell was a vacation for? After reading about every battle from Lexington and Concord through Valley Forge, right up to Cornwallis's surrender at Yorktown, Luke fell into exhausted sleep about three in the morning.

For the next two days he made a concentrated effort to come up to speed on the Revolution. He wanted to call Euphoria as soon as he found anything to report. It wouldn't do for too much time to pass. She might think he had lost interest in her. What a mistake that would be!

After Luke had read everything he could find about the war itself, he went back through some of the ancillary history on the makings of the war. He related to the animosity about the heavy taxation and soldiers forcing themselves into the homes of private citizens, billeting they called it.

The colonists lived through some rough times. King George the Second and King George the Third both limited printing presses and supplies to prevent communication among the colonies. Money from Britain, France, Spain, Portugal, and the Netherlands, as well as Indian wampum made doing business impossibly confusing. Insidiously, the British intercepted ships at sea and literally stole the colonists' cargo.

Anyone could understand why Thomas Paine's phrase "these are the times that try men's souls" struck a response with the colonists. On a personal level though, nothing he read about seemed familiar. Luke almost called Euphoria to tell her he'd failed to find any connection.

He came across a diary entry by a soldier who mentioned the belief that his life had been saved by a "smallpox party."

Bingo! Euphoria's exact words.

Luke phoned the research librarian in Phoenix immediately. Within the hour he had the amazing answer.

While Aaron putted golf balls across the teal carpet, Luke asked, "You going to need the car for the rest of the day?"

"Nah, I think I'll catch a movie in the rec hall."

Luke excitedly called the Crystal Cave, but the manager wouldn't let him talk to Euphoria, so he made an appointment for four o'clock to have a reading with her and chafed until the hour drew near. Aaron had already left for the movie so Luke wrote a note to say he'd gone to meet Euphoria and didn't know when he'd return.

Because he arrived a half hour early, Luke wandered around downstairs in the damnedest looking store he'd ever seen. New Age music played through a sound system, with notes that held so long they made him go bonkers waiting for the end of the musical phrase. The atmosphere carried a heavy fragrance.

The owners had gone all out to make the interior look like a cave with glittering stalactites hanging from above. Items for sale, like books, gems, jewelry, and tools for witchcraft, had been laid out on stalagmites. Maybe he had those terms backwards, but the store entertained him as well as anything could until the appointment.

The manager, a tall, willowy woman with nicotine-stained fingers grinned at him. "Are you Luke?"

When he nodded she said he could go up and pointed to an outside staircase. Luke hurried out the door and dashed up the wooden stairs.

Elegant in a long white dress, Euphoria stood at the top and called his name. She seemed surprised to see him, but not unpleasantly so. Luke got that hint because she gave him a quick kiss as soon as she ushered him in and closed the door of the tiny room, hardly bigger than a closet. The same music played as downstairs.

"Didn't you know I was coming?" Luke asked. "I gave my name to the woman on the phone."

"We don't get the clients' names, just their first initial. All I knew was L. Otherwise, some people might think our intuitions are faked or we're checking their records or something." Euphoria offered him a seat, and they both sat at an ice cream table, its chairs covered with lemon-colored cloth. She reached above her head and flipped a switch that turned off the music. "You came for a reading? That's not what I thought you'd do."

"Why?" Luke enjoyed the fact that he had disconcerted her.

Pushing aside a royal blue pouch that clinked with gems, she laid her hands on the table and looked at them a moment. "Well...I guess I thought you'd ask me for a date."

"Glad to know you'll accept if I do."

Euphoria gave him a sidewise glance, laughter shining behind her eyes. "I didn't say I'd accept."

"What a tease you are, but that's not why I came." Luke covered her hands with his. "Remember when you were trying to get vibes from the moss agate and you came up with the words 'smallpox party'?"

"Yes, it seems too bizarre to—"

"You were right. Smallpox vaccinations hadn't been invented yet. In fact, they came along ten years or so after the Revolution. But before it, they had a procedure called inoculation. It was a lot more dangerous and even outlawed in some colonies. People got together in someone's home. A doctor would come and inoculate the people with live, active disease pustules. Then he would stay for two weeks, tending them. Everybody knew some would die. Still, they had a whole lot better odds than people without the procedure. Know what people called those two-week stays?"

"Smallpox parties!"

"Yes, indeed, my sweet lady, you have hit the psychic mark this time."

"It must have been what we were doing in that infirmary. You and I. It makes sense now that those words, such an unusual combination, would come through for me. I should never doubt my impressions."

"There's more!" Luke leaned back and almost tipped the little chair over in his enthusiasm to play his trump. "One of the places where the procedure was outlawed—"

"Maryland!"

"Right you are."

"No wonder I felt so much danger." Euphoria stared at him as if they'd just discovered the fountain of youth.

Luke summarized the research he'd been doing and tried to give her a flavor of the times, at least from the political perspective. He saw her glancing at a wind-up kitchen timer. She must have set it before she let him in.

"I'm sorry, Luke. I've got a four thirty appointment." Euphoria squeezed his hand. "What do you think we should do next?"

Even though he hated to leave with so much to tell her yet, Luke rose. "That's your call. Can I pick you up for dinner, if I have a car, that is? Your daughter and my son seem to be monopolizing it lately."

A tiny nervous twitch crossed Euphoria's face. "How about tomorrow evening?"

"All right." Luke had forgotten she might have had a life before he showed up in Sedona on his white steed. "I'll look forward to it. Shall I pick you up here?"

"I'll meet you at Rosalia's at six."

Luke had no clue where that was, but he had twenty-four hours to find it. He didn't feel quite as grand as when he came in. The idea that Euphoria might have a steady man drooped his feathers. "See you," he said blithely.

On his way back to the condo with the top down, Luke stopped at a drive-through pizza place. Aaron liked pepperoni best, but Luke decided to splurge and get an everything Hawaiian to perk up his spirits. Pineapples rated as the top fruit of all time. He amused himself by speculating whether he'd had a lifetime in the islands. Maui or maybe Kauai. Probably Oahu. Definitely Oahu, he decided, before he started to condemn himself as far too frivolous about the idea of reincarnation. How could such a giddy one as he anticipate an adventure with a time traveler like dear Euphoria?

The woman made him so hot every time he looked at her that Luke had avoided her in part for the past four days so he wouldn't appear too eager. Maybe she did have another man in her life. So? Was Luke not her brave physician long time gone now returned and wanting to make love to her? That counted for something. That counted for a lot. She'd not be able to resist him. Luke had caught her imagination, he thought. He hoped. He would have to wait until tomorrow to know for certain.

After parking the BMW, Luke picked up the warm pizza box and trotted to the door. Just as he was about to turn the key in the lock, he heard a giggle, definitely female, issue from his condo. He stepped back in surprise. Then he heard it again. He'd heard that laugh before. Doubtless it came from Psyche and doubtless it came from the general area of Aaron's bedroom.

What the hell was going on? Should he barge in? Did his baby son know what he was doing? There must have been an angel sitting on Luke's shoulder because his second thought came through loud and clear.

Get a grip. Aaron can take care of himself.

Rather undone, Luke walked to the fountain in the front of the resort office, sat on a stone ledge, and opened the pizza box. Each piece had about three pineapple bits on it along with olives, onions, and green pepper slices. He took the pineapple bits from adjacent pieces and laid them all on one. He scooped up that gloppy piece and bit into the juiciest pizza he'd ever had. Man, it tasted good.

His son was getting laid. And by one sweet girl. Hallelujah. Luke should go out and light a bonfire by way of celebration. Single parenting had its drawbacks. He tended to express an excess of mothering to make up for the loss of Melinda. This situation tonight let Luke experience the bonding that only fathers can know with their sons, whether spoken or not.

Years of barely adequate and often duty-provoked sex with Melinda had crowded out the bittersweet memory of their first few months of married life. She'd been so willing and so afraid. When she conquered her fear of being hurt, she began to enjoy sex. For a while, it occupied her mind as much as it did Luke's, the glory months of their marriage that came to a stop when she got pregnant, never to return again. Once upon a time, Luke had felt rage about her emotional rejection. Now, it seemed like ancient history.

Luke hung out in the bar until it closed then slipped into his bedroom, full of pizza, beer, and happiness for his son. Luke had safely tucked away his feelings for Melinda. The grief had passed. Thinking of her this evening in past tense had been easy for him. The time had come for him to have a new woman in his life.

The next morning Luke awoke to the aroma of brewed coffee. In the kitchen, his generally log-headed son looked bright-eyed and anxious, but Luke took no notice.

"Hungry, Dad?"

"There's left-over pizza in the fridge."

Aaron laid a paper plate full of bacon strips in the microwave. "I know, but I thought we'd have a real breakfast, a man's breakfast." He cracked some eggs into a bowl and whisked them.

"Fine with me." Luke repressed a laugh and sampled the coffee, a bit strong but not bad for a beginner cook. They had some idle chat about whether to go back to L.A. for the weekend but both knew they wouldn't.

As Aaron set the man's breakfast on the small table, he said, "Hope you don't mind. I...uh...sort of promised Psyche I'd take her to Flagstaff shopping this afternoon. Are you okay with that?"

"Well, I've got a date tonight. With the mother."

"Okay." Aaron exhaled a long sigh.

Aaron lowered those soulful black eyes. He didn't normally try to manipulate, so Luke wondered whether he correctly interpreted his son's expression. What did it matter? The kid was only going to be young once. "How about you drop me off in town before you go?"

"Thanks, Dad." Aaron crunched bacon thoughtfully. "About Euphoria? She may have some things to do or work out or something."

Even though Luke quizzed his son about the enigmatic statement, Aaron refused to say more about Euphoria or about his own escapade the night before.

That evening Luke had high hopes that he might get laid, too. Like daughter, like mother, he promised himself. He invested a good deal of time in imagining what Euphoria would be like in bed. Would she anticipate his moves? She was psychic, after all. He hoped she'd have a wanton facet to her. The secret of her sexual behavior seemed tied in his mind to the other secret of a possible past life.

Though he felt rather silly admitting it to himself, Luke looked forward to finding out more about this mysterious doctor who performed illegal surgeries during the Revolution. It sounded more like a plot for a novel than his life. But the whole idea intrigued him.

Rosalia's turned out to be an open-air taco stand with picnic tables in back. Luke sat at one to wait for Euphoria and gazed at splendid Bell Rock. Many tourists did the same. No trees marred the nearly perfect shape as the ruddy dome rose above the other mountains against the cloudless western sky.

With a small smile, Euphoria slid in beside Luke, close enough that her thigh touched his. Her long dress of pale pink somehow reflected rosy highlights in her hair. She wore the same bracelets and necklace. She gestured toward Bell Rock. "Do you see any aliens?"

"Not yet but I'm hoping. I've heard this is one of their landing sites." Luke put his arm around her and turned her face up for a kiss. Her reddened eyes stopped him. "Is anything wrong?"

"I've been seeing a man," Euphoria said with her riveting policy of full disclosure. "We've been involved in a relationship for over a year."

"Are you sure you want me to know this?"

"I've told him it's over. I feel sad because I'm very fond of him, but you are on my karmic path." Euphoria looked suddenly exhausted. "I had to make a space for you."

Touched, Luke enfolded her. She smelled like peppermint, her hair soft against his face. "You didn't have to do that."

"Yes, I did." Euphoria's cheek moved against his chest as she spoke. "You needn't feel obligated. However it turns out, I had to be free for you to pass through my life. Or stay, whichever it turns out to be."

This could possibly be the most perfect woman in the world in Luke's arms at this moment. He kissed her trembling lips with the full force of his affection. He expected an erection but instead felt swept by a longing to protect her. Any person who made herself so vulnerable deserved the best from others. Luke intended to give his best. The long kiss bound them together in hope.

Afterward, Luke pulled away enough to look at her. "I don't know how this will end, but you can trust me."

"I know." Her tone reflected far more nonchalance than previously. That teasing grin returned. "I've known all along how you felt about me."

"This dating a psychic is not for the faint hearted." Luke squeezed her and felt a pleasing comradeship. Euphoria was his girlfriend. He had a girlfriend. How cool was that?

After they had tacos and beer, Luke bummed a ride from her.

Euphoria let out a hearty laugh. "This is the guy who buys a thousand-dollar bottle of wine and can't afford wheels?" Somehow she got more enjoyment out of that than Luke did.

In the parking lot, they found her Beetle of early Nineties vintage with curly designs painted on it.

Luke could have guessed she'd own a car like that. "Aaron and I should drive over to L.A. and bring my car back sometime soon."

"You could fly over." Euphoria rolled down her window, pulled out onto the highway, and headed toward Enchantment. "I'd go with you if you asked me, and we could drive your car back together."

With a good deal more bravado than he felt, Luke said, "Thanks, but no thanks." She pressed him for a reason. "I don't fly."

"You, a successful businessman, don't fly? That's hard to believe."

"Believe it." Luke didn't feel ready to go into all the details of the people in his family who had died in or because of airplanes. Besides, Euphoria would just say he was afraid. He didn't want her to know that. "It's early for you to be taking me home. Want to go somewhere?"

"How about back in time?" Euphoria gave him a challenging stare. The wind blew her hair around her face. She looked rather out of time herself, maybe a flower child of the Sixties.

"I'm game if you are."

Back in his condo, Euphoria turned into Miss Efficiency. While Luke found a requested pad and pen, she laid pillows on the couch in a tilt-back arrangement, turned the radio on, and filled glasses with water. She told Luke to go to the bathroom. That made him laugh.

Undaunted, Euphoria said, "If you are able to go into a trance, you don't want to lose it for some foolish reason like having to pee."

So Luke went. When he returned she had softened the lights. Violin music played in the background. She squirted her perfume in the air, pungent peppermint.

Euphoria sat on the coffee table with the pen and pad beside her. "Lie back on the pillows and relax."

"That might be hard to do with you so close." Luke gave her what he hoped looked like a sexy smile, but she was taking the proceedings seriously, so he thought he should too.

When Luke felt comfortable and closed his eyes, she touched his hand and began to speak in a soft, mellow tone. She told him he would always be able to hear her and answer her questions in English. She asked him to imagine a stairway going down. She counted thirty steps slowly then did it again.

At first Luke enjoyed her voice and pictured her pretty face. About the fourth or fifth time she went through the routine he began to lose track of the step numbers. He'd only had one beer so he was okay on that, but he wondered whether he had fallen asleep or not.

Luke's mind felt empty, a very odd experience not to have thoughts except the ones Euphoria put there. She said he would see pictures of people and events and not to question them. Just accept whatever came. She said it would be easy to travel through time. Luke floated along on a boat of tranquility woven by her words.

"Imagine a happy event when you were forty," Euphoria said.

Luke saw a surprise birthday party Melinda and the office staff had given him. He didn't remember the event the typical way. Instead, he saw a snapshot of it with himself in the picture. He could see blue balloons bouncing and Melinda hugging him. One of the secretaries handed him a package with a big green bow. Aaron and the computer technician sat at her console.

Euphoria spoke with gentle force. "You are flowing back through the years of your life. Stop when you see an unusual event."

In his mind's eye, Luke saw Aaron, a kid again, screaming as they sat in a roller coaster high above Disney's California Adventure. Aaron looked funny in a yellow and white striped shirt and Mickey Mouse ears.

"You are traveling on back through your life as Luke. You are becoming younger, a youth again. Let the years flow away. Stop when you remember an important event."

Luke burst out of the pool, a kid again. The diving teacher squatted nearby, a stopwatch in his hand. Angie sat with a spattering of other adults in the bleachers. With an expression of approval, she waved to Luke. He had just passed his diving test. He felt proud.

"Now, I want you to move on down the corridor of your life, back into the time of your childhood and babyhood. Stop when you remember some important event."

After a long stillness, Luke let out a babyish squeal. Incredibly, he pushed up bottom first from the floor, toddled to the television, and slapped happily at the screen. This perception didn't seem like memory but a reenactment of the moment.

Mommy Angie turned off the television and whisked him into her arms. He began to cry because the image went dark.

"Oh, is my sweet little Luke sad? *Top Cat's* over. Look at what I've got for you." Angie plopped him into a chrome-legged highchair and tied a bib around his neck.

Luke grabbed Cheerios spread on the tray and stuffed them into his mouth with both hands. He loved their sweet crunchy flavor. Putting things in his mouth was his favorite thing to do.

Daddy Russell, in Army fatigues, banged the screen door and dropped a metal lunch box on the kitchen table. He gave Angie a kiss on the cheek and opened the refrigerator door with oil-stained hands. "Well, what did the doctor say?"

"It's epilepsy. The test confirmed the original diagnosis."

"God damn it." Daddy grabbed an opener and popped the top on a bottle of beer. "What are we going to do?"

Daddy sounded so scary that Luke cried out.

Mommy took Luke out of the highchair and smoothed his hair with her warm hand. "Take care of him. Make sure he gets his pills every day. There's nothing else to do."

Her touch stopped Luke's tears. Daddy paced back and forth between the tiny living room and kitchen. He smelled sweaty sour. There was something wrong about him, but Luke didn't understand what.

Mommy took a covered cup from the counter and handed it to Luke. He slurped orange juice happily.

"Look," Mommy said, "he's holding his own cup like any normal three-year-old."

"I'm surprised he can do that. The kid's gonna grow up to be an idiot." Daddy took a long drink

"No, he's not. He's a smart child."

"Ridiculous." Daddy stared at Mommy with a very mean face.

Mommy told him, "The doctor says the best we can do for Luke is treat him like any other child. The seizures have caused him to get a slow start. We need to make sure he gets advantages so he can grow up and learn like other kids."

"It'll never happen." Daddy held out his arms. "We'd better find a place for him before he's old enough to know any better."

"A place? What the hell do you mean?"

"You're making me say it, Angie. You know what I mean. He's going into an institution. We have to do it."

"Russell, the child was watching cartoons today and trying to talk to the cats. He was following the action with his eyes. He's bright, and I know he can learn. So what if he's a little behind other kids. He'll catch up."

"We talked about this before. Don't fight me. God damn it, you fight me on everything."

Mommy stopped talking and got tears on her cheeks. "No, I won't agree."

Luke couldn't stand to see Mommy sad. He dropped the cup on the floor and cried. She held him against her breast.

"Even your mother agrees with me," Daddy said. "She wants to put the kid in. It's the best thing for him."

"That's her answer to everything." Mommy's hands trembled while she shifted Luke to balance on her hip. He loved to ride like that. He could see everywhere. "Just like she put my brother and me in the orphanage. She was having one of her nervous breakdowns. Well, I'm not having a nervous breakdown, and I'm keeping my boy with me, no matter what."

"That's it!" Daddy threw the beer bottle across the kitchen. It skipped once and rolled to a stop beneath the sink. "Nobody can reason with you. I'm finished." He stalked down the hall and into the bedroom.

"Good." Mommy sat in the wooden rocker.

Luke felt her heart beating as they rocked back and forth. He knew in his mind how much he loved her and hoped she could hear his thoughts.

Daddy banged the closet door and stomped around for a few minutes then emerged, carrying a duffel bag. He glared at Mommy. "I'm going to volunteer for active duty.

Anything to get away from you and the brat." He went out the door, and the unlatched screen clattered behind him.

Mommy clasped Luke to her and cooed, "Everything's going to be just fine. We'll go out west. We'll make a life for ourselves, and you'll always have a home with me." She looked into Luke's eyes. "Do you understand me, Luke?"

Whatever out west was, Luke wanted to go. He squeezed her cheeks and wished his hands were bigger. He wished he was bigger all over. He felt so helpless. "Luke go bye-bye."

Great silence suffused the moment point. Luke lost contact with his own mind and felt confused.

Euphoria's voice rescued him when it took on a commanding tone. "You are going back, back in time. The decades are flowing away. Centuries are turning. You are looking for an event around the time of the Revolution, an important event. When you find it, you will tell me."

Vast was the only way Luke could describe his own mind. He felt immense. He contained everything. He rested in an endless present. Very odd the way he needed nothing yet expected something.

Faintly from far away, he heard a baby crying. He strained to hear.

"Tell me what you are seeing." Euphoria's voice intruded, but with it came a clear picture.

Like a fly landing on an apple pie cooling on a windowsill, Luke's consciousness zeroed in. It was not himself as a baby that he saw any longer. "Two babies. They are crying." Joy filled him. They looked beautiful with matted hair and flailing arms and legs. "Oh, they are alive. They are healthy." Luke felt a huge sense of relief.

"Where are you? Look around you."

"I'm standing at the examining table in my infirmary. These are my twins, a boy and a girl. Our first child died, poor little Aaron." Luke felt great sadness, a loss so huge he had not known how to rise above it, but now he had something to live for.

"Look down at your clothing. What are you wearing?"

Luke thought that an odd request but complied. "I have on a white shirt with sleeves rolled up, knee-length trousers, and long white stockings. My hair is pulled back by a ribbon."

"Is anyone with you, a nurse perhaps?"

"Just me and the children."

"What year is this?"

"1767. I could never forget. A year like no other."

"Where do you live?" Euphoria's voice intruded.

Although Luke wanted only to gaze at the babies, touch them, bond with them in a physical way, he felt required to respond. "In the front of the house. My infirmary is in back."

"I meant what city do you live in?"

"Don't live in a city."

"A town, perhaps?"

It seemed like very hard work to answer. "I can't remember."

"That's all right. Do you know what country you live in?"

"We're subjects of the Crown, unfortunately. Maryland Colony. Is that what you mean?" Luke felt annoyed at the interfering questions when he needed to examine the children. "I'm looking for a mole or some identifying mark."

"On yourself, do you mean?"

"No. I don't know." Luke felt bewildered and lost focus.

"That's all right. We're going to leave this moment and go to another memory in the same lifetime. I'd like you to go back in time until you are a boy or young man. When you see a scene from your boyhood, tell me."

Pictures streamed past of a boy running in fog, riding on a schooner, swinging, playing with a hoop-shaped toy. They went by too fast for explanation. Then Luke fixed on a familiar scene. He saw two girls, maybe ten or twelve years old, standing in front of him. He realized that he looked down on them because he was taller, probably six feet or more. The girl with black curls wanted him to take her sailing.

The other little girl with brown hair and a plain dress shrank back, but she wanted to go too. Luke squinted to look at the girls. He should recognize them. Then he knew. The black-haired girl was his sister, the other Euphoria as she had been in another time.

How Luke recognized her he didn't understand. He felt a desire to know more and willed myself into a greater clarity.

Right away he thought of himself as a much younger man. He had just come home from a war he hated. He felt anguish about the horrible things people did to each other. The little brown-haired girl had been brutalized by an Indian in the way only girls could be. He hoped the little girl would get over her fear of men. He wanted always to be kind to her, and maybe that would help. He'd known her all her short life. She lived in the cabin in the woods. Luke knew a great deal about her, even her name.

A loud voice intruded. Someone yelled in Luke's ear. He felt pulled back from a very long way. He wanted to stay and learn more about the girl, the little sister, and himself.

"Luke, answer me," Euphoria shouted. "You will come out of the trance when I count three. One, two, three."

His eyes felt like they weighed a hundred pounds a piece, but he opened them anyway to see Euphoria bending over him, an anxious expression on her face. "Ah, so this is why you wanted me to go back in time," Luke whispered.

"Thank goodness. Are you all right?" Euphoria sounded befuddled now. "You stopped responding. I didn't know what happened to you. What were you seeing?"

"You. You were there. Now I know your real name. You don't have to tell me."

"You do?"

"Your name was Emily."

Euphoria gasped. "How did you know?"

Chuckling, Luke reached up and pulled her down into his arms. "You acted like you were afraid of me, but you secretly loved me. I tried to talk to you, but you were too shy and afraid. You're not shy in this lifetime, though, are you?"

"Oh, Luke, you were really there. How exciting." Her laughter rippled through him.

"You're the one who's exciting." Seeing her dear face then and her even dearer face now turned him on. "I want to make love to you."

"Now?"

"Unless you're willing to wait two more centuries." Luke crushed her in his embrace and kissed her sweet mouth over and over until an erection began to press against her through their clothes. Making love with her was going to be so much fun.

"My dearest Luke," she murmured, "please stop."

Luke couldn't believe his ears.

Hair a disheveled mess, Euphoria climbed off and stood, above him. As she straightened her dress, she said, "I'm sorry to dampen your enthusiasm and I really do feel a commitment to you, but this is just too soon for me. Only this morning, I..."

Mention of the other man deflated Luke's intentions. It crossed his mind to pull her down and ravish her. He'd probably get away with it, but he had promised to be trustworthy.

"I'll call you tomorrow." Looking embarrassed, Euphoria picked up her purse and headed for the door. "It's going to be lovely when it happens."

Eleven

Rule by Naming

Upstate New York

The boy's head hurt. He held his hands over his throbbing ears but couldn't shut out the noise. The Warsaw Concerto squawked through the sound system but not enough to drown out his screeching grandparents. He crouched on the tile floor in the dark laundry room and felt around under the cabinets for his Spiderman. It had to be there. It had dropped only moments before.

Finally, he felt its rubbery, wiry surface and pulled it out. After dusting the cobwebs off the red and blue action figure, he held it close to his face, unable to see the white eyes but knowing they were there and that he would be heard and understood. "This is a job for Spiderman. Go, Spiderman." He ran the action figure along the door to the knob, opened it, and slipped outside. He tried to close the door silently but the hinges creaked.

Grandfather yelled from the living room, "Where are you, Kendall? You get back in here."

"Leave the boy alone. He's scared."

"Shut the hell up, woman!"

The grass felt good on his bare feet as he ran across the yard lit by the moon and a streetlight down the way. He wished Grandmother would run away with him. Why did she have to argue with the old man and get him madder and madder?

117

"Kendall?" Grandmother's voice called. "Come back, honey, everything will be all right."

He wished they would stop using that silly name. It wasn't his, anyway. Tears slid down his cheeks. He wanted his mommy. He wanted his daddy. He wanted them to come and take him home. "Come on, Spiderman." He zoomed the action figure over his head as if it were flying then let it go.

Spiderman flew above his head as he dashed into the shed under a big tree. He loved the wonderful toy because it flew like it had batteries in it. Once Kendall got inside the shed, the action figure dropped to the ground at his feet.

In the dark he could smell the warm sourness of rabbit poop. He pulled on a string connected to an overhead bulb, which illuminated wire cages set on top of work tables. The rabbits were separated by color—browns, whites, and blacks—in different cages. On the opposite wall hung rakes, shovels, and brooms. He liked the way they looked with the same spaces between them.

"Hi, buddies." He felt happy to see the rabbits. He loved the quiet, cozy shed. His ears didn't hurt any more.

He picked up the action figure and wedged its suction cup through a square of cage wire. Inside, something wriggled beside his favorite rabbit. He opened the cage door and ran his hand over the soft reddish brown fur. He loved all the rabbits but this one especially. He loved them because they were so quiet and so nice to touch.

"Hi Karim, how you doing this evening?" he asked the rabbit. "You got something?"

When he gently edged the rabbit away, five skinny, little critters with their ears back against their heads rooted around near the big rabbit. They looked weird like little dark brown puppies or something. He knew they had to be bunnies though because they were so wonderfully quiet. Puppies made all kinds of nasty noises.

"I'm going to name all of you, and everybody will have to use your real name, not some fake one." He pointed to each baby bunny in turn and said, "Your name is Morfie. Your name is Almie, Your name is Tally, and your name is Loog." He thought long and hard but couldn't think of any name for the fifth bunny.

He picked up the unnamed bunny. It felt slimy and slick. He had trouble holding onto it, so he grabbed it around the neck with both hands, and then he had a terrific idea. "I'll call you Harry. I'll name you after Grandfather." He put just a little bit of pressure against the bunny's neck. The bunny's legs flailed. He squeezed harder and gave a little twist, and the bunny slumped on his hand. It sort of looked like a fat hot dog without a bun. He laid it under the mother rabbit. "Sorry, Harry." He looked at the bunny named Loog. "I'll do you tomorrow."

Grandfather's voice sounded loud. "Kendall, I know you're in there. Get away from my rabbits."

He closed the cage, yanked Spiderman off, and hurried toward the door. "Coming, Harry."

"Don't call me Harry, you little brat."

"This is a job for Spiderman." He zoomed the action figure in the air but it wouldn't take off on its own, so he held it above his head and ran toward Harry.

When he reached his grandfather, he began to bang Spiderman on his grandfather's knee.

"Quit that." Grandfather swooped him up in the air as if he were Spiderman.

It was no fun to fly this way. He felt afraid and yelled, "Put me down."

"Shut up." Grandfather stalked across the yard toward the house.

Grandmother stood on the back steps, crying. Her gray hair flew wild around her head, and her bathrobe hung open, showing her pajamas. "Don't hurt him, Harry." She took a long drag on her brown cigarette." Please, hit me if you have to hit somebody." Smoke trailed out through her mouth when she talked.

"Why don't you tell the whole neighborhood our business?" Grandfather stomped inside the house and dropped him. "Now, get to bed, you brat, before I do something you'll regret."

Twelve

The Price of Fear

Sedona

At Enchantment, Luke treaded water in a cove, one of many small swimming pools among artificial rocks overgrown with vines. Redwood tables and chairs beneath teal umbrellas dotted the terrace. People swam nearby but the décor so broke up the landscape that the illusion of privacy prevailed. Clad in black swim trunks, Aaron sat in a nearby deck chair, reading a spy novel on loan from Psyche.

That lovely girl's mother and the previous evening filled Luke's thoughts. He didn't know which fascinated him more, the seeming memory of his past life or the lovely Euphoria. Between them he could think of nothing else. He had a million questions. Had he made up all of the images? Was he so taken with Euphoria that he'd allowed her suggestions to parade themselves across his mind as truth?

If she had been his nurse in a long ago past, why had their paths crossed now? He had never believed in fate, rather that lives and fortunes befell everyone through free will. But things might be different if people came into this lifetime with baggage from another one. And more complicated.

Stretching out on his back, Luke floated in the placid water, gentle on his skin. He'd been smart to wear sun glasses as protection against the bright noonday sun.

What would Euphoria say about the regression when they finally got a chance to talk about it later this evening? Would she relent and let him make love to her? He would simply have to insist, or be so charming she would beg for sex. How fine would that be? All his questions could wait until after. Processing a past life regression sounded like the perfect conversation while lying in bed after lovemaking. He could see it all now. He conjured the image of a naked Euphoria writhing in the throes of a climax. The vivid image jolted him.

In point of fact, the images throughout the regression had been equally as vivid, clearer in his mind than some real memories. How could that be? His imagination seemed unruly these days. Maybe the atmosphere of Sedona caused that to happen, but definitely something had changed inside him. He remembered how his mother had described her visions as bright and clear images that commanded attention. Now he understood somewhat better why she had insisted on their veracity. He had to give her credit for making some correct predictions. He'd always thought his father left because of the epilepsy. Seeing the scene through his three-year-old mind had been poignant as well as amazing.

With much the same clarity, Luke remembered the emotions of that other self from the regression. He could swear he felt the grief of losing the baby and the poignancy of recognizing him reborn because of the mole on his shoulder. Those baby boys both had moles and one even bore the name Aaron.

How silly. Luke had a son named Aaron with a mole, so that name thing showed all this regression business as prefabricated nonsense. Damn, Luke dreaded the thought that he'd gotten as loopy as his mother.

Across the deck, Aaron slapped away a fly on his shoulder. Something looked wrong about that motion and jerked Luke out of his reverie. He didn't see the mole and swam the few strokes it took to navigate across the pool. "Hey, Aaron, what happened to your mole?"

Placing a finger on a line of text in his book, Aaron glanced up with a confused expression then rubbed his shoulder. "The doctor took it off at my last checkup."

"Why didn't you tell me?"

"Wasn't important." With a shrug, Aaron returned his attention to the page.

It amazed Luke that he hadn't noticed. That mole represented the sacred and beautiful connection he had made at the moment of his son's birth. How could it be gone and so casually gone, into the bargain? Luke considered himself guilty of taking too much for granted. He had grown accustomed to looking at Aaron without really seeing. Luke no doubt did the same in many aspects of his life. From now on he intended to pay closer attention to the details around him, to focus on the moments and not let his mind race away in scattered thought.

With a glance at his watch, Aaron slammed the book closed. "I've got a date tonight. Do you?"

"Sure." Luke grinned as he climbed out of the pool. "Want to double date?" Dripping water, he grabbed a towel from a stack of perfectly folded ones. He considered all this sharing great fun. He had hoped to get Euphoria alone, but what the hell? This chance to build memories with his son was important too.

"I'd like to have the car tonight."

"Hey, you had it last night," Luke teased as he sat in the chair next to his son and dried off. "I'll flip you for it. Got a quarter?"

"Nevermind, you can have it. I'll take a taxi." Aaron looked far more serious than Luke felt. "I'm going to fly home and drive the Jaguar back."

The concept of allowing Aaron to get on an airplane was very distasteful. "I'd rather you didn't. It's no big deal to share the car. Hey, I'll call Euphoria. She'll come and get me. You go on and have fun."

Aaron tapped the chair arms and took a deep breath. He looked as if he were trying to build his courage. "I'm going to do it because I want to. I'm seventeen, and I've never ridden on a plane."

"It's not that much fun, it's like riding an air bus." It gave Luke the shivers to think of his son getting on a plane.

"We need both cars, now that we've got...you know...friends." Rising, Aaron strode toward the condo.

Luke hustled along behind him, past palm trees and planters filled with petunias. "I don't want you on the road alone."

"Then go with me." Aaron glanced back, challenge written all over his face. He knew full well what he was asking.

"All right." Luke didn't seem to be making much headway. "We'll drive home tomorrow and then caravan back with both cars."

"That's two whole days out of our lives for no good reason. I'm not a kid any more."

"What does that mean?"

"It's a six-hour trip."

"If you drive like a lunatic. Eight hours is what it took us." Luke shuddered at how scratched and banged up the Jaguar could get on such a trip, almost as worrisome as the risk of having a banged-up son.

They walked the rest of the way to the condo in silence. Aaron waited while Luke unlocked the door then stepped inside and took hold of his bedroom door. "You know what, Dad, I think you're afraid." His eyes flared with anger.

"I'm just concerned for your safety." How lame Luke sounded.

"No, you're afraid. Why can't you admit it?"

"You'd better watch your mouth!" Luke had never mentioned his feelings about airplanes to anyone and wasn't likely to now, especially to some smart-aleck son.

"You're holding me back." With a pained expression on his face, Aaron walked into his bedroom and slammed the door.

Luke heard Aaron making calls and moving around in the bedroom. By all rights, Luke should be able to walk into the room, even without knocking. It wasn't a matter of privacy for study or friends. Aaron had insulted him.

Somehow in a manner Luke couldn't articulate he knew it would be a very bad idea to barge in. The balance of power had changed between them. It didn't seem possible that the boy he'd brought to Sedona could turn into a man overnight. Getting laid never had that great an impact on anybody. Something else was at work, and damned if Luke knew what.

After Luke changed into dress slacks and shirt, he opened a beer and sat on the couch. He tried in vain to read the newspaper. Another terrorist attack with sordid details couldn't hold his interest, so he fidgeted and waited until Aaron wanted to talk.

Finally, Aaron came out of the bedroom, carrying a shaving kit and the paperback. "I've called Psyche and postponed our date until tomorrow night." He sounded calmer even though his voice quavered. "I'm really sorry, Dad. I wish it didn't have to be like this. I'll see you tomorrow night." He went out the door.

Setting the beer can on the coffee table, Luke followed his son outside. "Damn it, Aaron. Don't do this." He wanted to take Aaron across his knee and spank him, but that was out of the question, considering he stood almost a foot taller. Luke had never felt more ineffective in his life.

Stiff-backed Aaron strode down the hill from the condo where a taxi waited. He said to the driver, "Take me to the airport." Without glancing back, he climbed in, and the taxi pulled away.

Luke regretted having given Aaron his own credit card, but the boy had never disobeyed before. He'd been the model of good citizenship and trustworthiness. Luke had considered giving Aaron financial independence a good thing, a reward for being the perfect kid. Having a piece of ass must have made him crazy, after all.

Pissed beyond words, Luke dashed through the shrub-fringed parking lot to Aaron's BMW and jumped behind the wheel. Leaving the top down, he screeched out of the parking space. He would outrun the taxi and talk some sense into the kid. He pulled the BMW onto the highway and followed the taxi, which grew vague in the distance, despite broad daylight.

Suddenly his preposterous actions struck Luke. Chasing down his own kid like an irresponsible parent? Forcing his will on his child like some schoolyard bully? He didn't know what he should do and wished to hell he'd had a father of his own so he would have some idea of what to do in this stupid situation. He needed to talk to somebody. Being a single parent sucked. Luke ached for just one good memory of a father who had shown him what it was like to be a man.

Bad as he hated to admit it, he'd probably better leave the whole business alone until some rational way of proceeding occurred to him.

The taxi veered south on the highway. Luke broke off pursuit and continued straight out of town. Once he entered the freeway headed for Flagstaff, he pressed the accelerator to the floor and felt the car kick into overdrive. Soon he was only aware of the wind searing his face and pine trees on the mountains zipping past. His anger submerged in the pleasure of speed.

As Luke began to unwind, he entered an altered state of mind where only he and the car existed in the universe. He experienced a wider view, as if he looked down on himself from a great height and saw himself riding from the past into the future.

He fancied he saw himself in a sailboat. An older man sat across the prow and gazed at him, an expression of concern in somber blue eyes. Luke felt comforted in a way that he had not felt since the last time his mother had hugged him.

The man looked familiar, definitely not his biological father, but perhaps an older version of Ty. Maybe the sailboat belonged to him. Ty had owned one. Still, that didn't fit. Figuring out who the man was and why he exuded love and fatherliness fascinated Luke.

The blare of a horn sounded in Luke's ear. A semi screamed past, so close he could see the driver shaking a fist in the air. Gripping the steering wheel, Luke swerved away.

Shaken, he exited the freeway at the outskirts of Flagstaff, turned in at a truck stop, and drank a cup of coffee. Feeling more settled, he headed back toward Sedona and Euphoria's house. He couldn't get there fast enough to feel her loving arms around him. He didn't know what had happened to him, but Euphoria could undoubtedly explain.

Although he had not visited her house before, he had little difficulty finding it in a tract subdivision right off the highway. All the small homes looked alike in a hackneyed southwestern style of stucco and red tile roofs. In the carport a black Harley Sportster was parked beside Euphoria's VW bug.

After he rang the bell, Euphoria opened the door right away. She wore a pale green gauzy dress, cinched at the waist, with the ever-present necklace and bracelets. Luke imagined how she would look with only the jewelry.

"Hello." Euphoria laid her arms around his neck and kissed him lightly.

"I'm glad to see you," Luke murmured and enfolded her, sinking his lips onto hers, hungry for their warm reassurance.

Her daughter's bright voice broke in. "Hi, Luke. Welcome to our home."

Reluctantly releasing Euphoria, Luke greeted a shorts-clad Psyche. Behind her stood a six-foot-four, muscular young man in rolled up sleeves. He wore a kitchen towel spread across his jeans. Aaron obviously had some competition. He had been replaced for the evening on very short notice. Luke worried that his son could get hurt by this fickle young girl.

"This is Jess Johnson," Euphoria said. "Luke Brock. Jess and Psyche have a project going." Her tone sounded conciliatory, as if she didn't want Luke to misunderstand her daughter's intentions.

As the men shook hands, Luke noticed an unidentifiable but pungent smell coming from the kitchen.

"Yah," Psyche said, "we're experimenting with some Chinese herbs to make a hot salad dressing."

"Ginseng and kava kava. Loaded with vitamins." Jess lumbered into the tiny kitchen, visible through an arch with vines climbing around it.

Jess looked like a guy who would be more at home on a football field than in a kitchen, but he seemed nice enough. Maybe his relationship with Psyche was purely scientific. Luke hoped so as he watched the two bend over the table littered with cups, bowls, and leaves.

This home might look like all the others on the outside, but Luke could bet it had the most distinctive interior. It was so like Euphoria. A bare-limbed tree stood flat against the corner. Someone had painted huge flowers and leaves on the wall as if they grew from the limbs. Another wall bore an ocean mural. Potted plants sat about on the floor and on the furniture, white wicker with green striped cushions. Crystals, mobiles, and other fluttery things hung from light fixtures and the ceiling.

Luke and Euphoria said good-bye to Psyche and Jess, left the house, and climbed in the car as twilight fell.

"Hungry?" Luke asked.

"Sure."

"Name a place. Just make sure it's a quiet one because I've got a lot to talk to you about."

Euphoria gave him a grand smile and touched his leg. "Oh, I do, too."

"Where to?"

"You got a blanket in the trunk?" When he nodded, she said, "To the Albertson's store," and pointed down the road.

"A picnic." Luke laughed. That could rapidly turn into far more than just dinner and conversation. "Great idea!"

They drove to Albertson's and bought take-out dinner trays, a bottle of Pinot Grigio, a corkscrew, and plastic utensils. Then they headed to Airport Mesa and found a secluded spot among junipers and pines where they spread the blanket on the hard-packed red earth. The desert had cooled after a hot day, giving the evening air a mellow softness.

City lights beyond the ridge cast shadows on Euphoria's face, but Luke could tell she listened raptly as he told her of the experience on the freeway. He didn't feel like divulging the fact that he'd been so out of it he'd almost hit a semi. He had a lot of nerve chastising Aaron, who couldn't do much worse at driving than Luke had tonight.

Euphoria sipped thoughtfully then said, "After people have a past life regression, sometimes more memories come spontaneously. That may be what happened."

"You mean I might remember more, even without being in a trance?"

"Yes."

"That just blows me away." Luke disliked the feeling of defenselessness he'd had in trance, as if Euphoria had been the one in charge. That he might be able to remember consciously pleased him much better.

"Did it have the same texture as the pictures you saw of the 1700s?"

"Now that you mention it, I think so. Who do you suppose the man was? Not me."

"It was your father, Thomas." Euphoria spoke with a certainty as astonishing as her words. "I remember him and your mother, Alice, I think her name was, but I'm not certain. They were very kind to me."

"I can't get away from the idea that I was making it all up. How can you be so sure?"

"I wasn't sure until you came along. When you were in trance and knew my name, then I felt much more confident of my own memories." Crickets chirped around them, undisturbed by cars in the distance. "I had a lot of trouble in that lifetime."

"Did it have to do with an Indian?"

Euphoria set down her wine glass and shifted away from Luke. "He...misused me." Her voice sounded ragged with fresh sorrow. "After two centuries, I still can't forget. People called me names, like I had done a bad thing. I was just a little girl."

Luke took her in his arms, hoping to give her comfort. "It's over now. No one will ever call you a bad name again." He wondered if that rape had any other influences on her. Maybe it had made her afraid of sex.

"It's made me careless of myself when I should have been protective. I've tried but deep inside there's still a feeling of worthlessness that hasn't gone away."

"You and I will make it go away." Luke didn't know what he could do, but he'd figure that out later. "I've got troubles of my own. We'll help each other."

"Oh, dear, Luke, how I love you." Tears coursed down her cheeks. "I loved you then but could never tell you. I felt so unworthy of you, such a smart and caring man, a genius even."

"I love you too." The words were out Luke's mouth before he realized what he'd said. He couldn't take them back, but he didn't really want to. His life had been so boring until this vibrant flower came into it. He'd lost track of how much he could feel. He was ready to risk with Euphoria. He smiled at her. "Now, where's the happy girl? She's inside you too."

"Do you want to make love?" she whispered.

"More than anything." Luke kissed her ardently and felt her tremble against him. He wanted to run his hands across her willing body and know what it felt like to be inside her, but he knew she had to respect herself before they could have an enduring relationship. "I think we'd better wait until you feel that worthiness, until you feel whole inside."

"Wait? But I thought you...but guys always..." Euphoria struggled against him. She seemed to have a bottomless well of tears in her tonight.

"My love." Luke hugged her. "I don't want a shallow relationship with you. I've had plenty of those. I believe we could have a good one. If we worked at it, that is."

A great sigh escaped Euphoria and she relaxed against him. "I know you're right. Thank you for that."

Luke hoped to hell he could hold off. He had an absolute longing to caress her boobs. They were practically begging for it. The last thing he wanted to do was remind her of that traumatic time in the past by acting like an animal. This lovemaking, when it did happen, would require more finesse than Luke had imagined.

After they finished the wine, Euphoria picked up the dinner leavings, wrapped them in the blanket, and policed the area. Luke teased her by calling her a recycling fanatic, she defended herself as a nature conservator. They stashed the blanket in the trunk and got into the car.

On the way back to Euphoria's house, she told him other details about the past life they had shared. He had married the printer's daughter and had twins, a boy and a girl. The printer's daughter was a hellion and made him miserable. Nobody liked her, especially not Euphoria. She also thought Luke had probably fought in the French and Indian War, not in the Revolution.

The little colonial town had been named Dutter's Landing. Euphoria had gone there to see if anything might jog her memory. Many of the founding father's homes still stood in downtown Annapolis with their history intact, but Dutter's Landing had been gobbled up by the metropolitan area and consisted primarily of high-rise apartment buildings. Nothing of two hundred years before remained.

All these details fascinated Luke, whether he could remember them or not. "Stop," he said. "I want to remember some things on my own."

Euphoria's hair billowed around her head in the wind, but she didn't seem to care and sounded triumphant. "So you do believe we had another life before this one!"

"I'm a man who relies on evidence. It's piling up here. If we did have a past life together, only one thing really bugs me, and I can't find a satisfactory explanation."

"The issue of the chance meeting." Euphoria read his mind, as usual.

"Bothers you too, does it?"

Euphoria's tone carried confidence. "The fact that you're on vacation means you volunteered to come here. At a subconscious level you probably knew I was here. At the very least you anticipated that something good would happen, otherwise you'd not have come to Sedona."

"That's right."

"I, too, knew something good was about to happen, so I was on the lookout for you."

"But that's cheating. You're psychic."

"Everyone is psychic to some extent. We can create events in line with our desires or perceive events about to take place. I call it divine synchronicity."

"Divine synchronicity? I'll have to think about that." Luke found the explanation rather glib, but that didn't mean it wasn't true. He had read Carl Jung's theories on the collective unconscious. In fact, they'd been a part of the religion training he'd received in his youth from Religious Science.

If there were an implicate order in the universe, some being or presence or force holding everything together, its work would probably reveal itself as magical from time to time to mere humans. He liked the idea. It seemed logical. Both he and Euphoria regarded their relationship as a gift from God, a very romantic notion for Luke to swallow, but he liked that idea, too.

When he and Euphoria arrived at her house, she glanced at the Harley parked in the driveway. "Tell me why Aaron cancelled the date. That wasn't smart with Psyche."

Luke hated having to explain. It felt like a confession. "He flew over to L. A. to drive the other car back."

"Hey, that's what I volunteered to help you do. Why didn't you go with him?"

Glad it was dark because he felt his face flush, Luke said, "I didn't want him to go either. He defied me."

"So what's new? He's a teenager."

"He's never done it before...and..."

Euphoria grinned. "Welcome to the real world of parenthood. You have been way too lucky."

Her reaction caught Luke off guard and made him feel a little asinine. If it weren't for the fact that Aaron was probably in an airplane as they spoke and at risk to get killed, Luke could laugh at himself. "I hadn't realized—"

"Your fear is holding him back."

Luke shot her a look. She knew. "That's what he said. I know he resents me and thinks I'm a coward."

"Are you?"

"No. Maybe. Well, shit. I guess I have been a little superstitious about flying."

"It's understandable with your wife's death."

"There's more, too, the guy my mom was about to marry, the one who would have been my stepfather. He died in a plane crash."

"And your grandfather."

Luke expelled a long breath, glad she'd read his mind. He hated having to recite the deaths of his family members.

With a knowing smile, Euphoria caressed his cheeks. "People have to do what they have to do. Aaron can't limit his life according to your fears."

"Oh, I know. My intellect is lagging behind my emotions on this."

"You'll get it. You're a spiritual master."

"A what?" Luke laughed aloud. "Me?"

"Maybe not yet, but you're on your way." Euphoria gave him a kiss that tempted him enough to reconsider her offer tonight. She pulled away casually as if unaware of the impact of her closeness. "I've got a lot of faith in you." She slid across the seat and stepped from the car.

Luke watched the lovely Euphoria walk to the porch and wave back to him. He could see the headline now. SCINTILATING PSYCHIC SENDS SPIRITUAL NOVICE TO SEXUAL NIRVANA.

Thirteen

Mind Matters

Upstate New York

The boy who named himself Kegan kicked at the pebbles in the driveway where he sat cross-legged. His stomach ached, but he hadn't felt like eating mashed potatoes and gravy. He really loved them most days, but not today. He felt too upset to eat. Some neighborhood children shouted as they played kickball in the street. He watched them for a minute, but he didn't want to play.

When Grandmother came out the front door and sat on the porch steps behind him, he didn't need to look up at her. He recognized the smell of cigarettes mixed with the lotion she put on her hands after she cleaned up the kitchen.

"Why don't you go play with the other kids?" she asked in a kind voice.

"I want to play with Spiderman."

"You'll get your toy back soon, sweetie."

He sank his elbows down on his knees, wishing she wouldn't call it that. It was an action figure, not a toy. "When?"

"Your grandfather just wants you to remember not to bring your toys to the table." Her voice sounded fuzzy and far away. "I know it's your favorite."

"Spiderman is very cool. I want him back."

Grandmother sighed. "I don't know which of my boys is more stubborn. Why don't you tell me what makes Spiderman so special."

"He can fly by himself. He doesn't even have to have batteries." At first the boy had thought he imagined that, and that there really were batteries somewhere inside, but once he took it apart just to make sure.

"Aha! Is that what you think?" Grandmother tossed the cigarette in the driveway, grabbed him, and pulled him up on the step beside her.

Even though he wasn't a baby anymore, it felt good to be picked up and held in her arms. "Have you seen him fly?"

Grandmother looked kind of pretty when she smiled even with the crinkly places around her eyes and mouth. She wore one of her muu muus, a funny name for clothes, but she had a lot of them. She bought them on the Internet and had them mailed all the way from Hawaii. They hung down straight from her chest and this one had big orange flowers on it. She coughed. "You think your toy can fly, but it can't. Not without you. You're the one making it do that."

"Me? Nah."

"Yes, my dear boy, you've got a gift."

He had no idea what she meant. "You mean like a present?"

With a glance back toward the house, Grandmother whispered, "You're making Spiderman fly. You can do it with anything. Here, I'll show you." She squeezed his shoulder and pointed at the driveway. "Now, look at those rocks. Pick out one that you really like."

He loved secrets and felt excited because Grandmother sounded excited. While gazing at the rocks, he noticed that they all were about the same size, not much bigger than his toe. They had lots of different colorings—gray, brown, white, even green and black. He picked out one of the big ones, light gray. It lay so close to his foot that he could have picked it up without bending over. "Okay, I've got one."

"Now, I want you to just look at that rock and not any of the others. Look at it so long and hard that all the other rocks disappear."

What a fun game, and more so because Grandmother wanted to play it with him. While he gazed at the rock, it began to look funny. It seemed to get larger and more important.

Her voice rattled in his ear. "Think only about the rock. Notice everything about it."

He did what she asked. One side of the rock seemed slightly bigger than the other side. That gave it a slanting top. The side that touched the ground looked like it had been chewed by a squirrel. He had definitely settled on a very interesting rock.

"Imagine it will do anything you want it to do because that is exactly right. It will." Grandmother sounded like she knew a lot about rocks. "Tell it you are the boss."

How small the rock really was. Of course, it would obey him. What choice did the little thing have? He stared at the rock until he felt filled up with the shape of it, the size of it, the color of it. In fact, the rock contained everything of importance in the world.

"Now, boy," Grandmother whispered in his ear, her breath warm on his cheek. "Tell that rock to move over in front of me."

He imagined the rock skipping up and dropping down in front of Grandmother's house slippers. *Go, little rock. You can do it. Jump.*

For a minute he thought the rock hadn't heard him, then it sort of tumbled across the other rocks and stopped in front of Grandmother.

"Yes, yes." Grandmother sounded very happy.

"Yippee!" He felt very glad and proud and happy.

Grandmother crushed him to her in a huge hug. He loved sinking his face into her squishy, warm chest. He felt amazed that he had actually made the rock move. He hadn't known he had caused Spiderman to fly. Now he did know he had done it and felt proud of himself. If he could move a piddling little rock, he could move a big one, and maybe even a bunny cage, or a car. This was wonderful.

"I love you, Grandma."

With a sob, she clutched him. "I love you too." After a special time of holding, she pulled back and looked at him. "I know you don't like to be called Kendall, even though that's your name. What would you like to be called?"

It surprised him to be living inside this tiny little body, as if someone had just plopped him down into it against his will. He felt angry without even knowing why, but he didn't want to end up like the bunny, all dead and limp. He wanted to grow big and strong, like he used to be, if he could only remember. "Call me Kegan, the mighty. That's my real name."

"Kegan, it is," Grandmother smiled. "But only between the two of us. Your parents, bless their souls, gave you the name Kendall, and we have to honor their memory. So when we're out in public, you will answer to the name Kendall Roberts, but just between us, only in private, we know your real name is Kegan."

He didn't understand what she meant about his parents and their memory, but it felt good when Grandmother ruffled the hair on his head. Having a secret name was good, very, very good.

"I've got a lot to teach you, Kegan, and you are an excellent learner."

Fourteen

To Soar Again

Sedona

Tormented by worry, Luke entered the condo after dropping Euphoria at home. He dreaded hearing bad news about his son when his cell phone rang but pulled it out of his pocket to see Aaron's smiling face shining in the lid. The boy was safe. Tension flooded away from Luke's muscles as he opened the receiver. "Hey, what's up?"

"Well, I'm home and figured you'd be worried." Aaron's happy voice sounded wonderful. "No problems. The plane ride was fun...sort of like a bus ride though."

Luke laughed. "Okay."

"The house is in fine shape, like we never left."

"Listen, son, I'm sorry."

"I know. Me, too. I shouldn't have rushed off like that and defied you."

"It's all right." Luke couldn't keep a tease out of his voice. "Just don't make a habit of it."

"I won't. See you tomorrow."

"Drive safely."

After he closed the phone, Luke plugged it into the battery charger, undressed, and dropped into bed. The silk sheet caressed his skin and he sighed with appreciation.

How lucky he was to have such a smart and devoted son. Luke wished Aaron's mother and grandmother could see their young man now. They would be very proud of him for turning out so well. Luke wished he could see their beloved faces once more.

Tonight he no longer felt sorrowful for the dead but grateful for the living, both his son and Euphoria. He felt glad he had thought to summer in Sedona. Now he couldn't remember why he'd decided to, but it had been an inspired thought. Local lore said nothing bad could befall one in this place, and much good would come, if one believed it to be so. Right now he did.

His mind remained alert while his body sank into a luxurious relaxation. The air seemed to become clearer and brighter. Thoughts of his mother filled his mind, so powerful they seemed to carry sensation. He could almost see her but not quite, almost hear her but not quite. He imagined her voice and waited with great anticipation to hear the words she would utter.

Angie slipped into Luke's bedroom and into his dream. She tried to tell him that Melinda was doing well, comfortable with her discarnate existence. Angie wanted Luke to know how happy it made her to see him in Sedona, finding a new love and dipping into life's mysteries.

Luke failed to respond to her, sleeping deep in delta waves. It seemed her headstrong son had a tight grip on his own destiny, not only in his choice of the psychic as a companion but in finding his own pace of self-discovery.

When he volunteered for the Plan before his birth, his goal had been to jumpstart his spiritual growth. His soul progress from killing and maiming men as a bloodthirsty warlord to healing them as a compassionate physician showed great strength, no matter how many lifetimes it had taken. Fifteen, maybe sixteen. Now he had the opportunity to build on that foundation. Euphoria was a perfect choice of companion.

"You chose her yourself, Luke. Can you hear me?" Angie waited but received no response. "I love you." She smiled at the irony of her concerns about interfering with his free will. He was strong and capable.

The next moment it seemed, morning had come. Luke awakened to light that streamed in through the still-open curtains. Disappointed that he couldn't remember his dream, he rose and made coffee. He had a feeling it would be a long day of trying not to fret while his son drove the Jaguar three hundred long and dangerous miles. If anything bad happened, he'd have a tough time forgiving himself for not going along.

When Luke sipped the instant fancy brew, it tasted bitter, and he wished he'd brought his own coffeemaker from home. To while away the time, he phoned his office. His secretary assured him that all the accountants were getting their work done and that she would call if any problems arose, either legal or technical. He gave her the date he intended to return for a series of July interviews and meetings. It occurred to him that perhaps he should make an unscheduled visit before that, just to check on everything personally. He had never been away from them before for any length of time and had little notion of their trustworthiness.

After finishing the call he noticed that his exuberance of the previous days had evaporated. Emotionally, he had dropped down to the low key at which he normally operated. He felt confident in his ability to supervise a business, but if he quit or if the business disappeared, what difference would it make to the world? Little except to the employees out of a job. He doubted Aaron, with his interest in science so high, would ever want to take over. Maybe Luke should hire a general manager and cast around for some other kind of work that would give him more satisfaction. He might go back to the law full time.

Luke could imagine living with Euphoria at some point in time if the logistics of the children worked out. Assuming he asked her to return to L. A. with him, how would she take to city life? Would she even be willing to move away from here? Not that it made any difference. Perhaps he'd gotten ahead of himself with this relationship still at its beginning stage. Too early to make such plans. He had come here to enjoy a vacation, and enjoy he would!

Nothing occupied his mind better than research, historical or legal. Flipping on the laptop, he searched the Internet for facts about Maryland Colony, what sailboats looked like in the seventeen hundreds, a bunch of stuff on the French and Indian War, and even some tomes on medicine of the times. It amazed Luke how fascinated he had become since the regression. His thoughts returned to it often. He loved the time period and imagined the pace of life would have been much more to his liking, all except for the Internet. What a terrific invention.

An undercurrent simmered beneath all the research and pondering about his life. Luke believed he had missed something in the night, a dream or maybe more seemed unresolved.

Late in the afternoon he called his son to get an update on the trip.

"Good timing," Aaron said. "I'm just driving into town."

Far faster than he should have, Luke thought. "So did you have any problems?"

"No, and not a scratch on the car. I'm headed straight to Psyche's, and I'll be home later."

Should Luke tell Aaron about the biker? No, Psyche probably would do that herself. This being an overprotective father could get suffocating. He had to allow his son the freedom to make decisions, maybe even mistakes.

After he showered and changed, Luke drove the BMW to the carwash, aware that the contents of his own mind had become unfamiliar to him, or at the very least he'd experienced some things that didn't fit his frame of reference.

Sedona had a reputation for bringing out the psychic in people, and maybe that had happened to him. His wife had definitely feared psychic things, yet his mother had sought them. He had no fear of trying out new perceptions but insisted on being in control when he did.

Luke drove to the Crystal Cave, knowing Euphoria generally worked until five. That gave him time to browse in the shop. He found some books on meditation that looked promising and bought them. Back outside, he sat on a park bench beneath an oak and dug into one of the books.

The more he read, the more he determined that he wanted to begin the practice of meditation. It suited him in part because he found no talk of God or angels or beings of light, just sitting down, going within, and focusing on learning more about one's inner life. That he could do.

Euphoria, scrumptiously feminine in pink blouse and skirt, joined Luke with a hearty kiss. Noticing everything, as usual, she remarked on the books.

Luke explained his new-found ambition to learn to meditate and the reasons for it, including the unsettling dream experience of the night before. "I keep thinking my mother was talking to me, and I couldn't hear her. Do you think it's possible to talk to the dead? Or have them talk to you?"

"I think it's impossible not to." Her bracelets slid down her arm as Euphoria gestured toward the sky. "They aren't far away. They're here, just on a different wavelength. You need to connect with your mother, that's what this is about, or she needs to connect with you. Let me see what I can get." She dug in her purse and pulled out the moss agate then took one of his hands in both of hers.

"Wait," Luke said, pulling his hand away, "you've worked all day. You don't have to do this for me, too."

"It's not work, Luke. It's my life." Sincerity filled her loving face. "Give me your hand."

Her touch drew Luke into her mindset. Not so much with a desire to believe the way she did but that her force magnetized him because he had no counterweight to argue against her. Of course, he wanted a belief system that mended the broken pieces of his life. Didn't everyone? But, more than that, he wanted one that explained the world beyond Sedona, the time beyond 2006. Right now he didn't have that knowledge, but he'd recognize a lie if he heard it. He hadn't gone to law school for nothing.

Beneath Euphoria's palm, Luke could feel the smooth agate warmed by both of them. He felt connected to her in a web of curiosity and longing.

With a sigh, Euphoria closed her eyes and sagged against the bench. Her eyes darted beneath her lids as if she searched for something. Tourists called to each other across the street at the old Spanish town. Cars drove by. Luke doubted that Euphoria heard any of the noise because her face held such a placid look.

After a time so long that Luke wanted to stretch and move around, though he dared not interfere with the trance, Euphoria whispered. He leaned forward so he could catch her words.

"Your mother wishes to tell you that she has spoken to you many times, but you have not listened. Just like in life. A little joke."

"You're in touch with her? Under these circumstances?" The idea of making such a contact seemed preposterous on the face of it, so why did Luke think it couldn't happen outside, late on a sunny afternoon in traffic? He needed evidence. That was why.

Perhaps caught up in listening to the other world, Euphoria didn't respond to his questions, anyway. She tilted her head and spoke insistently, "Only once did you hear her. Before the disaster. She warned you of a change in plans."

Luke remembered the night before the towers fell. The images of that time were frozen in his memory, never to diminish or change. And all preceded by the dream of his mother that had prevented him from dying. Maybe it hadn't been a dream at all. Maybe she had saved his life from the other side. But why? Logic would say she wanted him to be with her, but there was much he didn't understand. More by the minute, in fact.

"Your mother says..." Euphoria looked as if she strained to hear. "...to remind you of the time she came to get you before you got sick. That doesn't really make much sense, but I'm just going to trust it. She also says the Oldsmobile was a good car."

Euphoria had nailed a point of contention so genuine in personal detail Luke could laugh if he weren't in shock at the revelation embodied in her words. "Mom did love that Olds, the one we drove cross country when we moved to Arizona. She entertained some bizarre belief that the car would last a lifetime, but I argued that it took way too much effort to keep the thing running, so I convinced her to trade it in." Luke knew something had to be going on. He hadn't thought about that car in years, so Euphoria couldn't be reading his mind. Evidence appeared to be mounting that his mother or some part of her consciousness remained alive and had managed to communicate.

Falling silent, Euphoria appeared to listen to words that she did not voice. She looked wistful and desirable. Luke couldn't resist and gave her a gentle kiss. Her mouth felt so soft and yielding that he appreciated even more the vulnerability required to receive psychic perceptions. One had to suspend one's will in order to become a vessel. Luke doubted he'd ever be able to do so, but he recognized Euphoria's willingness and wanted to protect her during such moments. Not wanting to break her concentration, he fought the urge to take her into the shelter of his arms.

With a sigh, Euphoria came to herself and smiled at him, a smile so beguiling and naughty they might have been exchanging tokes behind the schoolyard fence instead of psychic emanations. "So," she said, "tell me about the time when you were sick."

Eager to validate her messages, Luke cuddled Euphoria against him. "I think I can corroborate your testimony about the sickness. It was 1975."

"How old were you then?"

"Fourteen. I was in summer camp not too far from here. That was the only time I ever went to camp and why I remember the year so clearly. Several other guys and I went with the camp counselor to climb the limestone cliff face at Montezuma's Castle and go inside, just like the ancient Sinagua Indians had. For some reason, I got very sick to my stomach, I headed off the trail and ducked out of sight behind some creosote bushes. My skin felt hot and sweaty despite the mild winter sunshine.

"Retching didn't improve things. I sat down on the ground strewn with dried seed husks and took off my sweatshirt, hoping another wave of nausea would pass. I'd waited weeks for that field trip. I hated being sick so much. The other kids called me a pansy. And even worse, I still didn't have any whiskers. I looked more like ten than fourteen.

"I struggled up, determined, and tied the sweatshirt sleeves around my waist. I retched again then took a chance and started up the trail. The other guys had already come out of the cave with the counselor. He was even skinnier than I, an Ichabod Crane look alike in an ASU baseball hat.

"Unsteadily, I pulled myself up the handholds and entered the prehistoric gloom. My head hurt so much I couldn't take any pleasure in seeing the cave, with its rough earthen walls and piles of bones and pottery lying about.

"The counselor called my name and I trudged outside then followed the guys down the hill. Once again I ducked out of sight to heave. I'd long since emptied my stomach of any food. All I could do was gag. I wiped my brow and hurried alongside. I described my symptoms in a hushed voice.

"The camp counselor said, 'Maybe we better call your mother to come and get you.' I could see the headline now. LUKE BROCK DECLARED WIMP IN FRONT OF FIELD TRIP EXPEDITION."

Euphoria gave Luke a glance that showed surprise at his words.

"Mom taught English and journalism in high school, and I loved the subjects. Guess thinking in headlines came naturally to me. Still does. Anyway, I hated it that I worried Mom so much. Wasn't the epilepsy bad enough? Now this. I'd just suck it up and be tough, so I told the counselor I'd be all right."

"The counselor said, 'If you're not any better by the time we get to Montezuma's Well, we'll let her know.' He and the other guys hiked down the trail. Stomach cramping and head aching, I straggled along behind them toward the school bus.

"There parked beside it sat Mom's beat-up, beautiful Oldsmobile. Just as beautiful with her long black hair done up in back, she got out of the car, stamped out a cigarette, and waved to me. Not long after that she quit smoking. In jeans and a sweater, she looked almost like a kid herself. I had so little strength left I feared I'd not make it to her side, but I managed to reach the car. I must have looked awful because she stared at me with horror all over her face. I said, 'I don't feel too hot,' and sort of slid down the bumper. Like someone clicked the lights out in my mind."

When Luke laughed at the memory, Euphoria said, "I don't see anything funny."

"Neither did I at the time. It turned out all right though. See, I'm still here." Luke noticed the glowing sun beginning to set through the tree leaves.

"Get to the point. How did your mother know to come and get you?

"Next thing I knew I was in the hospital in Flagstaff. Mom had driven me there. When I awoke she was sitting in one of those plastic side chairs with her hair all hanging down. She had slumped over, evidently falling asleep waiting for me to come to. I woke her up by asking why I had an IV tube in my arm.

"She said, 'You've just got a bad case of the flu. The medicine will fix you right up, so don't worry. You'll be home in no time.' I asked her, 'You knew the bus would be back home tomorrow. Why did you drive up here? Has something bad happened at home?' And she said, 'An angel told me to come and get you.' She called it a freaky little moment because she just knew, as if someone had told her that I was sick and she should come and get me."

Euphoria nodded in a knowing way. "I've had the same experience as your mother had. There's no explaining it or denying it."

"Yep," Luke said, "It takes two hours to drive up from Phoenix, and I hadn't even gotten sick by the time she left. She remembered how embarrassed she'd been before when she bought lottery numbers on a hunch and they turned out to be wrong. But she couldn't take a chance on my health, so she practiced what she'd tell me if she was wrong this time, that she had an irresistible urge to watch me throw up. I was gagging and she got up and positioned the plastic container beneath my mouth." His mother's lovable, cocky grin stood out in Luke's memory, bittersweet.

"She must have had a sense of humor."

"And how! She was good and kind and deserved to live. Not much older than I am now, but cancer just ate her up." Luke's pent-up anger spewed out with his words. "And there wasn't a thing I could do about it. I'd never felt more helpless."

In gathering twilight, Euphoria squeezed his hand. "Pretty bad, was it?"

"The last few months of her life were hell for both of us."

"How long has it been since she passed over?"

"Sixteen years, and still, when I close my eyes, I see her lying in bed, trying valiantly to breathe, wanting to live, hating what was happening to her."

"She doesn't want you to remember her that way."

The image of his mother before Nine Eleven popped into Luke's mind. "In my dreams she's fresh and vital looking, full of friendly advice."

"That's the way she wants you to remember her because that's the way she is now."

"Now?" The idea of Angie having a viable consciousness somewhere else intrigued Luke and distracted him from the surge of grief. "I guess I need to come to terms with the fact that she's gone." He knew he sounded lame, considering how long she had been dead but couldn't think of anything else to say. "How do you suggest I do that, Euphoria?"

"You don't have to come to terms with the fact that they're gone. They aren't. Your mother is still here. She has been talking to you. It's time you started listening or, better yet, talked back." Euphoria rubbed his hand with gentleness, her voice filled with compassion. "I think you've reacted like a civilian in time of war. You got shell-shocked from so many deaths so fast – your mother, your real father, your stepfather, your grandmother, your wife. As a result you never processed any of them."

Luke didn't recall telling her about all the deaths, but what did it matter? Psychics knew way more than people ever told them or wanted them to know. "There's no question that I did decide not to think about them."

"You can always change your mind." Euphoria made it sound simple.

What the hell? He had nothing to lose. "Okay. What do I do?"

Picking up the meditation book, Euphoria slapped the cover. "Start with this. It's a great way to open the channel."

A doubt about his own sanity crossed his mind as Luke waved the book and addressed the air. "Okay, Mom. I'm listening. What you got to say?" When Euphoria began to laugh, he couldn't help himself and joined her, relieved and hopeful.

Jumping up, Euphoria asked, "Are you hungry? I sure am."

"So am I. Let's have some Mexican food." As they started across the street toward the hacienda shops, arm in arm, Luke considered how much at home he felt with Euphoria. He wanted to hold her and kiss her and maybe go farther if it seemed right, more than anything he wanted to spend intimate time with her. He was getting very tired of restaurants.

If they went to her house, Psyche and Aaron might show up. If they went to his condo, Psyche and Aaron might show up. If he asked her to go to a motel, she might feel cheap, something he didn't intend. The logical solution came in a flash and was out of his mouth almost before it entered his brain.

"I need to go to L. A. to check on my business. Want to fly over there with me in the morning?"

A stunned expression crossed Euphoria's face. "Absolutely! If you're going to get into an airplane, I want to be there to see it."

Where had this new spontaneity come from? Perhaps recklessness described it better. Luke was beginning to scare himself. "All right, I'll charter a small plane from the airfield here, and we'll go tomorrow."

"How about Monday? I have two days off."

What in hell had Luke gotten himself into? He couldn't take the offer back now without looking like the coward of the century in front of this dear woman. On the other hand, whatever aspect of his mind that volunteered had probably done him a favor.

Luke needed to get over this fear. It limited him more each day and had almost alienated him from his son. He had stuffed a lot of emotions since that awful day when Melinda and so many others died. Flying would make a start. "Monday it is."

Fifteen

For Aulde Lange Syne

Los Angeles

Early Tuesday morning, Luke lit a candle in the center of the glass coffee table and settled against the leather couch, appreciative for once of its unyielding construction, which supported his back. Feet flat on marble, hands palms up on pajama trousers, he believed he had followed the directions in the meditation book accurately enough. His gaze swept the abstract paintings lit by the skylight and, through the patio doors, the palms and pool beneath a socked-in coastal sky. Then he closed his eyes.

Next direction, express gratitude. Luke could make a long list of items for which he felt grateful. The plane had not crashed on the way to L. A. He had sucked up his fear and not embarrassed himself. Spending a private day with Euphoria had turned out as enjoyable as he'd hoped despite the fact that they'd only gone grocery shopping, cooked dinner, and watched a DVD. One thing more for which he felt grateful, he had managed not to touch her in a sexual way last night. He wanted to remain true to his pledge to wait until she felt confident.

Inhaling a deep breath, he exhaled and let the tension out of his body. He noticed the breath going in and out. Notice and nothing more, he reminded himself. He sank into a pleasant place in his mind, untroubled, in fact, and very relaxing. He could understand why people got hooked on meditation. Whoops, was that a thought? Never mind, he just let it go and noticed the breath going in and out, in and out.

After what seemed only a moment but could have been far longer, Luke became aware of music coming through the speakers he'd mounted, hidden inside the walls, after Melinda died and could no longer nix the idea. The unfamiliar tune filtered through, a woman singing tones without words in a haunting way, as if her voice glided along canyon walls. The fragrance of herbs made Luke wonder if Euphoria had decided to make tea. When he heard the familiar tinkle of her bracelets, his eyes popped open.

At the near end of the corridor to the bedroom wing stood a smiling Euphoria. Her bracelets clicked as she flipped the light switch and illuminated herself, nude.

The leaf medallion nestled between her full breasts as she strode toward Luke. When she held up her shapely arms, the copper bracelets tinkled. She appeared as delighted to show her body to him as he was to see it. "This is what you wanted, isn't it?" she murmured.

The trance left really fast, replaced by an incredible passion to hold her, to know how it felt to have her softness melt into him. Luke nodded, not trusting himself to speak.

"It didn't take a psychic to figure that out." A tease filled her voice. Her pink skin glistened as she stopped beside the coffee table. "You like my music?"

"You are so...so... the word stunning isn't good enough."

"The music," she whispered. "Do you like it?"

"Yes." Now Luke really knew what it felt like to be grateful.

Her auburn hair fell off her shoulders as she bent toward him. "I want to make love. I know I'm ready. Are you?" Her sweet breath warmed his face.

"I am so ready." Luke's hands shook with anticipation as he pulled her toward him.

Her hazel eyes became a rich brown with the candle flickering behind her and gave her away. Love filled her face. "I've waited centuries for you. I can't wait another day."

Her arms enfolded him with a tender fierceness. Her lips on his filled Luke with an unbearable ache to join with her. Body and soul, she opened herself to him.

Luke plunged into her beloved familiarity, somehow new and exciting at the same time. He poured a lifetime of longing into his kiss. No matter what the future brought, he would never be alone in the way he had been before Euphoria. He would know her completely, and he would be known by her, holding nothing back.

After making love, they sat on the couch. Euphoria nestled in Luke's arms. She suggested they take a dip in the pool without their swimming suits.

"That would be wonderful, but we'd better not." Luke thought he saw the housekeeper peak through the window of her room across the pool in the other wing of the house. Not that he minded, but she was a bit of gossip, and he didn't want anyone thinking ill of Euphoria. "The gardener and housekeeper wouldn't approve of the idea. We took quite a chance that they'd walk in on us here in the living room."

With a naughty giggle, Euphoria said, "Guess they'll need to get used to your new-found activities."

"Me, too, but that'll be easy. I've never been so happy" Luke kissed her and sighed. "As bad as I hate to say it, I have to go to work now. That's why we came here."

Euphoria patted the couch and grinned wickedly, "That's why we came here..." obviously aware of the intended pun. "And where."

The thought that Luke should go to the office kept intruding into his awareness in a most unpleasant way. "I hope you know I need to go to work, but I don't want to."

"We'll both go."

Laughing and chatting like old friends, they dressed and caught a taxi to the accounting office, which like his home, still bore Melinda's taste and style. The secretary and most of the accountants had worked for him since before her death, and he had never brought a woman friend in before.

When he and Euphoria entered the office, the secretary ended a phone call abruptly and came toward them with a surprised look on her face. "My goodness, Luke, what are you doing here?" Her brows remained rigid in a way that made her appear to have had botox injections.

"Just dropped by to attend to a few things." He pulled Euphoria against his side affectionately. "This is my friend, Euphoria Clark."

"Nice to meet you." Euphoria's voice sounded warm and welcoming, as it always did.

"Ms. Clark." The secretary frowned and looked more flustered than a casual introduction should entail. She followed Luke into his office. "There's nothing the matter, is there?"

"Not to my knowledge." Luke glanced at his empty inbox. "May I see the end of the month report, please?"

The secretary looked worried. "I'm sorry, sir, it's not ready. We didn't know you'd be here until after the Fourth. We thought we had plenty of time."

Now Luke thought perhaps seeing his new girlfriend had not caused the secretary to act startled. The staff had accomplished very little, but no one could blame the secretary. He introduced Euphoria to several accountants, who rose from their maroon felt cubicles and greeted her awkwardly. Only the man cast an admiring look at her. Luke felt proud to have such a desirable woman beside him, one other men found attractive.

Assuming the women showed disapproval out of loyalty to Melinda, he didn't take their feelings too seriously. After all, five years had gone by. He had every right to move on emotionally. It didn't matter what they thought of Euphoria or of him. At the same time, he felt protective of her around these women, who could be catty. Euphoria must have read his thoughts because she gave him an appreciative smile that made him feel glad.

When Luke and Euphoria arrived at the last cubicle, Theresa Lopez, the most senior accountant, rose. Her face flushed as she nodded at Euphoria in recognition of the introduction then spoke to Luke. "I've been informed that you want to see the fiscal end of year report. Please accept my apology."

"Last Friday was the deadline." Luke shrugged, uncomfortable with the slip-up. "Good thing there wasn't a drop-in audit."

Theresa looked embarrassed. "We'll stay tonight and get the report ready. It will be on your desk first thing in the morning."

"All right, thank you." Luke doubted he concealed much of his annoyance. His employees were acting like babies with their daddy gone.

Euphoria seemed not to notice the cool reception and called out a cheery good-bye as she and Luke went out the door and into the elevator.

"Damn." Luke pushed the lobby button, trying to keep from feeling cheated at this turn of events. "I'm not going to be able to go back to Sedona tonight. Can you stay another day?"

"I'll call to find out. May I use your phone?"

The elevator doors opened. Luke handed her his cell phone and, while she talked to her boss, guided her across the lobby and outside. The June glooms had not worn off, and a gray pall hung over the city. Rain sprinkled as Luke and Euphoria climbed into a taxi. The weather made him feel gloomier.

Euphoria ended her call and returned the phone. "My manager says, what with the Fourth of July next week, clients are standing in line to make appointments. She can't do without me." Displeasure rang in her voice, and she snuggled up against Luke's shoulder. "I'm sorry."

"Me, too." Luke tried not to scowl. He didn't want to act like a baby himself. "It appears I've got some incompetent employees."

"Or worse." Euphoria's tone sounded ominous. "Check things out very carefully."

"You mean you think someone's trying to cheat me?"

"I don't feel good about it. Just be careful."

Luke kissed her out of appreciation. He found it comforting to have someone on his side. "I'll get back to Sedona as soon as I can."

"You're not fond of the work you do, are you?"

"Not really. If I could think of something else to do, I'd sell the business. Of course, it's very profitable. I don't know how I'd do without all this cash." He patted his wallet.

"I'll take you either way, rich or poor, but believe me, rich is better."

The comment surprised Luke. Although they'd not talked about their attitudes surrounding money, he'd assumed Euphoria was a modern-day hippie and didn't care about wealth. He had a lot to learn about her and about himself and about his employees, evidently. He wanted to lighten both their moods. "So working by the hour as a psychic, is that your get-rich-quick scheme?"

"It's just for the meantime. I've got plans." Euphoria sounded impassioned. "I'll always give readings because I love too, but eventually I intend to combine it with workshops and guidebooks. There's money to be made, teaching other people how to develop their own psychic natures. That's important work, too."

"Definitely seems like what you should do. You'd be good at it." Luke gazed at the gun-metal gray buildings as they sat at a traffic light through three exchanges. How he detested L. A.

"You'll eventually do something you love, too."

"I'm already doing it." Luke hoped the double entendre would entertain her. He cupped her face in his hand and gave her a lingering kiss. Her sigh filled him with longing, and he hated to let her go.

Luke directed the taxi driver to take them to the airport. He escorted Euphoria to the receptionist desk for the charter that had flown them in. Security procedures prevented him from accompanying her any further.

After a poignant good-bye, he went back to a house that seemed emptier than it ever had before. He would have new digs soon, one way or another, when Aaron went to college or if Euphoria moved in. All three would probably happen—his own little not-so-psychic prediction.

He dreaded tomorrow and having to deal with whatever problems had developed with the business. He'd felt envious of Euphoria when she spoke of her career goals. He needed some too. That part of him that took satisfaction and pride from his work had gotten lost along the way. He remembered fondly his first job as a junior lawyer in downtown Phoenix and his rise to full partner status, due exclusively to his persuasive arguments in the courtroom. Melinda had always said it was his boyish charm that swayed juries. He knew better.

After rummaging in the kitchen, he carried a ham sandwich and a beer back to the couch and stretched his legs on the coffee table. Recalling the incredible image of Euphoria bent over him in all her splendid nakedness made him shiver. What a lucky bastard he was! He'd have her and the job he wanted, the sooner the better. As he ate, darkness settled over the room. The pool light shimmered, creating a nice other-worldly ambiance.

On a hunch, Luke called information and asked for the number of the firm that he and Melinda had negotiated with for the sale of the business. Many businesses that had offices in the World Trade Center had not survived, but evidently Bolton's had. After the phone rang, he heard a forwarding connection, and the scratchy voice of an old woman came on the line. When she identified herself, Luke felt surprised. Maybe the firm had not prospered if she had to answer the phone. Well, he'd gone this far, so he might as well continue.

"Mrs. Bolton, I was wondering if you have any interest in expanding your interests into California? My accounting firm might be for sale for the right price."

"Who am I speaking to, please?" Her voice sounded professionally cool.

"This is Luke Brock. We were in negotiations before...uh..." He hated the casual label Nine Eleven to describe that horror.

"You've got a lot of gall to ask me that."

"Perhaps you misunderstood. I'm—"

"I know who you are. No, we are not interested in buying from you, now or ever."

"Mrs. Bolton, I don't understand."

"Your wife was having an affair with my husband." Mrs. Bolton caught a ragged breath. "Are you pretending you didn't know?"

Memory Luke had long ago suppressed rushed to center stage of his mind. He saw himself pull the covers down on the bed in the Holiday Inn. He saw the smear on the sheet, the disarray of his wife's clothes, the two wine glasses. He felt again the throbbing pain in his gut that could not accept such betrayal. "I'm sorry, ma'am. I—"

Mrs. Bolton hung up and the phone hummed in his ear.

Luke sprang off the couch. The beer can clanked as it overturned on the floor. He paced the room, back and forth to the patio door, feeling like a zoo animal frustrated by the denial of his wildness.

Why the fuck had Melinda betrayed him? How could she do that? Why had she not loved him? Luke hated her and wished she was here so he could hurt her as she had hurt him. He stopped pacing before a ridiculous painting of zigzag lines that she had loved. How could she love a painting and not him?

Luke drew a bead on the painting and banged his fist into its center. It fell to the floor, and he hammered the wall over and over. His punch crashed through the dry wall and plaster.

"Damn you, Melinda, damn you, damn you." He beat the rhythm of his words.

White hot pain raced through his hand and arm. He winced at his bleeding knuckles and hurried into the bathroom to turn on the faucet. Warm water coursed over his hand, and he watched his blood swirl down the drain. He grabbed a towel and wrapped it around his hand then sank down on the tile floor and laid his head against the cabinet.

Sobs he had repressed spun out of him. He cried for the years of being unloved. He cried for the years of being unloving. For the waste of the time of their lives. He cried because he could not take any of it back, could not love her now. He cried for his own unwillingness to accept the truth.

Had he turned into a lunatic? Luke had heard about repressed memory and always thought it was a bunch of nonsense. Sure enough, he had done it himself. That night five years ago, that awful night when he had learned of his wife's death and her infidelity, had gone out of awareness. He had pushed the knowledge down so deep he didn't have to consciously deal with it. Of course, he knew it was there, but if he didn't think about it he didn't have to feel the grief, the anger, the humiliation. He wished Euphoria was here so he could talk to her and the next instant felt relieved to be alone. Maybe he needed a shrink. No, this was way too private to share with anyone.

When he thought of the years he lived with Melinda, he felt discouraged all over again. They both had missed very much. The shallowness of their relationship offended him then and now. Euphoria had been right in saying that he had pushed down his grief. In fact, he had pushed it down so far he had no idea why he grieved. For his wife, for himself, or for his dismal marriage?

Over the years he had agonized as to why Melinda had not called his room the night before she died. If she had called, her death might have been averted. How, Luke did not know. Maybe if she had called and awakened him, then he would have gone over to her room and somehow prevented her from going into the tower. He would have told her about the dream of his mother. If Melinda hadn't gone in there, if she had overslept too, something she could have done if she'd been sleeping with her husband, then his son would not have felt such sorrow. It was wrong for a little boy to have to experience such grief.

Of course the answer to his question was embodied in Mrs. Bolton's hostility. Melinda had not called his room because she had been busy fucking Mrs. Bolton's husband. And if Melinda hadn't been fucking Mrs. Bolton's husband, Luke would have gone over there and crawled into bed with her and had some kind of unsatisfying sex.

No doubt Melinda found their sex life as uninteresting as he had. Maybe that's why she formed the liaison with Bolton, the one that placed her in the tower that awful day. That's why she was dead. Because she'd been trying to wrench value from life. Just like Luke. To be honest with himself, he had to admit that he hadn't enjoyed their sex life or their marriage for years, but Aaron's needs trumped his and his wife's.

At the moment he had no idea whether to name that belief noble or cowardly. He just knew that, given the circumstances, he'd do the same thing over again. What had the pundit said? Doing the same thing over again even when you know it's wrong is the height of insanity. Well, the pundit must have said it better.

Pulling himself up to the medicine chest, Luke sprayed his knuckles with antiseptic and wrapped his hand in a clean towel. Morose, he trundled into the kitchen, picked up a sponge and another beer, and headed back to the living room. Just as he finished wiping up the beer, the phone rang.

"Are you all right?" Euphoria's caring voice came over the line.

"Sure." Luke felt ill at ease with small talk even under normal circumstances, and these were far from normal. "How about you? Did you have a safe flight?"

"I kept having this image of you bleeding, so I just wanted to find out whether you were all right."

Luke held his wrapped fist up to the phone even though he had returned to his senses enough to know she couldn't see it. Or maybe she could. Dating a psychic required more presence of mind and emotional transparency than he'd ever given to a relationship before, but maybe doing so would benefit both of them. He valued Euphoria's authenticity. At the same time he found her exotic and exciting. And the best part…she was his. She had said so. If full disclosure worked for her, it might work for him too. "I got pissed and slammed my fist into the wall."

"You're insane, Luke. Did it help?

"Yes, love, I think it did."

"Want to talk about it?"

"No."

"I'll find out anyway."

"Probably." Luke's interest went a hundred eighty degrees. "What are you wearing?"

"Funny you should ask." Euphoria's silly laugh gave away her state of undress.

Luke imagined how she looked, and now he knew his imaginings had foundation in fact. "This morning…was fantastic."

After a long silence on the other end of the line, Euphoria sighed. "We're good together, aren't we?"

"Yes."

"Don't ever forget that."

"I won't." In the awkward silence Luke wanted to reassure Euphoria of his love. After all, he had blurted out the words to her before, but he felt strung out tonight. He would wait for a clearer moment to speak his feelings.

"Good night, my darling." Euphoria's voice sounded mellow with the wine of commitment. She had given herself completely.

Although he considered himself exceedingly blessed, Luke acknowledged that some little piece of him didn't feel ready to give assurances in words. He had thoughts yet to think. "Good night."

For five years, Luke had counted on alone time after Aaron went to bed. Tonight he needed that privacy more than ever so he could absorb new feelings of connection, the budding coupling with Euphoria. She was so fine and so good that Luke felt lucky to have her, but some pieces had yet to fall into place in his mind.

Never again would he deceive himself as he had about Melinda's infidelity. Never would he pretend something that didn't come from his heart. From now on, Luke would face whatever came, requiring the truth, alert to lies, especially those he told to himself.

The books had listed serenity as a benefit of meditation practice. Luke could use a dose of that now. He'd seldom felt less serene, in fact he'd let himself get extraordinarily agitated.

Regardless, it took two Bud Lites and a boring rerun of a Brazilian soccer match to even approach the quietude he had experienced early in the morning. Luke smiled at the idea that he should probably start dating the events of his life as BEE—Before Euphoria Era. and AE—After Euphoria. He deliberately removed his thoughts from her, turned off the TV with the remote, and assumed the meditation posture. He forcibly emptied his mind of thoughts.

Emotional exhaustion, physical tiredness, or the midnight hour might have contributed, but for whatever reason he settled into a quiet place and rested on a wave-less thought: *I am peaceful and calm.* Lethargy crept into his limbs, not unlike sleep except that he remained attentive.

It seemed that someone stood behind him, slightly off to the left of his shoulder although the couch actually sat against a wall, so that wasn't physically possible.

Luke had the sensation that someone mumbled the words "I'm proud of you" into his ear. Too relaxed to turn around, he strained to hear more.

"I'm proud of you," came a distant voice. Angie's had had a similar contralto timbre.

Unable to manufacture the normal sound of his voice, Luke squeaked, "Mom?"

"Yes, I came to say you're on the right track."

"That's good to know."

"You did well with Melinda. Don't waste time in anger. Forgive her and go on."

"Forgive her?" Luke's energy returned, so he asked aloud, "How can I?" He whirled around to look at his mother but saw only the wall and the table lamp beyond it. "Mom, don't go."

The familiar fragrance of Chanel, the one Angie always wore, filled the room.

His mother had come to him tonight. Now he remembered clearly how she had come to him on the night before the towers fell also. She had warned him. Maybe she had warned Melinda too. The idea oddly comforted him. Perhaps Melinda had not gone to meet her death completely without warning.

Astonished, Luke didn't know whether he had actually encountered his mother's spirit or wigged out entirely. He fell to analyzing her words and deduced the spirit of his mother had not said anything that she'd not said to him in life. He could be making the whole experience up.

But the perfume? How to explain that? He could still smell it.

Sixteen

Out of the Ashes

Los Angeles

The next morning Luke awakened before daylight, feeling raw from the emotional upheaval of the day before and alarmed about the task ahead. Euphoria hadn't made one incorrect prediction yet, and he'd noticed something off about his employees' demeanor. Female jealousy or protectiveness about his wife only went so far by way of explanation.

Partially restored by a shower and shave, he wanted to look professional and chose a pin-striped suit and a dark tie. He dreaded confronting a dishonest employee, and doing so in casual dress didn't work.

He caught a taxi driven by a Middle Eastern type, who droned on apparently oblivious to how difficult his thick accent made it for anyone to understand him. Luke cared nothing about the driver's opinions on the war in Iraq, the war in Afghanistan, the threat of war in Iran, or the financial corruption among Tsunami aid workers.

On getting out of the taxi, Luke laid a twenty-dollar tip in the driver's hand and said, "That's so you'll spare the next guy your opinions and give him the quiet I needed."

The taxi driver looked dumbfounded. Maybe that would teach the fellow to shut up, if he understood English well enough to know he'd been insulted.

Luke arrived at the empty accounting firm, flipped on the florescent overheads, and strode past the cubicles. His rubber soles squeaked on the checkerboard tiles as he crossed the floor and entered his private office. There in the center of the blotter on the oak desk lay the end-of-the-fiscal year report labeled 2006 with the accountant Theresa's byline, just as she had promised.

Loosening his tie, Luke settled in the overstuffed chair, rested his legs on the desk, and opened the report, determined to study it with care. A preview of the columns of figures revealed no irregularities. The bottom line gross of somewhat under four million, although less than last year, was not inconsistent with the low range of projections. Downturns in the stock market always resulted in a few clients' falling away. A closer reading showed consistent numbers in the daily expenditures for payroll and expenses. Perhaps Luke had worried unnecessarily. It would relieve him to learn so.

Flipping over a page, he glanced through a list of clients, not much new there. Business had been remarkably stable. His eye caught a name he didn't recognize, Consolidated Consulting Services, evidently a client Theresa had used numerous times. Considering the amount of activity, Luke should remember.

Rising, he strode to Theresa's files and tried the keys on his ring but none worked. Being locked out of one of his own cabinets annoyed him. He scribbled a note for her to bring him the file in question as soon as she came in. It was almost eight. She should be along soon. Crumpling the note and tossing it in the wastebasket, he sat on the edge of Theresa's desk to wait for her.

With his attention on high alert, Luke took another more critical look at the report. He discovered that the secretary had logged numerous hours of overtime. He remembered asking her to stay a few times back in the spring, but that couldn't have been more than ten or twelve hours. In May the secretary had logged twenty hours then twenty-five in June, hours Luke had not authorized. Theresa had paid the billed hours anyway.

When Theresa arrived, she stood in the aisle, clutching a small purse in both hands. "Is there something I can do for you, Mr. Brock?" Her voice trembled.

They had been on a first-name basis for years. When she spoke so formally, Luke's suspicions of wrongdoing escalated. Other employees greeting each other came through the door. He slid off the desk and gazed down at Theresa, wishing he could interpret the tight-lipped expression on her square face. He only stood five eight, but she barely reached his shoulder. She stepped back.

"I'd like to see the file for," Luke glanced at the report to make certain, "for Consolidated Consulting Services. I don't remember them."

"Oh," Theresa said in a small voice. "I don't know where it is."

"Maybe it's in there." Luke gestured toward the filing cabinet. "Get the file and come to my office. I need to speak with you privately."

Without answering she slipped her plump body past him. There was very little space in the cubicle, and she wore some nauseating perfume. Luke walked down the hall, nodding at good-mornings because he didn't feel like smiling. He headed into his office, puzzling over which subject to broach first—the mysterious client, the locked cabinet, or the unauthorized payment of overtime. He took the 2005 report off the shelf and did a quick comparison. All the numbers were higher the year before.

Luke waited several minutes and began to think Theresa had ducked out on him. Then she entered the room and handed him a folder. He set the reports on the table and picked up the file, just as she turned and headed back out of the office.

"Please wait." Luke didn't ask her to sit, so they both stood on the carpet between the desk and bookshelves. He felt awkward enough with the situation, he had no wish to act casual. She clasped her hands tightly together, while he leafed through the file, which contained letters from the president, a certain Clyde Martinez, and several invoices for consulting services billed at two hundred dollars per hour. The paperwork went back almost two years. Every invoice had been initialed by Theresa. "It appears you've employed this company several times."

"Yes, they've done quite a lot of work for us."

"What kind of consulting do they do?"

"Uh...software problems."

"What software problems? I don't remember any such problems." Luke had bought a whole new program a year ago. His patience waned with her evasive answers.

"I didn't think I should bother you with them. It was just some auditing glitches. You had more important things to deal with."

Anger bubbled up in Luke. He waved the file in front of her and shouted, "Theresa, there are thousands of dollars we're talking about here. You should have asked me."

Theresa backed away from him as if she feared he'd hit her. "I'm sorry, sir, I will in the future." She grabbed for the door handle and missed.

Luke strode to intercept her. "Sit down. I have another question." She sat abruptly in the guest chair, and he closed the door although he imagined everyone in the outer office could hear them. He didn't care if they did. "There's another matter. Why did you pay the secretary for overtime hours?"

With a defensive shrug, Theresa said, "I just paid according to the hours she posted."

Luke glared down at her. "It was your job to check with me."

"I thought you had authorized them." Theresa chewed on her lip.

"No, I didn't. You've been doing a lot of presuming. Why are you making decisions to spend my money without asking me? Until June I was here almost every day, and you never brought up the subject."

Her fingernails dug into the wooden chair arms, and she shook her head defiantly. "If you're dissatisfied with my performance, why don't you just let me go?"

Talking with a person who was unquestionably lying maddened Luke. "I hope it doesn't come to that, but I want to understand everything about this situation. You're not helping me. If you do, maybe we can get past this."

"You know, Melinda would never have allowed you to speak to me in this way. She understood."

Surprised that Theresa would invoke Melinda's name, Luke shrugged. "Try me."

Theresa gave a wry laugh. "Anglos don't get it, especially not Anglo men."

"Get what?"

"How hard it is to succeed in a white world."

Her brassy insinuation infuriated Luke. "Theresa, you've worked here for at least ten years. You make over a hundred thousand dollars a year. It's ridiculous to expect me to feel sorry for you because of your race." He'd not let her change the subject again. He shouted, "Get this Martinez fellow on the phone. I want to talk to him."

"No,' she screamed. "You can't talk to him."

"Why not?"

With a sob, Theresa cried, "Because he doesn't exist." She buried her face in her hands.

Astonished, Luke plopped into the desk chair and stared at her. Theresa's story poured out. She had stolen to support her husband when he lost his job, then he got back into drugs after being clean for years. Although she wanted to stop stealing and promised herself she would pay the firm back, one thing lead to another and she just couldn't. Then the secretary discovered what Theresa was doing and demanded money to keep quiet.

Under other circumstances, Luke would have tried to console Theresa, but this woman had stolen from him, how many thousands of dollars he had no idea. He felt sorry for her and her husband because he'd heard how difficult it could be to overcome a drug habit, but the fact that neither Theresa nor the secretary had shown loyalty infuriated him. What did he have to do to get his employees to treat him with respect? Probably an overboard reaction because, at least to his knowledge, none of the others had shown disloyalty. How much thoroughness would it take for him to make certain? Having to think in those terms made the future of the firm seem precarious.

"Please," Theresa said, her voice hushed, "I didn't mean to do it. I promise I'll pay the money back to you."

"All right. If that's the way you want to handle it." Luke had no faith at all that she ever would. On the other hand, nothing could be gained by prosecuting the woman. To do so might create some hurtful publicity for the firm. He stretched out his hand. "Give me your keys."

Snuffling, she reached into her purse and laid the keys in his palm. "Luke, I'm so sorry."

"I know that you are." Luke took care to remove the edge from his voice. What was done was done. He knew the course he should take. "You are dismissed from employment. I can't give you a recommendation, but I won't press charges. You may leave now on the condition that you don't take anything out of your office."

Wiping her eyes, Theresa rose. Her posture slumped. Luke watched her hesitate, as if about to head back to her cubicle. Then she squared her chubby shoulders, walked past the secretary without a glance, and stepped through the main door.

The secretary watched Theresa go then glanced back at Luke with a guilty expression.

"Come into my office," Luke told the secretary. "I have something to discuss with you."

171

Firing the secretary had certainly not been on his agenda today, but he had to do it, unpleasant though it might be. At first she denied any wrongdoing, then she threatened to call the EEOC. He told her to call anyone she wanted, and he would go to court and get an order to garnishee her wages on any other job she managed to find until the debt was paid. Not that he intended to do so, but that shut her up. Still, she flounced out of the office as if she had won.

Luke had never trusted the woman without understanding why, until this morning. Euphoria would probably tell him to follow his instincts. He vowed to pay more attention to his feelings about people. Something in the secretary had always come across as deceitful, and Theresa had also seemed devious sometimes. But in both cases, Melinda had hired them and believed in them, so Luke had accepted her judgment. From now on, he would honor his own.

After calling the other seven accountants into the conference room, he explained that he had found some irregularities. All smart people, they didn't have to know the details to understand the general idea. Luke told them to expect a special audit as soon as he could arrange it. When the books were flawless, he intended to sell the business. They all looked worried, but he promised to make retaining their employment a part of the package for any sale. He would make certain they all kept their positions and salaries if they wished to continue with the new owners. Then he gave them the day off, making a long holiday weekend.

The accountants returned to their cubicles, closed up for the day, and headed out the door in silence. No Happy Fourth well-wishing and no whispered gossip. The atmosphere was electric.

After the last person left, Luke phoned the best auditing firm in Orange County and made an appointment for the next week. He gained the assurance of a speedy audit. Then he arranged to meet a business broker to discuss what materials he should assemble in preparation for placing the firm on the market. The broker felt certain she could find a buyer but such things took time. Just what Luke already believed.

For safekeeping, he grabbed the reports and locked up the office. He would return to Sedona for the weekend and drive his car back. He jingled his keys, creating a merry tune, and stuffed them into his pocket.

Going down on the elevator it hit him that he felt terrific. His weariness had dissolved along with his dread. He had set himself on a new track, and all he had left to do was finalize actions already set in motion. In the future he would make certain his career supported his own wants and needs. He couldn't wait to tell Euphoria and Aaron.

Angie, shortly before her death, had probably been right in suggesting he should forgive Melinda. Maybe he had simply remembered their conversation and fashioned that into the psychic experience of smelling her perfume. Luke didn't understand very well how all of those processes worked, but he acknowledged that holding resentment against Melinda hurt no one except himself. He wanted to let it go. As a first step, he had to get rid of his wife's firm because it symbolized immersion in fulfilling her dream. Now, he had to create a life based on his own dreams.

As he exited the office building, Luke glanced up at the clear, blue sky and spoke in his mind. *Melinda, I forgive you for everything. Go in peace.*

Refreshed, he hailed a cab. He had no reason to return home and rode straight to the airport. A different Middle Eastern driver talked to him, but this time Luke could understand the conversation. He laughed and agreed that the American people should probably pay for a shrink for George W. Something had to happen to get Bush to quit antagonizing world leaders.

At the airport, Luke arranged for a charter flight then phoned Aaron and made plans to get together that evening. Luke tried but couldn't reach Euphoria. It annoyed him that he had to either go through Psyche at home or the scratchy-voiced manager at the Crystal Cave. He called his cell phone provider to have a new number added to his account and a phone shipped overnight to the condo. He intended to surprise Euphoria with it tomorrow. If she intuited the info about his gift, he hoped to hell she'd act surprised anyway.

Once airborne, Luke looked away from the cars and highways and buildings. Transfixed by the passing clouds and air traffic, he experienced a surge of exhilaration. Sitting beside the pilot, Luke felt as if they and the little Cessna flew in sync, sailing free. He enjoyed the ride enormously, something he would never have thought possible. The extent of his relaxation in flight surprised him. Facing his fear had been wise. Now he could put it behind him.

The wretched revelations of this day had wrought a miracle in him. It amazed Luke how bad could turn into good. He promised himself he would remember that lesson the next time a situation seemed grim. *That's a plan. Gotta have one.*

When they arrived above Sedona, the glow of the setting sun tinged the mountains with shades of mango, pomegranate, and apple, like fruit bins in the grocery store. Celery and asparagus trees lined the canyon around the tiny airfield mesa. The plane descended on a rush of hot air.

Luke felt happy to be back. Sedona felt more like home than any place he'd ever lived or visited, even though he had no idea why. He hurried off the plane, past small aircraft and vintage bi-planes, through the terminal, which looked like a glorified filling station.

Aaron stood beside his parked convertible, arms folded like an old man, a contrast to his shorts and T-shirt, which bore the hawk emblem of his high school. Luke wondered why the top wasn't down but didn't care enough to ask. He greeted Aaron with a quick hug, and they climbed into the car.

As Aaron shifted into reverse, he shook his head. "I never thought I'd be picking you up from the airport. I don't know what happened, but I'm proud of you."

"Thanks." Luke felt embarrassed to dwell on what he now considered a foolish fear. "I'm starved. Let's get something to eat."

Luke intentionally left out any mention of the potential sale of the business but summarized the irregularities at the office and the plans set in motion for the audit. Luke had no wish to make Aaron feel insecure, but the boy didn't seem quite as fascinated by the tale as Luke had hoped. In the intermittent headlights of passing cars and store fronts along the business district, he noticed a frown on his son's face.

Aaron pointed to a Mexican bistro with mediocre food. "Is that all right?"

"Whatever you want is fine."

Once inside and seated, Luke noticed very few customers in the other wooden booths. He hoped that didn't mean the food had gotten worse. He perused the menu. Aaron scowled so at his that Luke had a notion to wise off and say the food wasn't that bad. The set of Aaron's jaw, reminiscent of the time he had lost in the soccer playoffs, stopped Luke. The waitress came and took their orders.

"I'm not very hungry." Aaron ordered a beef *chimichanga* dinner anyway. After the waitress left, he said, "So, how did old uni-brow handle getting fired?"

"She was pissed, but that's her problem."

"I'll just bet she was."

Luke decided to venture into the subject to measure Aaron's reaction. "I may give some thought to selling the business. Would you be all right with that?"

"Whatever you think is best."

"I might go back to straight practice of law."

"Seems okay." Aaron's disinterest might have been believable from some other kid, but not this smart boy. He was shrewd like his mother and always considered the ramifications of things. He should be asking questions.

"How about you?" Luke asked. "Things going okay here? How's Psyche?"

"Beats me." With an exaggerated shrug, Aaron slid back against the seat.

"What happened?"

"She ran off." The anger Aaron had obviously tried to conceal erupted. "She ran off with some damned biker. Guess I wasn't good enough for her. Guess high school boys are too tame. Especially Hispanic ones, just a distraction. Her mom is all upset and trying to find her." Tears came to his eyes. He batted them back with a flick of his hand and gazed fiercely at Luke.

"Well, shit. I met the biker the other night." Luke's supposition had been right, the biker was trying to get into Psyche's pants, after all. Seemed like he'd succeeded, too. Euphoria would probably need Luke's support. It surprised him that she hadn't phoned to tell him. He'd have loved to go see her, but Aaron needed his full attention at the moment. "Get it out, son. Tell me how you feel."

"She said stuff, you know, when we were..." Aaron blushed.

"It's okay. I know you went to bed together."

Aaron's face turned even redder. "We've been going out for over three weeks. I thought she was my girlfriend. I wouldn't run out on her."

"I know you wouldn't. You're a fine fellow, very considerate and kind. Psyche is a foolish girl to pass you up. That's what you have to remember. You'll find another girlfriend soon, if not this year, then at college."

"But I don't want..."

The waitress brought *chimichangas* with big bowls of sour cream and guacamole and mugs of beer and coke. A black mark for this place. Didn't they know they were supposed to bring drinks and chips first?

Luke slugged down half of the beer and felt it burn all the way. That ornery little girl. She had hurt two people that Luke loved. He'd like to give her a good talking to and wondered if she had any concept of how much power she had over other people. He had suddenly lost his appetite.

Taking a big bite of his *chimichanga*, Aaron spoke as he chewed. "I don't want any other girlfriend. If I can't have Psyche, I'll just stay a bachelor all through school. I'll concentrate on my studies and get the best job in the best lab." He dipped a chip in guacamole and ate as if the food tasted wonderful.

Luke expected his son to recover fast from this first romance. Considering the strength of his attachment to the girl and his innocent trust in her, Aaron obviously had some things to learn about girls. On the other hand, he had so few members in his own family that he needed an attachment to someone, as much as Luke was coming to realize he did also. He hoped Aaron would find someone worthy of him.

"You gonna eat that?" Aaron pointed at Luke's dinner plate.

Shaking his head, Luke shoved the plate across the table. In some ways they were very different. Aaron ate to assuage his emotions where Luke lost his appetite. He finished the beer and ate a few chips while Aaron devoured the rest of the food.

Aaron dropped his napkin in the plate. "Want some ice cream?"

"Sure."

"We could take some to Euphoria. Do you know what kind she likes?"

"No, but I'll ask." As Luke pulled out his cell phone, he felt admiration for his son's loving soul to be thoughtful of Euphoria's suffering despite his own unhappiness.

After paying the bill, Luke and Aaron drove to the ice cream parlor and bought a half gallon of peach ice cream for Euphoria. That choice was just like her, delicate and pretty. Aaron ordered a hot fudge sundae so Luke drove to her house while Aaron continued to drown his anger in food. Euphoria hadn't sounded any different on the phone, so Luke felt curious as to her state of mind. He couldn't help wondering why she failed to mention something so important as her daughter's leaving home. Luke didn't want her to be tough. He wanted her to need his support.

When they arrived at her house and rang the bell, Euphoria opened the door immediately. "I'm so glad you're here." Eyes red-rimmed, she shuddered as Luke enfolded her. Her softness beneath the flowered gown offered no sensuality. She threw her arms around him like a kid.

Aaron stepped past them and went into the small kitchen area where he clanked dishes and spoons, dishing out ice cream.

Luke held her tight, glad she needed him, and kissed the top of her head. "I'll help you through this, whatever it takes."

"I know. I know." Nodding her head vigorously, she pulled away and stumbled to the couch where she grabbed a handful of tissues. She plunged her face into them and sobbed.

Going to her Luke put his arms around her waist. He wished he could protect her from the emotional pain. "We'll find her. Don't worry. Have you called the police?"

"Oh, no. I'd never do that." Incredulity spread across Euphoria's blubbery face. "Psyche told me she was going to ride with Jess for as long as it felt right. Even bikers need love, she told me. I've raised her to always follow her own heart. I couldn't go back on my word now." She wiped her eyes and nose, hurried to Aaron, and threw her arms around him. "I'm afraid she hurt you, and that I'm very sorry for." She reached up and kissed his neck.

"I'll be fine. Don't worry about me." Aaron patted her shoulder awkwardly. "You want some ice cream?"

"Yes, thank you for bringing it." All three sat around the table. Euphoria took both Luke and Aaron into her gaze. "I'm going to miss Psyche, but what's breaking my heart is that she did exactly the same thing to me that I did to my mother. Now I know how she felt. Guess you could call that Karma."

"Karma!" Aaron said at the same time.

Luke raised his spoon in the air. "Here's to karma!" When he took a bite, the ice cream slid down his throat, cool and refreshing. "She'll probably come back soon." He had no idea whether or not that prediction would come true, but he did know that he was following his own heart in loving Euphoria and selling the business. The future seemed an exciting possibility.

Seventeen

Growing Pains

Upstate New York

Lying on his bed, Kendall heard Grandmother and Grandfather down the hall in their bedroom. The yelling and clanging meant they were probably throwing things around again. The noise hurt Kendall's ears even though he covered them with his hands.

"You're not my boss," Grandmother shouted. "Never were, and I don't have to take it from you. My first husband never did that, and I treated him just fine in bed and out."

"I doubt that." Grandfather laughed loudly. "You goddamn better do what I say."

After some clatter Grandmother said, "Stop that, Frank. You're hurting me."

"What you gonna do about it, old witch? Put a hex on me?"

"I'll leave you, that's what."

"If you do, you'll wish you hadn't. This world's not big enough for you to hide. I'll hunt you down wherever you are and kill you and your brat."

Rising, Kendall slammed the door of his bedroom. Maybe if he ate lots of vegetables he would get strong enough to take Grandmother away. She had painted his room the day before, dark blue, his favorite color. He liked the smell of paint.

It was fun to go to the mall with her, just the two of them, but it wasn't fun to try on new clothes. She had bought him lots of them and new Spiderman sheets and comforter, pencils, crayons, rulers, and all kinds of stuff for school, and even a Mario Nintendo game.

Leaving the overhead light on to keep monsters away, Kendall crawled under the bed, yanked the comforter off, and dragged it under with him. He'd been good the other day, not because he wanted to please Grandfather but because he'd wanted his Spiderman back. And he had got it, too. He could be very good if he wanted to be.

"Come," Kendall said, and the action figure tumbled across the carpet and under the bed to him. He covered Spiderman and himself completely with the comforter. That way they would be safe from Grandfather and from monsters, no matter what. Spiderman could protect anybody.

Closing his eyes, Kendall imagined the super heroes battling it out against the aliens to save the planet. The super heroes would win, of course, and the aliens would fly away in their spaceships. Superman would chase them across the sky to make sure they never came back.

Finally, the house got quiet. Kendall pressed his face into the soft carpet and fell asleep.

In a dream, Kendall floated up through the comforter, through the bed, and through the ceiling of the room. He stood on the roof of the house and could see the sky all dark blue, almost black, and beautiful, like the walls of his room. The lights of the stores and the other houses looked dim compared to the stars.

Maybe he could fly. That thought made him excited. He spread his arms out like wings and then decided it would be better to crook them forward like Superman always did. "To Krypton," he whispered.

He lifted into the air and flew around above the house and even above the trees. He took off, shooting up into the air, just for the fun of it.

Then Grandmother was flying beside him, except she looked smooth and pretty, not wrinkled and sad. He could see through her, as if she was made of the plastic that covered new toys. She smiled at him and took his hand. They flew over the city and up, up, up, far away, maybe even to Krypton. He didn't know where to. It didn't matter. He loved to fly. Grandmother must love it too.

The next morning, Grandfather acted nice. He cooked bacon and eggs and toast and said that boys should have a good breakfast to learn on. Kendall felt so hungry that he ate fast. Then he went into his bedroom and put on scratchy new jeans and a Spiderman T-shirt.

Grandmother called from her bedroom. "Kendall, go brush your teeth."

Kendall walked along the hall, counting the tiles. He took his time because he didn't want to go into the bathroom. He hated to brush his teeth. When he arrived, he picked up his toothbrush from the glass where it stood upside down. He dabbed on a tiny bit of the nasty-tasting toothpaste, licked it slightly, then threw the toothbrush in the sink, grabbed a towel, and wiped his mouth.

Entering the bathroom, Grandmother closed the door and stood behind him, her hands on his shoulders. She had on the pink sweats that she exercised in. Her swollen eye gave her a monster face. She gazed at him in the mirror. "You look so handsome, sweetheart. All the children are going to love you. Eyes as black as your father's."

Memory of their conversation at the mall returned to Kendall. She had talked about a new school and new friends. That scared him. "Grandmother, I want to go to my own school. Please take me."

Grandmother picked up a comb and passed it through his black hair. She could make it all lie down, even the cowlick. "We talked about this. I know you don't like the situation. Neither do I, but there's nothing we can do. Your mother and father, God rest their souls, would have wanted us to do the best we could. Your father intended to provide for you. I know that he did. He just thought he had plenty of time." She took Kendall's face in her hands. "You look so much like him when he was your age. I still remember his first day of school."

Her eyes filled with tears, and Kendall wanted to stop her from crying. "You know what I dreamed last night, Grandma?"

"No, what?"

"I dreamed you and I flew up into the sky. We went far away to Krypton, I think, and we didn't come back here at all."

"My dearest Kegan, you remember?" Wiping her eyes, she smiled. "Are you sure it was a dream?"

Her words confused Kendall, but he didn't have time to ask anything because Grandfather called from the kitchen that the school bus had turned the corner onto their street.

"Go, now, son." Grandmother patted Kendall's shoulders. "And do your best in school. It's important."

Rushing to the front door, Kendall grabbed the new Spiderman backpack and ran outside. When the bus stopped, he climbed on, aware that the other kids stared at him. He didn't know any of them, and they didn't know him either. When the bus driver asked what grade he was in, Kendall mumbled, "First grade," then hurried to the back and sat in an empty seat. He didn't scoot over. That way no one could sit next to him.

Looking out the window, he hugged the backpack. Grandmother had been afraid for him to have it because of the skateboard that came with it, but he had talked her into buying that one. It seemed easy to talk her into anything.

He just had to look at her for a long time, put all his wanting into his thoughts, then say please. It worked every time, like it had with his mother.

In some ways Grandmother was easier to convince. Kendall missed his mother more than anything. His father too, but not as much.

Kendall understood that his parents had died, but he knew where they went. They walked around in a place that looked very big. It had white streets and fountains and trees in different colors, not like the green trees rolling by the window of the bus. Those trees in heaven glowed blue and pink and lots of colors. His parents didn't look the same there. They looked like colored lights, but still Kendall recognized them.

He liked heaven well enough, and his mother had promised he could visit whenever he wanted to, but he had to be asleep to go. That meant when he awoke he felt sad and angry most of the time.

His parents seemed happy, but he didn't see how they could be happy without him. That's why last night he had killed the last of the baby rabbits. Now they could go up in heaven and be with his parents.

First grade turned out to be a big surprise to Kendall. Even though he didn't really like the teacher as much as the one at his kindergarten, all the children liked him, and they mostly did whatever he asked them to do. On the playground he decided what games they played and he picked the sides for teams. The girls were kind of yucky and tattled to the teacher a lot, but they liked Kendall even more than the boys did. The teacher gave such easy assignments that he calculated the answers in his head and memorized the lessons without even thinking about it.

He knew so much that the school double promoted him, and he skipped second grade.

After a while Kendall stopped going up to heaven to visit with his parents in dreams. Heaven seemed boring unless the angel Emmons gave him talks about being a good boy. Then heaven was about as not fun as a place could be. Emmons reminded Kendall to listen to his teachers but to make his own decisions and other stuff best left to big people.

As days passed into months and months into years, Kendall excelled in music, tennis, and basketball as well as in coursework. He stopped missing his old school and forgot why he'd liked it so much. He kept a photo of his parents on the desk in his bedroom to prevent himself from totally forgetting what they looked like. He didn't intend to shut them out of his mind, but his life grew very busy.

After Kendall entered high school, he spent all of his time either in school, playing sports, or at his laptop. From long practice, he and Grandfather sidestepped so they hardly saw each other, a good thing because the bastard continued to pop Grandmother in the face every once in a while. That she allowed such treatment bothered Kendall.

To his relief, he found out that Grandfather was no blood relation. Grandmother had married him for unfathomable reasons. The fact that she stayed married to provide a home for Kendall made him feel guilty. Anything could set the old man off, so they all lived in a state of nervous tension. Despite the unsettling environment, Kendall always had all the latest toys and clothes and electronic gadgets. His friends envied him, and he enjoyed his status.

Grandmother was the most important person in his world, not only because of her role as guardian but also because she seemed to have an endless fount of amazing abilities.

Sometimes while awake she gave him instructions that developed his abilities. He came to know their scientific names. One she called psychokinesis. Kendall could move objects with his thoughts. Most people didn't even know the word, let alone have the ability.

Kendall used this skill in secret, practicing with Grandmother, except for the time he used it to drag Bobby Sims's pants to his knees in front of a bunch of girls. Boy, was that a hoot, especially when Bobby had to go to the principal's office. The principal even called Bobby's parents in, and they grounded him for weeks. Bobby never even knew who to blame.

Grandmother taught Kendall how to watch for instances of precognition in his dreams. She always said to think of his psychic abilities as simple tools, neutral in themselves, to be used to fulfill his desires. They joked about going to Las Vegas and winning big bucks by influencing the roll of the dice. He hoped they would someday.

Their journeys out of the body pleased Kendall most, even though she insisted he call them astral projections. After going to sleep at night, he and Grandmother slipped out of their physical bodies and met in their soul bodies, which shimmered a silvery color. They flew together through the astral world, spookier than the regular world because it had no sun. Trees and houses and everything else had a bluish glow to them.

Kendall and Grandmother sailed over the countryside of New York State and took trips. In some kind of magic that Grandmother seemed to easily weave, they flew to the Grand Canyon or to the Golden Gate. Kendall thought he had seen most of the tourist sites on the whole American continent without spending a dollar on plane tickets.

From time to time, Grandfather followed them in his astral body, but he always appeared disoriented and muddy, as if he had little notion of what he attempted to do. Grandmother ignored Grandfather, who generally fell back into his physical body and snored even before they left.

It occurred to Kendall that Grandfather could get hurt in this state. He seemed weak on the astral plane, the opposite of his generally powerful demeanor when awake.

Eighteen

Many Happy Returns of the Day

September 11, 2018

A few days after school started for his senior year, the day of his sixteenth birthday, Kendall sat playing Dungeons and Dragons on his laptop. He heard a knock on his bedroom door.

Grandmother's voice came through. "I've got a surprise for you." She sounded excited.

Expecting a birthday check or something, Kendall opened the door. "What's up, Grandma?"

"Come on, let's go, Kegan," she whispered. She only used his old secret name on special occasions. He felt glad he had told her as a boy of what he considered his true identity. He doubted he would tell her now if she didn't already know because he seemed to be losing his connection to the old Kegan self, the great and powerful warrior of his dream life since childhood.

As they hurried through the house and out the front door, he noticed she had a big shiner, and she limped a bit as if her back bothered her. The old bastard had really hurt her this time. That meant he had probably coughed up a lot of money. He always had before. At least, he had the decency to feel guilty afterward. Kendall couldn't understand the lack of control that provoked such violence and subsequent guilt because he always monitored his own behavior. No surprises, ever. Kendall felt grateful for his intelligence and self-control.

Outside, beneath a maple tree, its leaves tinged with yellow, a taxi waited in front of the house. Kendall felt keyed up and climbed in beside Grandmother. He didn't care where they went.

Kendall hoped that they were finally making the getaway he had wanted for so long. He felt certain they would be all right. Just getting away from Grandfather meant the most. Kendall could get a job, and Grandmother, at seventy, wasn't too old to earn some money herself. Maybe she could get a job at a MacDonald's or something. They hired a lot of old people. He and Grandmother would get along fine by themselves.

"Now this is my surprise," Grandmother patted his knee. "For your birthday. You will never forget this day."

More than ever now, Kendall believed that they were leaving. He wished he had known so he could have brought his computer and guitar, but he'd just have to buy new ones.

The taxi pulled up in front of the bank. Kendall and Grandmother went inside. Grandmother handed over a check, signed by Grandfather, for a hundred thousand dollars. She said, "Open an account in the name of Kendall Roberts, please."

Looking as surprised as Kendall felt, the wimpy little bank teller, his bowtie wiggling with each breath, gazed at the check while his fingers flew over the keyboard. In seconds he jerked a printout off his machine and stuffed it in a welcome folder, which he handed to Grandmother. She placed the folder in Kendall's hand reverently with a smile that made her creased face glow despite the bruises.

"Thank you, Grandma, from the bottom of my heart."

As they left the bank, Kendall's astonishment gave way to concern. It crossed his mind that maybe Grandmother had fallen ill. What appeared as a sudden extravagance might instead be an attempt to provide for him after her death.

Back in the taxi, Kendall asked, "Are you feeling all right?"

"Of course." Her face twisted in a naughty grin. "What did you think this was? Your inheritance?"

"I can't help it." Kendall gave her a quizzical look. "I've got to ask. How did you get so much money?"

"I got the old man a good one this time. I made him feel really guilty."

"You provoked him? Why can't we just go away?"

"He owes me from a past life. We've been on this seesaw for eons. For the first time, I've got the upper hand financially, and I intend to enjoy it."

Stumped, Kendall had no rebuttal to her use of reincarnation as a rationale for her behavior. "But why did you give me so much money?"

"Let's just say I did it more for myself than for you. For my peace of mind. Are you all right with that answer?"

Kendall nodded although he didn't agree inside. What choice did he have? She seemed intent on dim-wittedness despite her generosity. He wanted the money more than he could even imagine. Withdrawing the printout, he tucked it into his shirt pocket for safekeeping. It represented a security he had longed to experience.

"What's your favorite kind of car, dear?" Grandmother asked.

His friends might answer with something flashy like a Corvette or Jaguar, maybe a hybrid like a Tango or Jupiter. Kendall didn't have to think twice. "A Lexus sedan. Classy, durable, and safe."

"You got it," Grandmother appeared to be enjoying giving him these gifts as much as he appreciated receiving them.

They went to the Lexus dealership, and Kendall picked out a stunning gold one with a sun roof. Nobody at the high school had anything close even though some of the students had quite a bit of money. Certainly not the teachers. Even the principal drove some ordinary thing like a Toyota.

Kendall could have any girl he wanted in the backseat of this Lexus. Finding a girlfriend to have sex with was becoming more important every day. Although he hadn't made up his mind definitely which girl he wanted, the time would come soon, with his new-found wealth. He longed to enjoy a girl's body and to witness that envious look on the faces of his teammates when he walked on campus with the foxiest girl. Plus his secret fantasy was to find out if he could unhook bra straps without using his hands, just with the power of his mind.

Amazingly, with Grandmother paying cash, it took hardly any longer to buy a car than it did to check out at the supermarket. The salesman handed her the key and the remote, and she dropped them into Kendall's hand with a smile. "Happy birthday, dear boy, and many happy returns of the day."

"Thank you." Staring down at the Lexus insignia, Kendall felt great pride.

It was such a delicious feeling to sink into those golden leather seats and see the array of dials in front of him. Soon, he and Grandmother sped off the lot in the Lexus with him in the driver's seat. At the first intersection, he turned onto the freeway. Kendall could go on for hours, enjoying the physical pleasure of the car. She'd probably had this planned all along when she overrode his protest and insisted he take driver's training at school. He'd made an A, of course. He made A's in everything.

Grandmother seemed to love the car too. She rubbed her gnarled hands across the seat as if she were stroking a cat. "Take us somewhere nice. I've got some things I need to tell you."

"I'd rather just keep on driving. We don't need to go back home at all. With all this money, we could get an apartment in another town."

His pleading look didn't work this time. Grandmother folded her arms and shook her head. "Find a place to park."

Kendall headed off at the exit and drove directly to a waterfall and parked across from it. Pine trees lined the country road. He leaned over and kissed Grandmother on the cheek. "Thank you so much. This is super generous of you."

Although she flushed, Grandmother gave him a serious look. "I know you've not had it easy. Neither have I, but there's more to life than some jerk of a man. You will have the good things that life can bring, no matter what happens to me. You are provided for now, no matter what."

Her tone alarmed Kendall, like that of someone who was about to die or commit suicide or something. Maybe she had lied to him about her health. "What did you want to tell me, Grandma?"

She clenched his hand in hers. "I want to tell you about your past." Her voice sounded hoarse from the brown cigarettes she smoked.

That seemed very ordinary. "I know all about my father and what a good son he was and how he was the light of your life."

"I don't mean this lifetime." Grandmother's eyes glowed with contagious excitement. "I mean the time before you came to us."

She had his attention now. Kendall sensed there'd be no going back from whatever she was about to say. He felt suddenly nervous.

"I was born with the caul. The gift of second sight. You were too." Grandmother whispered, so low that he could hardly hear her against the tumbling water of the falls. "The day you were born, the stupid doctors just wiped it off you and destroyed it. They think they know so much with all their science. They should have given it to your mother to keep. That would have been luckier for all of us."

"A caul?"

"A hood over your eyes. You know, the placenta? I wasn't a bit surprised though because of a dream I had where an angel told me you would become my student in the psychic arts. He said you were coming back too soon and needed more guidance than he could give you. Of course, I knew your mother was pregnant, but I had no notion she and your dear father would die and I'd end up literally raising you."

"That caul? Is that why I can move things with my mind?"

"Yes, and there's more." Her voice took on a haunting tone. "Much more. You can remember the past, your own past lives."

Kendall had known since childhood of Grandmother's belief. Even though she didn't go to church, he had noticed her whispering to herself occasionally and assumed she prayed. He had an intellectual understanding of reincarnation. He had done a term paper in English on *The Vedas* and Hindu beliefs. Fascinating mythology, he had written without giving it much thought. He drummed his fingers on the steering wheel, distracted by her tone. He hated the itchy feeling that this whole day had gotten out of his control.

"Listen, my boy." The grip Grandmother had on his hand tightened. "Close your eyes and listen."

Compelled to honor her, Kendall did as she requested.

"In your last incarnation you did something very important. You committed a violent act that hurt a lot of people." Her words pierced his mind. "This was important work for the world. You volunteered to do it to advance your own soul. It was a part of the Plan to teach people to love each other more. You had a short but valuable life."

Kendall had no conscious reaction to what she had said. He didn't understand at all.

"It's no accident, dear boy, that today is your birthday."

A vivid image of a tall building flashed in his mind's eye. Kendall gasped as the building seemed to come toward him with inconceivable speed. Screams of horrified people assailed his ears. His fingers bled with the force of his hold on the steering column. The cockpit vibrated around him. Pride filled his heart and soul. Mission accomplished.

Startled by the realism of his imagination, Kendall wondered if he could have been there. Of course not, he had seen video of the actual event many times in history class and on TV documentaries. How ridiculous to think anything else could cause his imagination to go awry. "Nine Eleven? It couldn't be true!"

Because Grandmother failed to respond to his words, Kendall opened his eyes. Her face looked rapt and her eyelids fluttered she was so deeply entranced. He feared she had gone off her rocker and would likely make him crazy too. He felt impatient with her and protective of her at the same time. She had sacrificed much for him, but she went overboard with some of her beliefs.

Grandmother emitted a long sigh and appeared attentive to a world far away. Her cheek twitched as she said, "I see you a long time ago in Ireland. You are a forlorn child, burdened with pain and torment. Someone hurts you, someone you trust. You grow up in spite of odds that would send a lesser youth to his grave. This was a long time ago, in the 1700s. You feel responsible for your brother, but you are not capable of taking care of yourself, let alone him. Still, you try. You take your brother to England in the hope of a better life. Money is the most important thing to you because you don't have any. Poor child." She sobbed as if the tragedy of the story she told was too much for her to bear. "I see you hiding in the woods. Do you remember?"

Her words transported Kendall back into his own imagination. A cold wind tore across him, not of the warm autumn afternoon in New York, but of a wintry England ages ago. He quavered among trees in a dark wood. A wave of fear overwhelmed him.

"Yes, I sense something. I don't like this. I'm afraid."

"Stay strong, my boy. You can see it, remember it, and rise above it."

"I'm about to do something I don't want to do," he whispered, caught by the fragile images. "I feel like I can't help myself. It's like I have to do a very bad thing. I must be a criminal. Oh, no."

"It's all right to remember. You're safe. I will always take care of you."

A new hatred filled Kendall. He would get revenge for awful things. He couldn't remember what they were, but he knew he needed vengeance. He waited for the bitch, who would soon walk into the trap he had set. Then her coddled little boy would become his victim, as he had been a victim. Somehow that would right the wrong. It had to. He had no other way. Unknown others needed retribution, too.

"Colin," Grandmother said, "your name was Colin in that lifetime. Such a brutal one, and your soul can't let it go because all your enemies had reincarnated there again."

The fervor of Colin's needs swept over Kendall. He feared Grandmother spoke the truth. He had wanted revenge, and now he might be able to get it. He could see them as clearly as he had seen the rabbits in the cage— Lugh and Alma and Taliesin, even Morfran. Those names must have come from deep inside his subconscious; otherwise he would not have named the rabbits for them as a child. Something sinister fit.

Perhaps he had incarnated this time so he could finally have his revenge. Such a moment might not return for a millennium. Over and over, they had defeated him. In this lifetime, it all had to end. If they had reincarnated too. If.

Grandmother shook his shoulders and cried, "You saw it just like I did!"

Tears spurted out of Kendall's eyes. He felt dismayed because he'd not cried since he was little, but he couldn't help himself. "I saw myself, yes, I saw myself. How is this possible?"

Grandmother tenderly wiped the tears from his face. "I don't know how it's possible. I don't know if it's a gift or a curse."

"This is insanity. What's past is done and gone. And even if it's true, I don't have to act on it if I don't want to." Kendall had bought the arguments for free will in literature class and history. His accelerated academic program focused on such issues, and he had argued the side of free will in a debate, winning handily over the fate team, primarily because of the intractable quality of an immutable future.

"All past all present and all future are here with us now. That is why you can't change your reaction. If you learn anything from me, learn that."

"It can't be true. Everyone has choice over what they do with their own bodies. It's American law." Kendall thought it no more probable to solidify the future than to change the past.

"It is written in the Akashic records. They are the memories of all our lifetimes stored on the astral plane, and they cannot be negated. Someday, you'll have to fulfill your destiny." Although she looked sad, Grandmother sounded determined.

It was pointless to argue with her. Besides, vague images flitted across Kendall's mind and distracted his thought process. He remembered the pretty place he'd imagined meeting his parents. How gullible he had been as a child in thinking he had gone to some honeyed place to visit his parents. "If that's true, heaven must be a bad place."

"Doubtless that is true. Earth, where all of heaven's intentions play out, is an exceedingly bad place."

Twisting in the seat, Kendall flipped the key in the ignition. Rolling down the windows, he gulped crisp, wonderful New York air. He didn't care that the temperature had cooled considerably and the sky had grown gray.

More than anything, he wanted to get away from the burden of hatred all these memories provoked. He wished he could shoot hoops right now or study for an exam. The last thing he needed was to deal with the emotions of some berserko in the eighteenth century, but once they had lodged inside him he feared they would fester until they burst.

Kendall needed control over his own destiny. He felt weary as if he'd aged a hundred years instead of one year on his birthday. "I'm hungry. Let's go eat."

When Grandmother nodded, tears stood in her eyes. They both cried as he drove along the highway toward town, MacDonald's, and normalcy, he hoped. Lightning checked across the sky, and big drops of rain fell on the windshield. Things hadn't gotten bad enough in life. His perfect car had to get rained on?

"One more thing," Grandmother said.

Kendall shivered, uncertain of how much more he could take from her.

"You know how we sometimes meet in dreams and go flying?"

"Uh, huh." Despite trying to dismiss the experience as fantasy, Kendall knew it to be real. Grandmother had just confirmed the reality beyond doubt.

"Well," she spoke in a conspiratorial way, "if I ever just disappear while your Grandfather is flying with us, don't pay me any mind, all right? Just go on flying. Uh, for the fun of it."

"All right." Kendall thought that a most unusual request, but so far her behavior had been anything but normal today. He owed her his life, everything. He would do whatever she needed. She loved him, the only person who did, he supposed. Why had the idea of love come into his mind? He didn't understand its dynamics too well.

The pictures in his mind wouldn't let Kendall go. He couldn't conceive of himself wanting to actually kill four people he didn't know, any more than he could imagine himself flying a plane into a building to kill thousands of people on purpose. Something Grandmother said niggled at him. "How could world peace come out of such a terrible act as Nine Eleven?"

"I didn't say it did. I said that was the original Plan. Up there." She pointed skyward. "You might live long enough to see the fates allow it. Probably not, but it's possible."

Kendall intended to assimilate the information his grandmother had given him about his past lives, but his stomach ached, and filling it took priority. They stopped at McDonald's and dashed through the rain to get inside where they pigged out on fries and chicken sandwiches.

When they returned home, Kendall went into the kitchen for a candy bar, and Grandmother followed him.

Ten beer bottles lay on the table, lip to lip, their bottoms to the center in an arrangement that looked stupid and bizarre at the same time. The empty bottles formed a pentagram, the shape of a witch's star. A Dresden cup sat beside them filled with brown glop, a makeshift spittoon.

"My mother's china!" Grandmother's face contorted. "How dare he mock me. The son of a bitch will pay for this."

Unquestionably, Grandfather had consumed the beers during this evening because two six packs had sat in the fridge that morning. So it looked like the old bastard had taken far more than a few nips.

If Kendall and Grandmother had arrived home earlier, they would probably have suffered through an angry diatribe. Instead they walked to his bedroom door and peeked in to find a snoring drunk.

Grandmother reached up and put her arms around Kendall. She drew him close to her in a loving way, something she rarely did. It embarrassed him a little even though he enjoyed her nearness. She kissed his cheek. The kiss warmed him and gave Kendall a sense of belonging for which he felt grateful.

"I love you," she murmured.

Kendall had seldom heard those words before. He didn't doubt that Grandmother loved him, but he knew through her actions, not her words. Girls at school wrote notes saying they loved him and passed them in class, but they just did that because they wanted his attention. He didn't know how to respond to Grandmother. He probably should say he loved her too. It seemed like the polite thing to do, but he couldn't. He felt too overwhelmed, too wounded by all that had transpired during the day. "Good night, and thank you again," he whispered.

He needed to get to bed. To lie down and seek oblivion. When he walked into his own bedroom, he noticed that the comforter lay askew, as if someone had already turned it down for him. He had wanted to go to bed, and his bed covers had responded.

After twisting the lock on his doorknob, Kendall dropped on the bed, exhausted. He glanced up at the overhead light and thought *dark*. The lights went out. Peeling off his clothes, he fell into bed. He had slept in this bed every night for ten years. How reassuringly ordinary it felt.

A review of the events of the day had given him the sense that his life had changed irrevocably, but there was much he didn't understand. With all the surprises Grandmother had foisted on him, Kendall tried to settle down. He loved her and hated her at the same time. She gave him a great deal physically, but she expected too much of him. Yesterday he would have said he had no particular belief about past lives, but tonight he knew he had experienced something incredible when she spoke, as if she had opened his soul and read its contents.

Grandmother should explain things better. He didn't understand her logic leading to the conclusion that he was bound to fulfill her prophecy. So exhausted he hoped he didn't wake up until next week, Kendall fell asleep finally,

In the blackness of the night, Kendall became wakeful, aware of himself in his astral body. Shimmering white and young looking, Grandmother hovered above him. They wore astral sheaths of silver light reminiscent of pajamas. She smiled at Kendall in the old way, as if the events of the day, the bank account, the car, the past life memories had not happened. Glad to forget them for now, he smiled back and floated up to her. They sailed off into the west.

Other astral travelers flew about. One young boy, looking confused, glanced down at his naked astral body then whisked away at top speed. He evidently hadn't intended to go out of his physical body and probably didn't even know how he got out of bed. The expression on his astral face amused Kendall.

Grandmother pointed behind her. Kendall looked back and saw Grandfather, in a discombobulated state, following them. His astral body looked fragile and flimsy as he bobbed along. Kendall thought Grandfather was really out of his element and ought to stay home and drink and watch TV.

As they flew over the autumn treetops in a pale blue glow, Grandmother held out her hand to Grandfather, as if having him for company delighted her. Grandfather took her hand, and she motioned to Kendall to fly alongside, so he did although he dreaded doing so.

Time had a way of compressing in the astral. Kendall wondered whether or not Grandfather would want to see the Grand Canyon. Well, who wouldn't in the astral or in the physical? Grandfather appeared to be following, regardless, and Kendall flew with him, aiming toward the west.

Kendall glanced up to give Grandmother a smile, but she had gone. Only he and Grandfather flew above a mountain range. Kendall went to a great deal of trouble to keep from having to be alone with Grandfather in the waking state. No way did he want to compound the problem by companionship in the astral. He intended to end this excursion right now and headed back toward home.

Then something odd happened. Kendall noticed that Grandfather stopped moving. He appeared to hover in the air, then his ghostly image started to dissolve.

Kendall looked down and realized that they flew over their house. He could see through the roof down into the bedroom. There Grandmother stood, the real flesh and blood Grandmother, stabbing a knife into the real flesh and blood Grandfather's chest. Over and over.

Oh, God, she had done it. A part of Kendall had always known this moment would come. Another part, the part still a kid in this lifetime, hoped that it would all go away. But it wouldn't. Grandmother had murdered Grandfather. Already blood flowed all over the bed clothes.

Kendall had understood the potential, had known what Grandmother could do, given certain circumstances, but in his innermost heart, he had not really believed it would all fall out like this.

Bewildered, he tried to reenter his physical body and missed. His astral form fell into the wastebasket near the bed.

Weeping in his soul, Kendall crawled out of the wastebasket and into his body. He fell asleep, knowing he shouldn't, knowing a dead man lay in the next room, knowing whatever befell his grandmother, they were joined in an inexorable knot.

In a way that didn't make sense to Kendall, he felt the guilt of murder, though he hadn't done it.

Nineteen

The Shape of the Future

Sedona, 2021

In the gold tunic he customarily wore at roundedness events, Luke leaned against the podium in the hotel conference room. In barrel chairs spread out in a semi-circle across the room sat eleven participants. They wore white gowns he had issued to them at the beginning of the five-day intensive. They gazed with rapt faces, indicating they expected a miracle from his wife as Luke did.

In the center of the room, Euphoria, in a green-for-healing gown, passed her hands over the head and shoulders of an arthritic old man, who lay before her on a massage table. His crutches stood propped against the table.

The old man shuddered as if he actually felt her hands even though she did not touch him. She worked by soothing and smoothing the patient's aura. She always taught that technique as the most important requirement for healing. She continued the passes over his entire body then began again.

Since Euphoria made it a habit to give Luke an aura cleansing at least once a week, he could empathize with the impact on the old man, something similar to an electrical charge, exhilarating and calming at the same time. Luke would never argue with the efficacy of the treatment, especially when combined with meditation to balance chakras, the centers of spiritual power in the human being.

Together those techniques had eliminated his dependency on prescription medicine for epilepsy, a state of wellness Luke had never even considered possible a few years ago, B. E. E. Before Euphoria Era.

Luke and Euphoria limited enrollment for each session to twelve. They'd learned over time that any larger a group lessened the impact of the spiritual connection they attempted to make. The nub on the floral carpet had worn shiny, and Luke noticed the food tasted flat this past week. He intended soon to build their own retreat and get away from the shabby commercial area.

Kneeling before the patient, Euphoria whispered, "The swelling diminishes more every day, and you feel healthy and happy. I thank the Divine for your return to health."

The participants hushed with anticipation.

The old man's eyes opened, and he gave Euphoria a glassy stare. He began to rub his knees, broke into a huge smile, and stood up. "It's gone. I'm cured."

Euphoria picked up the crutches and handed them to him. "Keep these with you. Just in case the symptoms return."

"Don't you believe in your own ability?" the old man asked.

"There is often a period of adjustment. Your legs aren't accustomed to bearing your weight. It's better to be safe."

The old man ignored her and wobbled to his seat. Following him, Euphoria propped the crutches beside his chair and surveyed the room. "I believe that's everyone." She sat in a chair near the podium and nodded toward Luke. "Your turn, darling."

"I'm ready!" Luke bent over Euphoria, intending to give her a quick kiss. Her great love for him flashed on her face. She alternately rendered him passionate about making love to her or about sharing teaching duties with her. He was joined with her day and night, work and play. They spent all their time together. His marriage had been a thirteen-year-long romantic encounter.

Luke kissed her, probably longer than prudent, to convey the scope of his love. He knew her well enough to imagine that she received his thoughts telepathically as he thought them. Once he'd gotten used to that facet of her gift, it gave him joy.

A titter of laughter came from the audience, reminding Luke of how transparent his thoughts had become. Or the whole room had become telepathic. Breaking the kiss, he caressed Euphoria's cheek then stepped to the podium. He grinned at the audience. "Do you blame me, gentlemen?"

Both men and women applauded. Euphoria smiled happily and turned on the sound system. She didn't appear one bit embarrassed, certainly because she understood as well as Luke that the quality of their relationship played a large part in the success of their trainings. They often received notes from previous participants thanking them for modeling marital love.

When he heard the subtle violin music, Luke said, "Let us begin."

A few moments of clatter followed while the participants left their seats and stretched out on the carpet beside their chairs. They seemed eager. Quiet descended on the room.

"Close your eyes and center yourselves." Luke modulated his voice with his best courtroom persuasion. The meditation to balance the chakras was his favorite part. "Breathe in on the count of four. Hold for a count of four. Breathe out on the count of four. Hold for a count of four." He waited while the same little miracle happened. Everyone, including Euphoria, breathed in unison. "Imagine a beautiful, rich red light swirling through your root chakra at the base of your spine. See it brighten and grow, filling you with a sense of safety and security. This is the elemental fire of creation fueling your body with power and warmth."

Luke continued through the six remaining chakras, orange for the sacral, yellow for the solar plexus, green for the heart, pale blue for the throat, indigo for the third eye, and purple for the crown chakra.

With only the even-toned music for accompaniment and the deep, abiding breath of life going in and out on a wave, he felt the incredible energy of Divine power fill him. Once enough time had elapsed for the energy to crest through each individual's chakras, Luke led the meditation to its conclusion and waited for the others to rouse themselves. "Thank you for attending our roundedness event. The god in me greets the god in you. *Namaste.*"

Just like always, men and women, who had been strangers at the start sometimes hostile, fearful, or grief-stricken, felt buoyant by the end of the training. They kissed Euphoria and Luke good-bye, promising to write and hugging each other, tearful but happy.

Luke wished he could bottle the good will and send it to the warring continents. If only they could experience such abundance, they might reconsider the wars that had gone on for so many years. No matter what the American government did, conditions continued to worsen.

Terrorists had bombed major cities along the Atlantic. The press had recently predicted that the Capitol would move to the Southwest. So far, the government had made no announcement, but media rumors almost always turned into facts.

Every attempt to secure visas so Luke and Euphoria could travel to Europe and the Middle East had been denied. It didn't seem that the ban would change any time soon with Christian battling Muslim, Jew battling Muslim, Shinto battling Christian. Shinto had even tried to engage mainland China's Buddhists in war, something akin to fighting Jello because the Buddhists refused to fight back.

After a cell of Muslim terrorists assassinated the Pope, the Church fell into disarray because of internal corruption and scandal. Only the South American Bishop carried any Catholic clout in the ever more religion-centered governments of the world.

The religious chaos had helped to ruin missionary attempts, even by people with spiritual messages not affiliated with any religion, such as himself and Euphoria. He understood the reservations of Congress and the President, but the resultant restrictions on travel and cooperative ventures felt like persecution.

"It was good, today," Euphoria said.

"What?"

"The program went well. I think we helped all of them somewhat, don't you?"

Luke nodded his agreement and waited for Euphoria to gather their music disks, paper handouts, and Tibetan bowl and bells into a rolling bag. He carried it outside in the warm May air, and they climbed onto a crowded city bus. They had to stand and hold onto straps.

A million residents now claimed tiny Sedona as their home. With traffic so heavy, it was too beastly to even try to drive along the narrow streets any more. Even with the population growth, Luke still loved the craggy red mountains overhead. He didn't blame people for wanting to live here. He doubted he would ever move away, no matter how crowded the area became.

Their route snaked along the narrow old highway, past restaurants, art galleries, motels, and rows and rows of condominiums built into the sides of mountains in an architectural style reminiscent of prehistoric Sinagua Indian cliff dwellings. The Sedona city limits meandered all the way to the freeway despite recent Navajo Nation efforts to annex the territory.

The bus dropped Luke and Euphoria down the street from their white stucco bungalow. Its red tile roof glistened against the sun setting beyond it. They strolled, hand in hand, up the gravel street. When Luke had moved in with

Euphoria after Aaron went to college, the house seemed very small. Accustomed to the massive L. A. house, he still felt glad they had kept hers and built the second story for an office and extra bedrooms.

A smart move, one of many he had made, including selling the accounting firm and opening a one-man law practice in Sedona. Now he could choose the cases he took, and with the roundedness trainings going so well, he wanted to devote less and less time to law. Teaching spiritual concepts suited him. His mother had always loved teaching, so he had taken to it naturally. He recalled his old habit of casting thoughts into headlines. SURPRISING SON PICKS PARENTAL PROFESSION.

From the visits that his mother continued to make from the spirit world, Luke knew she felt proud of that choice. He considered those visits a compensatory gift. Even though he had lost her in his twenties, at least he could continue to feel her love and appreciation. In the workshops, he always tried to impart the miracle of that gift for bereaved people.

After supper and a shower, Luke felt marvelous. The last day of a workshop always revitalized him. Euphoria joined him in bed with a bottle of merlot. Nude, they cuddled while they shared it.

"Are you ready for this weekend?" Euphoria asked.

"Absolutely."

"I dare you to make one prediction about it."

Luke knew her game to help him build confidence in his psychic abilities. She often said she hoped to make him as good at telepathy and precognition as she. It might happen someday but hadn't yet.

"We are going to have a new family member soon." Luke cast a teasing eye upon Euphoria as if revealing a great insight. "I know, a daughter-in-law!"

"Be serious."

"Okay, but it's not easy with your naked bod in my arms." Trying to ignore it, Luke emptied his mind for a moment to allow the fragile knowledge to come through, not because he wanted to but to please Euphoria. Then he went with the first well-formed thought as she had taught him to do. Comfortable with receiving subtle psychic perceptions, he'd learned to trust in his growing abilities. "We'll meet a most unlikely person, someone we've never heard of, who will change our lives in a way we can't predict at the moment."

"That sounds right, even though we probably do know all of the wedding guests. I'll keep an eye out for a person who suits the description." Euphoria reached up, kissed him, and pulled him into the magical aura of herself.

They made love fired by the chakra meditation augmented by wine. The energies flowed through them, their passion a divine fire all its own, fueled by remembrance of their past lives together.

After a while, Euphoria fell asleep in Luke's arms. He still marveled at her perfect fit. Cuddling with Melinda had never quite satisfied him, more a touching of bodies than an intertwining. Maybe because they had been the same height, probably more because Melinda never completely relaxed. Silly though it might be, Luke was glad for Euphoria's short stature. Her body fit his perfectly.

Just as Luke entered sleep, her movement awakened him. She kicked off the blanket, rolled away from him, and sprawled on her stomach. Not an unconscious desire for escape in his estimation, but a bodily display of her birthright requirement for freedom. He grinned at her round butt, visible by moonlight, and pulled the blanket over her.

With a sigh, he allowed his mind to settle, opening a space for sleep, for subtle knowledge or whatever came. He felt comfortable with the range of his consciousness and enjoyed each state, whether of trance, meditation, prayer, emptiness. He trusted his spirit. It would never betray him. He trusted the spirits of his loved ones in the Afterlife. They would never betray him either. He fell into a wakeful serenity.

"Hello, honey."

A mellow feminine voice sounded somewhere in Luke's mind or behind his head. He couldn't discern which, but he recognized the tone. No one had called him "honey" in all the long years since his mother's death. Luke calmed himself to hang onto this connection between the worlds.

"Mom, it's good to hear your voice." Luke didn't know whether he whispered or thought the words. It didn't matter.

Angie spoke into his mind. "Please tell Aaron that I will be there in the church on Sunday. Others who love him will be present too. His mother, both of his grandfathers. We are proud of our boy and send our love."

"He'll be very happy to hear that." Luke felt momentarily sorry for both himself and his son because so many of his relatives were dead.

"I am alive, Luke. Try to remember that."

Delighted to be fussed at by his mother from the spirit world, Luke laughed. "I stand corrected. I meant to say made their transition to the spirit world."

"This message is for you. We are coming back. The three of us. We are coming back."

"You are?" The possibility that his mother would reincarnate filled him with awe.

"Look for us."

"I will." Luke trembled with an emotion he couldn't identify. He wondered who the others were, but all awareness of his mother slipped away and he fell back to sleep.

The next morning Luke and Euphoria rose early for the weekend trip to the Valley. They dressed casually for the rehearsal dinner, she in a yellow, belted dress and he in a forest green silk blazer and black slacks. He packed their suitcases in the trunk of the new Jaguar while Euphoria hung his tux and her peach satin gown in the back seat for the wedding tomorrow.

Luke held open the driver's side door. "Want to drive?"

"Not really." After they climbed into the car, Euphoria sank back against the seat and closed her eyes. "Maybe I'll just take a little siesta."

"Sure, get some rest. I'm going to dance your legs off at the wedding."

"Okay, you're on."

Her words sounded right, but something seemed off. Luke worried that she might become ill. The crow's feet around her eyes, normally almost invisible, looked pronounced in morning light. Despite what Euphoria said to the contrary, the workshops wore her out, especially the healing sessions. Although as lovely as ever, lately she seemed tired more often than not.

After they returned home, he would broach the subject of a vacation. At least she had this incredible car with its white leather interior for a carriage. If the day ever came that Luke couldn't enjoy a new car, he'd know his life had lost purpose.

Red mountains and crags turned into scrub desert on the descent. While Euphoria slept, Luke negotiated the traffic, thicker every year. The trip that used to take less than two hours now consumed at least four because of congestion. Something had to be done about the burdensome growth of the state into one of the most populous in the union.

Luke veered off at the Carefree Highway and headed for Cave Creek with dense traffic the entire way. Finally, near noon, they arrived at the Glass Tower. It looked more like an office building than a resort. People in business attire, colorful jumpsuits, moved about outside with others visible inside through the glass walls.

Since Luke had phoned ahead, Aaron and Vera waited at the turnaround. They waved exuberantly as the car pulled up, then they stooped to peer into the darkened window. They made an incongruous couple. Aaron stood six feet tall, trim and muscular, black hair contrasted with his white jumpsuit.

Vera's blonde hair even piled up in an exotic style for the occasion barely came to Aaron's shoulder. To her credit, she had chosen to avoid the popular clothing and wore a long gown with little puff sleeves and gloves, all powder blue, exactly the shade of her eyes.

Aaron jerked open the car door on the passenger side as Vera squealed, "Welcome, welcome."

Euphoria stepped out of the car and enfolded both of them. "It's good to see you, my darlings."

The valet, a young man in a tux, opened the door on Luke's side. "May I take care of your vehicle, sir?"

"Thanks." Luke nodded toward the trunk. "We've got luggage."

"I'll see to it." The valet handed Luke a plastic token.

Once out of the air-conditioned car, Luke hurried around the front end. The suffocating heat hit his skin as only Phoenix in the summer could do. Once upon the driveway he threw his arms out and joined the group hug. His cheek crushed against Vera's soft skin. She smelled of watermelon.

Vera treated him to a glorious smile that lit her cute face. She was a study in pastels with delicate coloring and a good-hearted manner. "We're so glad you're here. Isn't this a wonderful day?"

"I don't think so," Luke said in a teasing tone. "It's hot as hell."

"Oh, no, silly, I meant the occasion." Vera chewed gum vigorously.

"I knew what you meant." Luke laughed aloud. He glanced up at Aaron's lips stretched to their maximum smile and felt glad once again that his son had found this terrific girl.

All four strolled into the lobby with the restaurant on one side and the pool across the way, visible through walls of glass. The absence of borders to space took some getting used to. In a way Luke found it charming because of the intimacy it created.

After Luke signed in at the desk, they stepped into the glass elevator with chrome posts. Their ascent took on a rather dizzying quality since the elevator faced outdoors and hotels across the street. Through the slightly opaque glass compartment, Luke watched the earth rush away from him. His stomach took a dive when the elevator stopped at the forty-seventh floor.

Once Luke and Euphoria entered their room, the view came close to being terrifying. With the one-way mirrored glass wall, Luke fancied he could see the entire Valley of red-roofed housing developments, buttes, shrubs, swimming pools, and skyscrapers.

He couldn't avoid noticing that this resort would make a fine terrorist target, but it was too late now with the plans set. That they would spend most of their time on the main floors in the common rooms consoled him somewhat. Any pilot could thread this glass needle with a speeding plane and cause devastation for miles around.

Euphoria stood beside him and gazed out the window. "Kind of scary, huh? Don't worry. We'll be safe."

Luke shuddered and chastised himself for negativity. After he and Euphoria had freshened, they rode back down to the banquet room. Since the two of them had not been needed for the rehearsal, they had arrived just before the scheduled luncheon with the other guests.

Steering Euphoria by the elbow, Luke entered the round banquet room, set off from the other areas of the hotel by banks of purple flowering vines at eye level. Their roots grew in clear tubes of gurgling water. The flowers smelled fresh and pretty in the climate-controlled air. The indoor / outdoor blending had a dazzling effect, crowded and private at the same time.

Against the trellised flowers stood bridal-white table rounds with place settings of bone china and crystal stemware filled with pink wine. Pastel balloons floated high above the parquet dance floor in the center of the carpet.

At one of the tables, Vera and Aaron engaged in noisy conversation with their maid of honor and best man. Luke recognized both as fellow graduate students at ASU where the bride and groom had met and fallen in love.

Melinda's brothers and sisters with their children and grandchildren, boisterous as usual, occupied several tables. Luke felt glad that Aaron and Vera had invited Melinda's family. They hadn't been required to but obviously had wanted all the relatives present. Mama Chacon sat at one table in a wheelchair.

"Where are we supposed to sit?" Luke whispered.

"Over there." Euphoria indicated another table where a well dressed older couple sat. "With the in-laws."

"After we say hello to Mama." Luke called out, "Hello, Mama. It's good to see you." He knelt beside her wheelchair and patted her vein-creased hand. Her hair, pulled back in a bun, must have been done up by one of her daughters.

Mama gazed into his eyes for a long moment as if trying to get a fix on reality. He would hate it if she didn't recognize him. Her face twisted up in a garish kind of smile. The stroke had damaged her ability to move much of the right side of her body, but she clutched his hand with surprising strength. "My dear Luke. Isn't this a wonderful day?"

Smiling at the same phrase Vera had used, Luke said, "Yes, it is. I'm so glad you could come."

"I wouldn't miss it. To see my Melinda's son marry."

"Hello, Mrs. Chacon."

"Dear Euphoria." Mama gave Euphoria a look of great fondness. The two women had bonded when Papa Chacon died and they sat through the wake together. Euphoria had given assurances over and over that Papa's spirit attended all the ceremonies, glad to be free of his poor disease-ridden body.

Euphoria kissed Mama on the cheek. "Would you like me to come to your room afterward and give you some healing?"

Luke guessed that the touch must have alerted Euphoria to some inner condition. She never asked how anyone was feeling. She could always tell from touching them.

"Well," Mama sighed, "if it's no trouble."

"It's no trouble at all. I'm glad to help."

"Please do." Mama's eyes filled with tears, and she said to Luke, "I'm so proud of Aaron, aren't you?"

"You know I am."

"He takes after his mother, don't you think?"

Actually, Luke had done the bulk of the raising, and probably would have even if Melinda had lived. Any credit should go to him, but he ignored the unintended insult out of pity for the poor old woman. "Yes, indeed Aaron does take after his mother."

Involuntarily Luke looked at Aaron, speaking excitedly to his new bride. He had the same animated gestures and proud tilt of the head as his mother.

Mama sobbed. "I miss her even now, after all these years."

How different their lives would have been had Melinda lived. Luke doubted their marriage could have survived. They would all have experienced another kind of pain with divorce. And what if he had been in the tower, too? What would have become of Aaron then? Sad as it was to contemplate, Melinda's death may have been the best thing that could happen. He regretted the thought. He had much yet to learn of the purposes for incarnation.

"I wish," Luke said, "Melinda could be here, too, in the flesh, but I know she is here in spirit. I'll bet Papa Chacon is here, too. Don't forget that, Mama."

With a startled smile, Mama scanned the ceiling.

Luke kissed her flabby cheek, glad to have given her comfort. "We'll see you later." He and Euphoria crossed the noisy room to the table with Mr. and Mrs. Valdez and greeted them. Waiters moved about the room, filling water glasses and setting *hors d'oeuvres* on the table.

Mr. Valdez, a large, florid-faced man, who looked very much on his way to a heart attack, brandished a cigar as he stood and shook Luke's hand. "Ola, Senor Brock."

"Good to see you again, Mr. Valdez. Ma'am." Luke bowed to Mrs. Valdez. "Welcome to the family."

Far more attractive than her husband, an older version of Vera, with a warm and tender face, Mrs. Valdez said, "Gracias."

"Hello, again," Euphoria said as she and Luke took the two empty places reserved for them. She picked up her place cards with her name written in filigreed script and spoke to Mrs. Valdez. "Very pretty."

Several weeks ago, when Luke had volunteered to help pay for the wedding, Vera had warned them that her father had tremendous pride and would never allow any help. Operating from their home in Castile, he had made a great deal of money buying and selling condominiums on the Mediterranean.

Mr. Valdez had paid for everything, including all the Chacon family hotel rooms, despite the fact that most of them lived in Phoenix and really didn't need to stay at the hotel. Mr. Valdez wanted everything done properly, as if the wedding took place in Spain.

The best man, an East Indian in a magenta jumpsuit, rose from the wedding party's table and strode across the dance floor to a microphone that stood beside a table of young people. "Thank you all for coming and celebrating this joyous occasion with my very lucky lab partner, Aaron Brock." The best man spoke in cultured British English. "I want to wish him and Vera the best of luck in their life together."

Applause broke out all over the room.

"All of us at the university wish our compatriots the best of everything, and... " Grinning, the Indian glanced at the table of young people. "We promise to be sober tomorrow and make it to the church on time."

Laughter followed. Once the various groups of guests had begun to chatter, Vera walked to the table of students. One of the girls made room on her chair, and Vera sat down with them.

"Excuse me." Luke slid out of the seat, aware that time alone with Aaron would become more and more precious as the weekend went along.

With a pang, Luke realized the easy access he'd always had to his son would probably diminish for the rest of their lives. They had obligations to Vera and Euphoria that had to come first. Luke strode across the dance floor, aware of his pride in Aaron, not only for achieving a doctorate, but for believing in the good life and for finding a good person to share it. Aaron had an optimistic soul and deserved a delightful marriage like Luke had found with Euphoria.

"Hey, Dad!" Aaron's little boy trusting and loving nature, pre Nine Eleven, shone once again in his eyes.

Luke clapped his son on the shoulder. "Great shindig."

"Yeah."

"I just wanted to say—"

Aaron raised one arm protectively across his body as if shielding himself from a blow. "Don't get mushy, Dad. I know how you feel." His voice carried good-natured mocking.

Chuckling, Luke admitted to himself that Aaron understood his father very well. "Seriously, I just wanted to say how glad I am you had a change of heart."

"About what?"

With a wave of his hand, Luke indicated the ring of tables filled with people of assorted races. "About people of other...types, uh persuasions." He hesitated to refer to the word prejudice, but at one time he had feared his son felt some.

Recognition flashed on Aaron's face. "Right. I remember when I used to worry about passing for white." He seemed to laugh at himself. "Now I'm worrying about whether or not I can pass for Castilian."

"I doubt it. That Mexican blood is pretty strong in you."

"Who would have thought I'd find a Hispanic girl who looks whiter than I do?"

Luke wondered whether his son had made much progress, rather exchanging one prejudice for another. On the other hand, Aaron had chosen an East Indian as a best man, and he had friends of all races at the university. Regardless, Luke loved his son. "You've made a great match. I'm proud of you."

"Hey!" Aaron's black eyes glittered with ornery glee. "I told you not to do that."

"I managed to slip it in, anyway." Luke hugged Aaron, whose sturdy, muscular back gave a sensation of strength and durability. He would make a good family man. Maybe not perfect, but good. Oh, well, no one was perfect, at least not those still alive on the earth.

"Thanks, Dad." Aaron withdrew from the embrace, looking pleased.

A waiter crossed the room, carrying a stool over his head. He deposited it behind a standing microphone near the table where Vera sat.

A tall, black-haired young man rose from the student table. He grabbed at the microphone, as if to keep it from falling. Another student handed him a guitar.

"What's going on?" Luke asked.

"Oh," Aaron said. "That's Vera's teaching assistant. He's going to sing at the wedding tomorrow. Looks like she's talked him into doing a little preview. He's very good."

Something in the way the musician moved caught Luke, like a hawk soaring lazily but capable of a high-speed plummet at any moment. "He looks familiar. Do I know him?"

"I doubt it. He's from New York. Kendall Roberts is his name. I'll introduce you later."

Surprised, Luke thought he knew all of Aaron's and Vera's friends, at least those close enough to receive an invitation. Luke remembered his prediction to Euphoria earlier about meeting someone new today, too vague for verification.

All the wedding guests quieted and turned their attention to the striking-looking youth who strummed on the guitar. He looked elegant in a silver shirt, black trousers, and boots with spurs. He had the slender, lithe body of a swimmer, lean cheeks, and dark eyes that gazed without focus over the heads of the audience.

Luke felt intrigued by Kendall Roberts but put off by the haunted look he had about him, as if he had suffered great sorrow in his short life.

Twenty

The Better Part of Valor

Damn! The microphone stand had moved on its own.

Propped on the edge of a stool, a confused Kendall eased the microphone stand back into place. He knew he'd not thought he wanted it to move, but he had experienced some stage fright, an uncommon reaction for him. That nervousness must have destabilized his mind enough to tip over the flimsy microphone stand. Or perhaps the alcohol had caused the problem. If he had known in advance that Vera wanted him to sing, he wouldn't have drunk any wine. Booze made the voice thin. Now he had to worry about random psychokinesis too? He tapped the microphone softly and smiled at the audience with what he hoped looked like a disarming expression.

Picking up his guitar, Kendall strummed, waiting for the audience to quiet. The circle of tables and the half wall of flowers created an effect as if people in other rooms far away could hear. He feared the acoustics would be terrible.

As Kendall gazed around the ballroom, he nodded to Vera and her party, ignoring the tables where he didn't know the people. He couldn't help but notice two tables filled with Latinos, of a variety of ages, including many young children. Even the youngest boys were elaborately dressed in little tuxes with cummerbunds and the girls in long gowns with streamers in their hair. The parents didn't try to control the children, who moved from table to table and made a lot of distracting noise, laughing and shouting. Kendall knew from table talk that these were Aaron's relatives, so it didn't surprise Kendall that they acted like inconsiderate clods.

An old woman in a wheelchair seemed to command a lot of attention from the children with her scratchy voice. Although Kendall couldn't decipher her words from the distance, the fact that she continued to blabber annoyed him. Why in hell didn't she shut up? Then maybe the kids would too. Did all grandmothers think they could manipulate and dominate their families? He wished the old bitch would shrivel up and blow away.

Finally, she shut up, the room quieted, and Kendall sang a love ballad, *Destiny's Child*, popular twenty years ago. Vera had asked him to perform one of his own compositions, but he didn't because he'd not polished it enough for public performance. Many of the little kids didn't pay attention to his song, but the adults all seemed to listen with approval. He ended with an old standard that Vera had specifically requested, *Black Is the Color of my True Love's Hair*, in the perfect range for his baritone.

The mournful quality of folk music suited Kendall's mood, often anxious and depressed. Its popularity showed that others experienced similar emotions. He wondered how much like him they were inside and if they had the brains to analyze themselves.

Everyone clapped, even the kids. Some of Aarons' relatives whistled and hooted, not very tasteful behavior but better than booing. Vera applauded, a wide grin on her face. Kendall wanted to please her, and it appeared that he had done so. She and her amiable dolt of a fiancé left their chairs and headed across the dance floor.

Kendall bowed his head, gratified that he had performed well. He might get more gigs out of this exposure. He needed the money. "Thank you very much," he said into the microphone then took his place at the table with the other students.

Someone had refilled his wine glass while he performed. He doubted the waiters considered him under age, but he wouldn't likely mention the fact. Most people forgot about accelerated student enrollment and took him for at least twenty one. He did look older, maybe from being both emancipated and almost an orphan at seventeen. He liked the wine even though he knew he'd better not drink too much because his body wasn't used to it.

Poor old bastard Grandfather hadn't known how to hold his liquor, and look what happened to him. The fact that Grandmother sat in prison serving a life sentence wouldn't give Grandfather back his wretched life.

The sexy brunette from chemistry class sat next to Kendall at the table. She reached up and kissed his cheek. "You have a beautiful voice. So soulful."

"Glad you like it." Kendall knew she had a steady boyfriend somewhere out of state and wondered just how serious she felt about that long-distance relationship. He liked brunettes a lot. He picked up his glass and sipped the wine.

With a happy grin, Aaron tapped Kendall on the shoulder. "Great songs. Would you come with us?"

Vera stood beside Aaron, an expectant smile on her face. "We've got some people we want to introduce you to." She always acted so cheerful and kind that she almost restored Kendall's faith in people. He'd had a cautious but warm friendship with her ever since the day the department chair had assigned him to Vera last fall at the start of his freshman year.

"Of course. I'd be delighted." Kendall gave the brunette a wistful look. "Excuse me. I'll be right back."

The brunette cast her eyes down in a flirty way. "I can't wait."

As Kendall edged away from the table, Vera grabbed his arm and guided him across the room.

Aaron followed them, laughing. "I'm right behind you. Got to protect my interest, you know."

"Oh, you silly man." Vera hooked her arm through Aaron's and pulled him and Kendall toward her. "My two tall, dark, and handsome men."

The three approached the table where four adults sat, and Kendall felt growing discomfort, as if the air thickened. For a moment he imagined he saw the room destabilize and take on the eerie blue of its astral complement. Just as quickly his vision returned to normal. He didn't know what to expect and remained on guard.

"Mama, Papa," Vera said, "I'd like you to meet Kendall Roberts. Kendall, my parents. He helps me in the lab, work he does exceptionally well, and he's a very sweet boy."

Embarrassed by her praise, Kendall murmured, "Very happy to meet you." But he hated being spoken of in a childish way, even by Vera. He shook hands with both of her parents. They seemed warm and open. He liked them right away and wondered if his mind had played a trick on him.

Vera indicated the others. "Mr. and Mrs. Brock, Euphoria and Luke," she blushed "I mean Mom and Dad Brock, I'd like you to meet Kendall."

They both rose with smiling faces. Aaron's father grasped Kendall's hand and shook it, saying something unintelligible.

A current charged up Kendall's arm. He felt trapped by the grip. Hatred welled up in him, and he found it difficult to listen to the words Aaron's father spoke. Not surprising, it took a moron to sire a moron, neither one good enough for the likes of Vera and her parents.

Such feelings didn't come close to explaining the anger, actually rage, that threatened to unnerve Kendall. He'd as soon murder the man as shake his hand. Where had this response come from? Perhaps that murky place he thought of as his own memory? Kendall must analyze this reaction later. Right now it took all his concentration to remain polite and at least pretend to be calm.

Euphoria touched Kendall's arm, lightly, like dusting it with a feather. Her movement carried her sickening perfume to Kendall's nostrils. He felt like a fly desperately trying to extract its legs from a sticky spider web.

"We enjoyed your music." Euphoria sounded insincere.

It seemed to Kendall that she attempted to distract him from his confused thinking. But how could she know he had become discombobulated? Could she read minds?

Giving him an odd smile, Euphoria made an almost imperceptible tip of her head. He fancied she communicated to him that she understood.

Kendall had no doubt that she had read his mind. His sense of self-preservation kicked in. He closed his thoughts to all intrusion and deliberately said something innocuous. "I hope we have good weather for the wedding."

That brought a general laugh and comments about the summer heat, but the tense moment broke.

Somewhat relieved, Kendall determined to remain wary. Aaron's parents threatened him in a way that defied logic. These two might be dangerous. They might hurt him in some way. Kendall would take pleasure in eliminating both of them from the face of the planet, but he veered off the thought, unwilling to let the woman intuit anything else about him.

Mrs. Valdez asked Kendall, "Are you from Arizona too, dear?"

"No, ma'am, I grew up in New York, not the city, upstate."

"Oh, I've never been there. Is that where your parents live?"

"Well, actually, my parents have passed on. I don't have any relatives except my grandmother, but she's in...uh...a nursing home." He created an imaginary picture of a dear old woman in a rocker, just in case Euphoria could read Grandmother's true location.

"Oh, you poor child." Mrs. Valdez's face scrunched up, and she sounded as if she wanted to apply for the job of grandmother.

Mr. Valdez gave his wife a withering look. "So, young man, what are you studying at the university?"

"I'm a life sciences major now."

Vera bragged. "He's going to medical school after he graduates."

"If the money's there, I will." Kendall couldn't depend completely on his bank account with tuition and living costs so high. He intended to budget every dollar and live frugally so he wouldn't have to sell his Lexus. The damned State of New York had frozen Grandfather's assets once Grandmother, his only heir, went to prison for his murder.

"Kendall's a smart fellow," Aaron said. "Most likely he'll get scholarships and grants all the way through. We've recommended him and intend to stay in touch even after we go to California."

"I can't thank you enough," Kendall said. "You and Vera have been especially kind to me." He appreciated the vote of confidence from Aaron, someone who could have been likeable had he not already snagged Vera.

Kendall intended to keep his fascination for Vera to himself. In his fantasies, she became his lover as well as his mentor, the devoted older woman who always put his needs first and taught him to love. He glanced at Euphoria to see whether she registered his thoughts. Apparently she had not because she jumped up and squeezed Vera and Aaron around the waists.

"Oh, my dears," Euphoria cried. "I forgot to tell you. Psyche sends you hugs." She squeezed again. "And her congratulations, and so does Jess."

A reflective smile spread across Aaron's face. "How is Psyche doing these days?"

"Oh, fine." Euphoria gave him an indulgent look. "They appreciated the invitation, but they can't get away right now with the crops needing tending. It's just getting summer warm or planting warm or whatever they call it in Oregon."

Aaron disengaged himself from Euphoria's hug and pulled Vera against him, wrapping his arms around her waist. "Tell Psyche thanks and we said hello."

Vera stared up at Aaron, her head tilted far back. Kendall knew that quizzical expression. The same way she studied test tubes to interpret results, she tried now to interpret something in Aaron's face. Kendall would bet money there was a story about Psyche worth hearing.

Euphoria whirled around to face Kendall with a questioning glance. Then she turned her attention across the room.

The noise level mounted higher than wine could account for.

"Help us!" a girl screamed. "Mama!" She leaned over the old woman slumped in her wheelchair.

"Oh, God." Luke bounded toward the wheelchair. Several of Aaron's relatives gathered around it.

"Mama," Aaron cried and hurried to her with Vera following him.

Dashing to the wheelchair, Euphoria knelt, touched the old woman's carotid artery, and spoke to Luke with a grave face. "Call nine one one."

Luke took out his cell phone and dialed. It seemed like every kid in the place began to cry.

The old bitch appeared to be in bad shape. Kendall regretted that he'd wished her ill. He'd only wanted her silence. Had he caused her collapse inadvertently? Euphoria might have wondered the same thing. What else could explain the way she'd turned around and stared at him? Knocking over the microphone stand with his mind might not have been an isolated event.

Kendall remembered how Grandmother had taught him to focus his thoughts to move the pebble in the driveway. That skill had grown as he grew, and he took it for granted, just as he did their travels in the astral world. Then, when he saw how his astral projection had facilitated Grandfather's murder, Kendall had decided to stop using his abilities. Grandmother, now in prison, could no longer tempt him, especially since he'd not visited her during the entire school year.

At the time of Grandfather's death, Kendall had sworn to never use psychokinesis or do astral projection again. He wanted to live in the world like ordinary people did.

Now it appeared that the psychokinesis was out of control. Kendall needed help. He wondered whether he could ever have a normal life.

Twenty-One

This Fragile Frame

Mama's collapse and the arrival of paramedics at the rehearsal dinner had a very sobering effect on the celebratory mood. Aaron's handling of the aftermath had made Luke proud once more. While the paramedics took Mama away, Aaron calmly took the microphone and thanked everyone for attending. He asked them to sign a list with their cell numbers and keep their phones on so he could contact them later with a determination of whether or not the ceremony would proceed as planned the next day. He seemed so detached and professional that it was amazing to think that he meant his own wedding.

All Mama's relatives trekked to the hospital behind the ambulance.

On a plastic couch in the waiting room, Luke hoped to hell the poor woman wasn't suffering. She'd been in the emergency room for hours.

With her legs curled up beneath her, Euphoria lay asleep against him close enough that he felt the weight of her back heavy against his arm each time she took a breath.

Facing them on an identical couch sat a worried-looking Aaron with Vera beside him. The arms of his suit jacket hung from Vera's shoulders while she sipped coffee from a Styrofoam cup. Her rumpled blue gown billowed around her. The table between them held many empty coffee cups, an attempt to overcome the effects of the wine.

Nearby waited Ray, Sylvia, Rosa, and Priscilla, Mama Chacon's living children, Melinda's brother and sisters. Their spouses had taken the youngsters home earlier when a nurse announced that it would probably be a long time before definitive news came about Mama's condition.

Luke had talked with his first wife's siblings and tried to give them encouragement. Only Rosa unsettled him. Despite the fact that she was short and weighed over two hundred pounds where Melinda had been tall and trim, Rosa looked like Melinda in the face. They also shared the character trait of acting vulnerable one minute, brash the next. Luke had reassured Rosa and the others that he would remain with them and support them, no matter how long it took. They had prayed together for Mama's recovery. With all the words said, nothing remained except the wait.

Near midnight a middle-aged woman in a business suit came from the direction of the emergency room operating theatre. She strode to the waiting room and addressed the whole group. "I am a non-denominational chaplain. I would be happy to call your own clergyman or pray with you myself."

A look of dismay crossed Ray's face. He and Rosa stood up. "How is Mama doing? She didn't—"

"The doctor will come to tell you as soon as he can."

"Ma'am," Rosa said, her voice pitched low and controlled. "Do you suppose you could call Father Ambrose?"

The chaplain sighed. "He only comes for extreme unction. He has reinstituted that sacrament at the time of death. He's the only priest left in Phoenix."

Luke regretted the distressing lack of leadership in the Catholic Church. Splinter groups and distrust among the members left a great need in local communities that other people of faith had been unable to fill. Old timers like Mama refused to accept the demise of their religion.

From what the chaplain said, Luke deduced that the crisis had passed with Mama's health. Because Ray and Rosa looked downcast, Luke went to them, squeezed their shoulders, and smiled. "Here's the good news. Mama isn't sick enough to require the priest's presence."

An Arabic doctor strode down the hall, pulling his surgical mask beneath his dark beard. "Chacon family, please?"

"Yes, sir." Ray said, and everyone else stood up.

The doctor cleared his throat. "Mrs. Chacon has had another stroke, but the prognosis is, well shall we say more positive than negative. We brought her back this time, and hopefully she will have several months of life yet."

Relief rippled through the room.

Tears stood in Rosa's eyes. 'May we see her?"

"You may all visit her but only a few at a time. And only for a minute. She asked to see Aaron first." The doctor gave Ray a quizzical look. "Is that you?"

"It's me." Aaron happily waved to Vera, Luke, and Euphoria. "Come on."

"Room Seven." The doctor pointed down the hallway from which he had come, walked to the vending machine, and threaded in a five-dollar bill.

"Thank you, doctor," Rosa called out and choked on her words.

Ray took her in his arms. "Mama's all right. You just go ahead and cry now, sis." Rosa sobbed loudly.

With a concerned glance at Rosa, Ray, and the others, Luke said, "We'll only be a minute." It surprised him that Mama wanted to see Aaron first, but that didn't mean preferential treatment. Mama always treated her progeny with great fairness.

Hurrying down the unadorned tiled hallway, Luke caught up with Euphoria, Aaron, and Vera. They turned into Room Seven where Mama lay asleep, a white sheet drawn up to her chin. Someone must have taken down her bun in the emergency room because her gray hair lay around her ashen face.

Luke stood inside the door with Euphoria. The soft beeps of the monitors took him back in memory to the painful days of his mother's illness. Now, it appeared that he would soon lose this dear lady, as well.

That Angie lived in another dimension gave Luke some consolation, but he would have much preferred having a mother here to live the days as a part of his life. Bereavement seemed the most poignant of human experiences. Although the excruciating grief had long since dissipated within him, loss remained an undercurrent of every other emotion.

"Mama," Aaron cried and strode to the bed. He took her hand and caressed it. "Mama, it's Aaron."

Opening her cloudy eyes, Mama gazed at her grandson in a bewildered way. Luke wondered how much quality she might find in life after two strokes but prayed she would find some.

"Dear Aaron," Mama said. "I want you to go on with the wedding tomorrow." Although hoarse, she sounded far more alert than she looked.

"No, it's all right. We'll wait until you can attend. I..." Aaron glanced at Vera. "We want you to be there."

"Yes." Vera took Mama's other hand. "We talked it over and agreed. We can go on to Los Angeles and start work. Then, when you're better, we can come back and get married."

Mama's hair flapped as she attempted to shake her head no. "I will not allow it. You will get married tomorrow. As planned. If you postpone because of me, I will be very angry."

Only the left side of her face turned up into a smile, but Luke thought it a fetching smile, nonetheless.

"Promise me," Mama whispered.

Aaron raised a questioning eyebrow at Vera for a moment. When she nodded, he said, "Okay. We'll do as you wish." He kissed Mama on the cheek. "You get well soon. We'll be thinking of you tomorrow."

"Thank you," Vera whispered in Mama's ear.

As Aaron headed out of the room with Vera, he told her, "We've got a lot of calls to make."

Luke and Euphoria took their places beside the bed.

"Now, Luke," Mama said, "you make sure those young folks keep that promise, even if I go in the night. You'll do that for me, won't you?"

Euphoria grasped Mama's hand, the one with no mobility. "There's no cause for concern. You will still be here tomorrow."

"How do you know?" Mama sounded surprised.

"None of your departed loved ones are here." Euphoria's tone carried complete conviction. "If they had come to take you home, I would be able to see them or sense their presence in the room. There's no one here but you, Luke, and me."

Relieved, Luke relaxed and let a bit of playfulness come out. "You've got to hang on for a while longer because Father Ambrose is way too backed up to fit you into his schedule."

"You rascal." Mama's attempt to laugh ended in a cough. "I don't know whether to feel happy or sad about continuing to live. I miss Papa and Melinda. I would be content to go and be with them, but it's in God's hands."

Luke kissed Mama's cheek, glad for its feverish aliveness. "Stay as long as you can for your sons and daughters. And for us. You are mother to more of us than you know." He turned to Euphoria. "Let's go so the others can come in."

"Just a minute." Euphoria laid her hand on Mama's forehead, took a deep breath, and closed her eyes.

Divine healing energy passed through Euphoria's body into Mama's. Luke could almost, but not quite, see it.

As Luke and Euphoria left the room, Mama mumbled, "Holy Mary, Mother of God, pray for us sinners now and in the hour of our deaths."

Once they'd said their good-byes to the Chacons, Luke drove his family back to the hotel. Although Aaron and Vera chattered in the backseat, Euphoria fell asleep. She roused when the car turned into the hotel driveway. They walked inside and rode up the open-air elevator with its splendid view. The stars twinkled above and Phoenix twinkled below.

They all had room assignments on the same floor, but Aaron and Vera stayed in different ones. Luke wondered whether they had honored that convention for the edification of Vera's parents or whether the young couple had not yet consummated their love. Luke realized he didn't know many details of their relationship and with chagrin thought the separate rooms could also be for his edification.

After kissing the young people, Luke and Euphoria went into their room. Luke closed the door, and a nightlight automatically turned on.

Dropping onto the bed with her clothes on, Euphoria sighed, "I'm just exhausted."

"Can I help you take off your clothes?" Luke grinned, too tired himself to do more than talk about sex. Euphoria nodded and smiled weakly, allowing him to take off her dress, bra, and panties. Then he disrobed and crawled in beside her.

Pulling the cool sheet over them, he cradled Euphoria and hoped she'd feel replenished in the morning. It worried Luke that on several occasions lately she'd seemed more tired than the situation called for. "Let's get some sleep. Big day tomorrow."

"Your prediction came true. That young man, Kendall? He might be the someone new in our lives."

"Maybe but I doubt. He's just a kid."

"I sensed a lot of hostility, even fear coming from him."

Luke recalled feeling unsettled at meeting the young man, but hostility seemed too strong a description. "Maybe he just had stage fright. A lot of performers do. I think I'll keep an eye out at the wedding tomorrow for another contender for the title."

"He's bad trouble. We need to watch out for him."

"What kind of trouble? What did you sense?"

Yawning, Euphoria settled into the pillow and closed her eyes.

Luke assumed Euphoria hadn't answered because she was trying to formulate her thoughts. Instead he heard her even, diaphragmatic breaths going in and out at a slow pace. They would have to talk tomorrow. He kissed the top of her head and prayed his customary gratitude. "Thank you, Divine Spirit, for my people, my life, and my work."

Luke matched his breaths to Euphoria's, a trick that helped him fall sleep quickly and avoid his propensity to mull things over excessively late at night.

The trick worked. In moments he fell asleep.

In a dream, Luke knelt before a fireplace, stoking it with a reed. Large hands grabbed him from behind and dragged him across a dirt floor. His screams to stop had no effect. A big man slammed Luke onto a bed, jerked off his shirt, and tied his hands behind his back.

Across the room a woman lay tied up the same way. She swore at the big man, who didn't seem to notice. The big man laughed and waved the shirt in the air then ran out the thatch door.

In helpless rage, Luke jerked himself awake. He wished he could dismiss the dream as caused by overwrought imagination. He eased out of the sheets so as not to awaken

Euphoria, took a carton of milk from the small fridge, and quenched his thirst in a satisfying way. Dreams with such strong emotional content required analysis or they would just reappear in new guise. He might as well figure this one out.

Once back in bed, Luke settled into an easy clarifying state between sleep and wakefulness, a welcome movement of mind into altered consciousness. Had the negativity Euphoria felt earlier in the day triggered his dream?

The fireplace and the thatch door cast the dream into another time. He remembered the memory of the doctor during the Revolution. Could this be the same lifetime? Perhaps an episode from the previous childhood? Luke recognized Kendall as the big man in the dream even though they looked different now. The tables had turned, big to small, youth to adult for Luke and Kendall, but such a strong negative reaction could have its seeds in a previous lifetime.

If so, maybe Kendall owed Luke. On the other hand, what cruel act might Luke have perpetrated in some far distant past to provoke the eighteenth-century violence? No pat answer presented itself. The dream had left only unanswered questions.

Morning crept in. Aaron's wedding day. Casting brooding thoughts aside, Luke left Euphoria to sleep until the last minute. He showered in the gleaming stainless steel bathroom. While shaving he assessed his image in the mirror. He had to admit sixty years didn't look bad on him. Still muscular, stocky, but not fat. A few crows' feet maybe and gray in his dark blond hair added a distinguished quality. He'd lost what Melinda called his boyish charm, but people took him seriously now. The mottled green and brown eyes looked just as girl-catching as ever.

A wisp of memory returned to Luke. The boy in the dream had the same hair and eyes. Some reincarnation theories said souls had trademarks, traits that tended to repeat in different incarnations. The eyes and hair might be his.

"Morning, Luke," Euphoria called from the other room.

Feeling devilish, Luke lunged out of the bathroom door onto the carpet before the bed where Euphoria sat nude. He held out his arms in a stagy pose so she could see him in his altogether. "Ta dah!"

The look of carnal appreciation that crossed her face tickled him. She rose and stepped toward him. "You are gorgeous, my darling husband."

Her soft skin against his felt homey and sexy. Luke crushed her against him and poured his delight with her into his kiss. Euphoria responded with only a shadow of the ardor she normally exhibited. He pulled away enough to look at her face. She smiled at him, but something felt wrong. Her hazel eyes looked washed out, their sockets dark.

"Are you feeling all right?" Luke asked.

"I'm okay. Just tired."

"That's what you say every day."

"I'm probably a little rundown." Euphoria pulled away and stepped into the bathroom. "When we get home tomorrow, I'll do some self healing. I'll be back up to speed before you know it."

Following her, Luke stood in the bathroom doorway, his hands wedged against the frame. "Haven't you been doing self healing all along?"

"Well, maybe some." Euphoria picked up her toothbrush and squirted toothpaste on it. "Don't worry about me. I'll be all right."

If he didn't know her so well, confident of her full-disclosure manner of relating, Luke would swear his wife was hiding something from him. He couldn't help but worry. "I'll tell you what. Let's stay an extra day and go out to the Mayo Clinic tomorrow. Let them check you over. Just to make sure."

"I'd rather not." With the toothbrush poised in midair, Euphoria sounded defensive.

"Euphoria, I don't want anything to happen to you."

"I said I'm fine!"

"Are you hiding something from me?"

"I can heal myself, and I will." Euphoria grabbed the door and started to close it. "We're going to be late. I have to get ready." She slammed the door.

Luke rescued his fingers just in time. Pissed at having such an intractable wife, he yelled, "I don't know why in hell you can't ever do what I ask."

Twenty-Two

The Path of Submission

Kendall couldn't think of a way to handle the dysfunction in his psychokinesis on his own. He knew something had gone wrong when the microphone fell. The thought that he might have almost killed that woman made him even more nervous. Not that he cared about the old bitch personally but he could not tolerate being out of control.

Nevertheless, Kendall felt irritated with himself for needing advice. He hated the idea of asking his grandmother at all, but who else could he turn to? The prison personnel monitored all of her phone calls, letters, and email. Having some half-witted prison guard privy to Kendall's business appalled him.

Grandmother had come to him in her astral body many times since she'd gone to prison, but he had managed to keep from going out with her. He didn't want to see her at all, in or out of the astral. For some reason he didn't understand, he could control the astral projection but not the psychokinesis.

The morning after the wedding, Kendall rose early, packed a suitcase, and took off driving to New York. He didn't take his guitar or his laptop because he intended to come right back after he accomplished his mission. He slept in the car beside the road, then ate and washed up in MacDonald's to save on expenses.

Once he arrived at the prison, Kendall's resolve weakened. He hated to go inside. Not that he didn't think Grandmother belonged there. Even though old and female, she was as dangerous as the others housed in maximum security. Guess being female didn't count for much when one got too handy with a butcher knife. The few times he had come to visit her before he left for college, he had disliked being in an environment with so many stupid or mentally twisted people. It was like plodding through a muddy river bottom trying to keep one's boots dry.

Kendall left the car in the parking lot away from the mulberry trees. He knew what the droppings did to car paint. After showing his ID at the reception desk, he typed Grandmother's name into a computer, then sat down to wait in an austere area where the only other occupants were a woman and two little boys.

A TV set blared news about bombings in Hong Kong. With so much destruction, the Chinese government feared the city could never secure the money to rebuild. When gory pictures came on of the survivors, the woman jumped up and changed the channel to *Barney and Friends*. Even as a child, Kendall had laughed at the idiotic purple dinosaur, but *Blues Clues*? Now, there was a program a smart kid could enjoy. Funny, how he could remember watching those programs but couldn't remember his parents at all.

The receptionist called Kendall's name and gave him a visitor's pass, which he stuck on his shirt. He walked through locking gates one at a time, listening to them clang. The whole building resounded with grating noises. Never would he get caught and end up in such a dismal place. When he arrived at the visiting area, he took a seat in a booth, like a small closet with white walls.

In a gray wraparound dress, Grandmother walked up on the other side. No more muu muus for her. She'd wear government issue for the rest of her life. It appeared that she seemed so close he could touch her, but Kendall knew not to try because of the glass pane between them. A female guard stood behind her against the wall.

"Well, would you look who's here!" Grandmother's voice sounded mechanical through the microphone imbedded in the glass. She sat, gingerly as if her back hurt. She looked a lot older.

"How are you doing, Grandmother?"

"Please, try not to pretend you care."

Kendall couldn't read her—maybe hostile, maybe hurt. "All right, I won't."

"Good then. Cut to the chase. What'd you come here for?"

Relieved, Kendall leaned toward the glass so the guard wouldn't hear and whispered, "I'm having trouble controlling the PK. I don't know what to do."

The guard moved closer. "Speak up please."

Grandmother's expression changed into something similar to her old fondness. "What's happened?"

Kendall didn't want the guard to know his business. "I can't tell you details."

"Tell me in the astral."

"No. Not a chance."

"Well, then. Thanks for coming." Grandmother rose, as if to leave.

"I drove all the way across the country to get your advice." Kendall gazed at her for a long time, investing all his thoughts with his wanting, just like he'd done as a kid to get his way. "Please, Grandma!"

With a sigh, Grandmother sat down, and for a moment she looked loving, like a grandmother should. "My dear boy, you have so much ability, but you need to focus it. I could show you how to do that if you would let me." She leaned forward and whispered, "At night, you know."

Kendall shook his head. "Isn't there anyone else? I just don't trust myself with you."

"Aurum Solis. The Grand Master lives in London. He will know what you need to learn. You'll have to go there and submerge yourself in the mysteries. The magical philosophy."

"To London?"

The guard stepped forward. "It's time."

Kendall had thought they would have longer.

Rising, Grandmother placed her hand on the glass. "Dear Kegan, I would have had all this otherwise for your sake."

"Good-bye, and thanks."

Although Grandmother leaned heavily on the guard, she stumbled as she left the room. Kendall doubted he would ever see her again, at least not in this lifetime. He didn't really want to, especially not in this place, but he felt depressed anyway.

Her solution, the trip to London, would consume what little money remained in his savings account. He'd have to drop out of school, a sacrifice he refused to make. He had to get a graduate degree to generate a large income to secure his future.

What's more, visualizing himself becoming some kind of dark lord of sorcery scared him. Never could he commit himself to that kind of godless cult.

There had to be another way. He would handle this problem himself.

Hurrying outside to his car, Kendall headed back to Arizona. He drove onto the freeway and set the cruise control for ninety-five. The mindlessness of the task of driving allowed his mind to roam free.

The solution dropped as if from the sky. Perhaps an angel advised. "Go to the Imam. He will help you."

After Kendall returned to the university, he bathed and donned different clothes. Somehow he knew cleanliness was important. He walked across campus to the beautiful blue and white mosque. Its golden dome sparkled against the cloudless desert sky.

Inside the unlocked front door, about a dozen young men had arranged themselves in lines as they knelt in prayer on the blue and white floor. The bright, clean sanctuary, empty of furnishings, reassured Kendall.

Somehow he knew what to do, not the words, but the moves.

In unison with the other men, Kendall covered his ears then crossed his arms over his chest.

"God is greater," they said.

"God is greater," Kendall repeated and waited while they prayed. He bowed forward at the waist and placed his hands on his knees. "Glory to my great Lord. God hears those who praise him." He rose while the others chanted, "God is greater."

Kendall fell to his hands and knees, bowed his forehead to the comforting, cool tiles, and murmured, "Glory to My Lord, Most High. God is Greater."

Finally, the decision was out of his hands.

Twenty-Three

To Have and to Hold

Luke arrived home in Sedona after dark, anxious to share with Euphoria the details of his solo night flight. From absolute fear and revulsion regarding airplanes, he'd turned into a passable student pilot. The instructor, a hotshot in his twenties, had teased Luke about hiring on as a pilot with America West. He doubted they employed fifty-seven-year-olds, but it amused Luke to dally with the idea of changing careers again, especially the challenge of one that involved flying around the globe.

Of course he wouldn't. Not a chance he would give up the roundedness events. He loved teaching and he loved partnering with Euphoria, conceivably the best healer west of the Mississippi. Even though she'd refused to see a doctor, in recent weeks she seemed to have regained some of her old energy. Thankfully, she felt better.

This successful flight deserved a Bud. Luke flipped the light switch in the kitchen and illuminated counters, appliances, and tile floor policed like an Army barracks, tidier than Euphoria usually left them.

A letter-sized envelope hung above the fridge door handle suspended by a magnetic chip clip. He pulled off the envelope, which bore his name written in Euphoria's flowing handwriting.

Odd to receive a note, very unlike her. Euphoria, the deluxe communicator, honest and transparent. She always called if she ran late and never went anywhere without informing him. She had consideration for mere mortals such as himself whose psychic senses operated infrequently. He'd had no forewarning that she wouldn't be here when he got home and felt disappointed despite the fact that he'd seen her early this morning.

Breaking the peppermint-scented seal, he pulled out the single page, and read:

My darling Luke, we have had a great love, one not to be duplicated in many lifetimes. Passion still undoes me when I think of you, and it always will. Yet I must make a space for another on my karmic path. However it turns out, I have to be free for new energy to pass through my life. You are my best self, the soul of me. I know you will understand. Euphoria

Another man? What the fuck was that about!

Luke dashed upstairs and into their bedroom. Euphoria's clothes, cosmetics, herbs? All gone. Even her stash of boxed, out-of-date shoes from the top of the closet. Damn, he never thought it possible that she would leave him. What else did she take?

Hurrying into their office he opened desk drawers and file cabinet drawers, searching then slamming them shut. He discovered absolutely nothing missing. Euphoria had walked away from her husband and her business too.

The daybook lay open to next Saturday—a couples workshop. Is this what they had to teach? Abandonment?

Enraged, Luke threw the daybook across the room. It clattered against the wall and fell to the carpet, a childish reaction but for the moment most fulfilling.

Grabbing the daybook, he smoothed its pages, closed it, and smashed it harder against the wall. This time it lay where it fell. He went back downstairs and jerked a beer out of the fridge.

Luke drank and paced from the sink to the window. All along he had thought their marriage wonderful, that they loved each other. That all was well. How could he have been such a chump? This is the way that other chump felt, the one Euphoria threw over because "Luke was on her karmic path," he whined in imitation of her tone.

In all these years she'd never even mentioned the name of the man she left. Guess Luke Brock was about to go down in her nameless history next. Not some airy fairy love forever horseshit.

He got another beer.

I must make a space for another. What a line. She was contemptible. Euphoria, the contemptible. She hadn't needed to look far for a new man. All the male participants in their workshops always fell in love with her. She probably had offers all the time that she failed to mention to Luke. Well, now he understood why.

What in hell was wrong with him to cause his wives to leave him, and not just leave him but to screw other men? People used to ask whether anything could be worse than Nine Eleven. Hell, yes, try joining it with the image of a stained sheet in the damned hotel bed.

Now, Euphoria had done it to him all over again!

Pausing mid-pace, Luke thought of the ludicrous moment years ago, the day he'd introduced his mother to Melinda. What a lunatic he had been, assuming they would love each other as much as he loved them. In that disarming way she had about her, Melinda asked Angie which was worse—the death of a spouse or divorce. At the time he'd thought Melinda cute and clever. Now he considered her a mean little shit, careless of anyone else's feelings. Guess he was about to find out the answer to her question.

Luke had gone through the entire episode after Melinda's death sober, knowing beer could ease his mind, at least temporarily. But, Aaron at twelve didn't have alcohol to soften the pain, so Luke didn't either. This time, the hell with it.

Slugging down the beer in a bitter gulp, he opened another, tramped into the living room, and dropped on the leather couch, the white one he'd brought with him from California, from the wreck of a marriage to Melinda. How fitting to sit on it while this marriage went down in a tornado.

One thing would turn out differently this time, in spades. Luke had allowed himself the luxury of repressing the pain. That had done nothing except produce avoidance. Eventually he had to feel it anyway. He would never push grief or anger away again. He had loved Euphoria, and she had ultimately treated him like crap. He would face this cesspool of emotion and get over it. Damn straight, he would.

As he drank, a glance at the entertainment center across the room told Luke something out of the ordinary, but he couldn't figure out what. A spot on the green and white striped wallpaper looked discolored. Their wedding portrait had hung there ever since their wedding day. At sixteen by twenty it was far too large to go into an album. Besides, the photographer had caught Euphoria's essential quality of joy, and Luke had looked as proud as any man ever and handsome enough to deserve her. A wonderful capture of both of them on their best day.

Why did Euphoria take it? What would the new lover think? He wouldn't like it at all. So why?

"Oh, dear God!" Luke ran back to the kitchen and reread the note. Perhaps her phrase *new energy* had not meant a man at all. A sickening feeling in his gut told him the answer. Illness.

Pulling out his cell phone, Luke punched the number one. It rang several times. Why in hell didn't she answer?

"Hello, Luke." Euphoria sounded defeated.

"Where are you?"

"In a motel outside Tonopah, I think."

The image of his wife with another man in a motel room enraged Luke. "Oh yeah, who's with you? Find a new karma connection, did you?"

"No one's here. I'm by myself."

Luke felt relief in spite of himself. Would he rather have her sick than with someone else? "Are you really leaving me? Talk to me, woman."

"I am leaving you. The marriage is over because I can't participate in it any more." Her voice sounded thin as if she were having trouble breathing.

"But why?"

"I'm just not able to. You've got to trust me on this."

"Trust? Are you out of your mind? There's another man, isn't there?"

"No, darling. There never will be."

"Euphoria, this is insane. Give me your location. I'm coming to get you."

"I don't want you to. I'm going up to stay with Psyche until her baby comes. From then on, I don't know where I'll go. I'll keep you informed. That's all I can promise."

"Not good enough. I want you to come back. You're sick, aren't you?" The silence on the other end of the phone shouted the answer. "Tell me the diagnosis."

Euphoria expelled a long sigh. "Congenital heart valve disease."

That sounded so bad that all Luke's anger melted into love for his precious wife. "You know, darling, I take my wedding vows very seriously...in sickness and in health."

"I know you do. So do I. You're my only husband, and I can not bear for you to have to endure this. And also...oh, Luke, I'm a failure as a healer. I can't heal myself, and I'm so ashamed."

"Don't give up, Euphoria. We can fight this. Let's go to some different doctors. Try some energy healers. We'll get this handled one way or another."

"I've made up my mind." Euphoria took several labored breaths. "I'm going to file for a divorce. No amount of shouting on your part will change anything. It will just make us both more depressed than we are. I'll call you every day, but don't come after me. I have to do this my way." With a sob, she cut off the phone call.

Euphoria kept her word and called every day with an update on her location if not on her health. It took her four days to make the drive to southwestern Oregon. Three days would have been plenty, so she probably felt worse than she admitted.

Luke lay awake most of the nights of her journey. Sometimes he slipped into nightmarish dreams that he couldn't recall in the morning. On the weekend, he taught the roundedness event by himself, not too inspiring either to himself or to the participants, most of whom acted disappointed at not receiving healings from Euphoria.

With workshops booked at least one per month through the winter and the spring, Luke would have to convince Euphoria to come back or make a decision about continuing to teach alone. He could probably find a substitute among the psychics in Sedona, but the possibility of doing so distressed him. He resented having to deal with the situation. His wife should be here. The idea that she might die ripped him apart.

To find out more, Luke considered calling Psyche on her house phone in hopes that Euphoria wouldn't know. Outfoxing a psychic was next to impossible, but not knowing the details of her condition drove him nuts. All Luke's attainments in mental telepathy, precognition, and dream recall seemed to have gone down the rabbit hole.

As to divorce? Out of the question. He didn't want to go on alone. Euphoria might feel humiliated about the failure to heal herself. He could understand the damage to her professional pride, but this attempt to save him from grief was preposterous.

Luke would have his wife back again if he had to go drag her back by the hair. He'd pound his chest and howl to make it more dramatic. Oh, to have it so simple as to display those Neanderthal reactions.

The right thing to do was to honor her wishes. After all, Euphoria was an intelligent woman, far more than just capable of making her own decisions, doubtless several lifetimes ahead of Luke in spiritual development. If the situation were reversed, Luke would expect her to comply.

How could he remain in Arizona while she lay ill and possibly dying a thousand miles away? If he merely allowed her to disappear out of his life, he'd never forgive himself. He needed to see her and stop the divorce. He loved her and wanted to be with her whether that meant searching for cures or accepting her death. He hoped she would relent if she saw him.

With his flight instructor, Luke rented a light aircraft, a Cirrus three passenger, and flew up to Grant's Pass. He would try to change Euphoria's mind. If she didn't relent, he'd figure out a way to make himself leave her alone.

After an hour's drive in a rental car, Luke knocked at the door of a white wood frame house set in a stand of trees leafy with autumn foliage. The farm had a few out buildings, lots of drying grass and corn stubble, a few goats. A black Labrador bounded around the house, barking.

Nervous as a guy on a first date, Luke petted the friendly dog. "Hey fella."

Psyche opened the door. With an enthusiastic hug, she pressed against Luke, her firm belly so huge he had to lean over to kiss her cheek.

"Oh, Luke, we had a feeling it would be you. Welcome to my home."

When she waved her arm, her auburn pony tail swished across her bottom. In her maternity smock, she looked like an egg about twice the size as the last time he had seen her.

The cozy living room looked like Euphoria had decorated it, with mobiles and checkered pillows.

Luke felt encouraged by Psyche's hospitality. "How's my grandbaby?"

"Just fine." Psyche's pretty face glowed as she caressed her belly. "I know you'll love him."

"You're right on that. How's your mother? Can I see her now?"

Psyche's expression went gloomy. "Not very well. She's lying down. I'll get her." She waddled down the hall.

It crossed Luke's mind that the baby she carried might be one of the people who intended to reincarnate. Maybe Angie or Melinda or any of the other dead multitude in his family. He shuddered at the prospect of having one of them for a grandchild. He was getting more like his mother as time went by, whether he intended to or not. Luke gave up that line of thought. It seemed pointless to spend his time conjecturing on such subjects.

After tapping on the bedroom door, Psyche opened it and called inside. "He's here, Mom. You want to come out?" She returned to the kitchen with an indulgent smile. "She wants you to come in."

While he strode down the hall, Luke said a quick prayer for the right words to persuade Euphoria to come home with him. If necessary, he would overwhelm her with the power of his charm. He'd done it before. He could do it again.

His cheekiness dissolved when he entered the room.

In a battered four poster, Euphoria sat propped up against pillows, a quilt across her legs. Their wedding photo stood atop a worn wooden bureau.

Euphoria gazed at him from dark-circled eyes. Her hair had lost its sheen and clung to the sides of a weary face. Her hand traveled up to her chest, and she gasped for a breath.

Hiding his shock at her haggard condition, he smiled as he crossed the room and sat beside her. He kissed her lightly. "Hello, love. I couldn't stay away."

She returned his kiss with a dry mouth. "I'm not doing very well today, but I'll be better tomorrow," she whispered. "Maybe you can stay till then."

"Definitely, I'll stay till then." On the bedside table sat two vials of capsules and a glass of water. "You have medicine, then?"

"Sometimes it helps more than others." Euphoria pressed against her chest again, obviously suffering.

God, Luke thought, this was way worse than he had expected.

"Don't worry, darling, I'm not going to die today." Euphoria gave him a small but genuine smile.

"Am I that transparent?"

"'Fraid so."

They both laughed, and things felt a trifle more normal.

Picking up a vial, he read the label. "Dr. Sears of the Mayo Clinic." At least she had followed Luke's advice even though she had done so without his knowledge. "What does Dr. Sears recommend?"

"Surgery with a very low likelihood of improvement. You know how I feel about surgery...it's a violation of the body, makes it more difficult to heal on its own."

"Perhaps you need to make an exception here." Her obstinacy amazed Luke. With other people she always recommended a combination of allopathic and alternative therapies. "We can try a variety of techniques, whatever helps you get well."

"You know what I teach...illness is a manifestation of our thoughts. Heart trouble is a classic case. It occurs because of longstanding emotional problems, lack of joy primarily. That's me."

"You are joy." Luke felt grateful for the happiness she had given him.

"No, I named myself Euphoria to counteract deep, negative currents I didn't want to acknowledge in my psychological makeup."

"You were born with this affliction, Euphoria." Luke tried to keep annoyance out of his voice.

"Exactly. That's the point. It's my karmic path. I have to make myself whole or die in the process."

Frustrated, Luke leaped up and went to the open window. A breeze carried the faint smell of manure. Through lace curtains he saw two goats run and butt at each other. They locked horns and danced around, trying to free themselves.

Luke wanted to shout at Euphoria to come to her senses. First he needed to understand. Walking back to her he stroked her shoulder through flannel pajama tops. "Tell me how you feel. What are your symptoms?"

"Tired, short of breath, palpitations, weakness, the feeling of weight bearing down on my chest." Euphoria tipped her head. For a moment the haunted look fled, and her vibrant self returned. "Sometimes I think I'm under psychic attack. Same symptoms. What do you say to that?"

For the life of him, Luke could come up with no answer. He'd heard of psychic attack, of course. Even the trees in Sedona spoke of it. People, when angry or out of malicious intent, sent negative energy to another through their astral bodies. They intentionally or unintentionally attacked the person they hated. In either case, the victim generally lost energy, got nervous, felt afraid, or became ill.

Such situations gave the psychics in town a lot of work. They reversed the attacks, for a fee, of course. Luke had mixed feelings on the subject. He imagined a lot of gullible people tried to find relief. Some normally honest psychics considered their ignorance a windfall.

Many of the people who believed themselves to be under psychic attack actually threw their own ambivalent energy back at themselves with negative thoughts. It was complicated, and Luke didn't understand very well. A lot of these situations apparently happened in the astral world, a place he believed existed but had never consciously visited.

"You're serious about this psychic attack, aren't you, Euphoria?"

"Deadly serious, if you'll forgive a pun."

Her forlorn expression belied the attempt at humor. Luke felt sorry for his courageous wife, misguided though her leaving him had been. "I want to hold you." By answer Euphoria held the quilt up, and he climbed in. She felt listless and weak when he enfolded her. "Here, take my strength." Luke kissed her warm neck.

"I need it," she whispered and snuggled against him.

"You think Dr. Sears is wrong about your condition?"

"I wish, but no, I think a psychic attack is making all of this much worse than it needs to be. The medicine should be having more effect."

"Who would do this to you? Everybody loves you, not just me."

"I think it's because you love me that I'm being attacked." Euphoria pulled away enough to make eye contact. "Someone who hates you wants to get at you through me. That's one of the reasons I thought I should get away from you, but it didn't help at all. I've seen him here. He hovers around while I'm sleeping."

"Him? Someone who's passed on?"

"No, the young man at the wedding, the singer."

"Why would he hate me?"

"I don't know, but he does."

The dream where Kendall as a grown man had beaten up Luke as a child came to mind. Perhaps some kind of metaphorical turnaround or maybe a past life with unfinished business. Luke's subconscious mind had tried to bring forth important information. Evidently Kendall knew more details.

No way would Luke let some angry soul hurt Euphoria, in the physical or the astral plane. "I'm going to find him and put a stop to this. Whatever it takes."

Twenty-Four

Vows of Vengeance

Relieved to exercise his cramped muscles, Kendall bounded out of the lab and down the stairwell of the Bio-Design Institute at Arizona State. Feeling starved, he stepped out onto the portico. The night air tickled the back of his neck. A shiver of dread ran through him.

Amber lights illumined the trunks of palm trees lining the walkways of the deserted campus. He pulled a cigarette out and leaned his book bag against a glass column. When he lit up, his hands shook far out of proportion to any fear of getting caught smoking.

"Kendall Roberts!" a man's voice shouted.

Kendall glanced around the other wing of the building, at first not seeing anyone. Then he noticed someone among the trees. Maybe one of his profs? Who else would call him by name? The voice evoked unresolved hatred in Kendall.

"I want to talk to you." The words didn't sound like a request. More like a command.

When the man stepped out of the shadows, adrenaline swept through Kendall. No mistaking the disgusting swagger of Luke Brock. The cocky look on his face infuriated Kendall. "What do you want?"

Luke stopped on the sidewalk about three feet away. "I came to give you a warning." His tone carried authority as if Kendall had no right to disobey.

"How'd you find me?" No doubt the old man had asked Aaron and Vera. One of them must have ratted Kendall out and given his address away.

"Leave my wife alone."

"I haven't seen your wife since Vera's wedding." Kendall realized then that the wife had some psychic power. She might be the one to fear.

"You know what I mean." Luke scowled. "In the astral."

Trying to hide his surprise at this change of subject matter, Kendall scowled back. "I don't have a clue what you're talking about."

"My wife is sick, and you're tormenting her. She's not going to be able to get well. Is that what you want? To kill her?"

Kendall had tight rein on all his psychic powers these days. He knew he was innocent of these charges, but he itched to slam a fist into Luke's too-proud jaw. "I'm not doing anything to her. Even if I was, you couldn't prove it."

"It's me you want, isn't it?" Luke clenched and unclenched his fists. "Then why take it out on her. She's innocent. Leave her alone."

Innocent, hah! That witch of a woman? Kendall had fantasized about how lovely it would be to watch her go up in smoke, but he knew he'd not astral traveled since becoming a Muslim. This was way over the top. He needed to get out of here, away from these allegations.

"Listen, you bastard, I'm not bothering your wife in any way in this world or the next. Now you leave me alone or I'll do a lot worse to you." He headed toward his book bag, intending to depart.

"I remember you from a long time ago. In the 1700s back in England. You tried to kill me then, and I was just a little kid."

The book bag fell over all by itself. Kendall's psychokinesis was still erratic. Regardless, he could not deny his need for revenge. He turned back and faced his old enemy. "If you remember, then you know it's not over between us."

"You'll never destroy me, Kendall. You might as well give it up and save your soul."

"Never!"

"You've got a chance to undue the damage in this lifetime. Look at you. Smart, talented, a great career ahead of you. Why throw it all away on vengeance?"

"Because I hate you." Kendall grabbed the book bag, slung it over his back, and took off at a run.

"Why do you hate me?" Luke didn't ever give up. "You stay away from my wife!"

The sound of his tennis shoes thudded in Kendall's ears. Rage fueled his run all the way to his apartment building where he rounded the back side and climbed the fire escape stairs two at a time. At the landing he stopped and looked back. His hated enemy had not followed him.

Kendall collapsed on the landing. He had repressed his problems along with his psychic abilities. The book bag's falling over proved that he didn't have his powers under control. Truthfully, he could have been astral traveling without conscious awareness. Maybe he had gone after Luke's wife, after all.

Luke must have some past life recall too, otherwise he wouldn't have mentioned the eighteenth century. Now what would the scientific community think about two people who shared the same past life detail? It sounded like a possible avenue to prove the theory.

Much as Kendall would enjoy going off on the intellectual trip, debating reincarnation logically, he knew he needed to get emotional control or he could lose his chance for revenge again. Like he'd lost it in the 1800s and on Nine Eleven. He'd wanted to kill Luke and the others both times but didn't have a clear idea of why. He felt like a pawn in a game commanded by the jinns.

Since joining the Moslem church, he'd been afraid to share his problems with the Imams. If he tried to make them understand he didn't know what they'd do. They didn't seem to believe in reincarnation. They might kick him out, and he needed them, the only refuge from his inner self.

Why did he want to kill Luke and the others? Kendall couldn't even identify who the others were, although he felt fairly certain Euphoria was not one of them. He had wanted to kill them ever since he could remember. It was like a prime directive in his soul. He even knew their names— Lugh, Alma, Taliesin, Morfran. Why didn't he recognize any of them in this lifetime? Except Lugh, back with almost the same name.

Kendall felt like a prisoner of his own destiny. Did he have to murder Luke to save his soul? Or would he lose his soul?

Exhausted, Kendall laid his head on the book bag and stretched out on the fire escape landing. He felt no hunger despite a day long fast. Nor did he wish to say praises to Allah although he'd already missed two prayer calls. He needed answers.

Two long and difficult years had passed since his grandmother had forced him to view his past lives and tricked him into assisting in his grandfather's murder. Kendall had expended a great amount of psychic energy to repress the images as he had tried to repress the astral projection and psychokinesis. All of these abilities he'd obviously been born with, but he'd felt too insecure to use them after the horror of his grandfather's murder.

Now things had to change. Kendall had the opportunity to fulfill his karma, but he refused to do so blindly. He must understand the whole truth. He would have the whole truth, no matter what.

Closing his eyes, he directed his consciousness deep within him to show him the cause, the reason why the hatred continued despite the passage of lifetimes. Grandmother had said he could remember on his own, and remember he would.

Moments ticked by, the air paled, Kendall lost awareness of this lifetime.

Finally, the treacherous bitch was dead!

A gust of wind from the northern sea fluttered the death wrappings, revealing Alma's pale blue eyes that stared vacantly toward the heavens. Beside the stone altar, the sconce flame flickered in the dusky afternoon. The young Druidess, Caitlin, officiated. Tears streaked her face as she prayed to the Goddess.

Even now, in the gray corridor of the underworld, the arrogant Alma held a grip on Kegan's hopes for the kingship. "May you return in your next life as a rat, hated by men!" he muttered under his breath.

Longing to make his claim, Kegan rose and somberly marched through the circle of stones and down the hill, away from the tor. Broadsword pointed toward a sky filled with thunderclouds, he took up a position between two leafless oak trees that served as entrance to the holy place.

Old men, warriors loyal to King Lugh, crones in hooded capes, young women with huge bellies dragging wide-eyed children by the hand— all the clan members filed by the altar. A few knelt and prayed. Others cried.

Kegan cast a disdainful eye on the mourners. How could they revere the dead bitch who had used her influence to make her own son king? Not to mention that she banished her lover, Taliesin, on a whim and murdered the valiant Morfran. Alma's sniveling son was too weak to punish his own mother. That's not the kind of king the clan needed. What if the Abinges attacked?

The cowardly king, the last of the mourners, stood before the altar. His blond hair flapped in the wind like a child's. Behind the chalky stone on the tor, Caitlin, the new high priestess, dipped her fingers in the silver cauldron filled with honeyed mead. After anointing the forehead of the corpse, the priestess raised her arms in prayer. All across the hillside, mourners bowed their heads. Kegan gazed at the threatening sky, letting the gust cool his flushed face.

The priestess brandished the sconce and set fire to the death wrappings. A great wind blew out the flame, and the clansmen gasped. Were they so gullible they thought it was a message from the Goddess? Thunder echoed beyond the bare-limbed trees. With Caitlin's second effort, the flames caught. Amid prayers from many voices, the acrid odor of burning flesh soon filled the air.

Gagging at the stench, Kegan chafed to issue his challenge. He remembered the dismal day when he felt compelled to pledge his allegiance to Lugh's sovereignty. The whole clan, caught up in superstitious adulation, believed Alma spoke for the Goddess in naming her son king.

Lugh had usurped Kegan's rightful place. The Goddess must have chosen Kegan. Why else would She have orphaned him, except to test his mettle? If there were a Goddess at all, Kegan would be victorious. He prayed to Her for intercession. He was strong and smart like a wolf. He deserved his chance. He should be king. He would be king!

Filled with self-righteousness, Kegan strode toward Lugh and planted the broadsword in the earth between them. Hands on hips, Kegan glared at the brat, privileged since boyhood. "Prepare to do battle, Lugh. I challenge your reign!"

Lightning shimmered across the slate-gray sky.

With shouts and cries, the clan members scrambled behind stones and peered out. Tear-stained faces suddenly looked curious and excited. They would know in a moment whom the Goddess smiled upon. The wretches would soon bend their knees to Kegan.

Tears glistened in Lugh's darkly mottled eyes. He spoke in a steady voice, "I am the rightful king. Withdraw your challenge or prepare to die."

"Fight me, you son-of-a-bitch!" Kegan jerked his broadsword out of the ground and swung it in a high arc that cut down toward Lugh.

"You villain!" Jumping clear, Lugh drew his own weapon and leaned into a ready position. The flickering flames of the pyre behind him shadowed his face.

Kegan wanted to taunt past all bounds. "I speak truly because your mother was a bitch in heat, never satisfied to fuck one man."

The ill-begotten king lunged.

Reckless with the nearness of victory, Kegan sprang back and thrust his weapon overhead. He willed all the power of his soul into his taut arms. He brought the blade down, intent on splitting the usurper's skull.

While lightning crackled above, Lugh raised his sword and leapt. The blades clanked so hard, the reverberation knocked Kegan's sword out of his hands. Panicky, he reached for the fallen blade.

Like Cu'chulainn, the hound of hell, Lugh bellowed the clan's battle cry and kicked Kegan's chest. The boot's impact sent surges of pain through Kegan and he collapsed on his back. Lugh straddled him and pinned Kegan's sword arm against the damp earth.

In terror, Kegan struggled helplessly. The Goddess had abandoned him.

"No one vanquishes the king." Face contorted, Lugh hacked through the bone and sinew of Kegan's wrist. "I only let you live as a warning to others."

White hot pain seared Kegan. Horrified, he watched as blood spurted from his handless arm. He didn't want to die.

A towering shadow of evil, Lugh rose above him. "Leave this land and never return. You are anathema."

"Help me," Kegan cried and reached out. The clan members surrounding them ignored him but clapped Lugh on the shoulder with great praise.

Summoning one last measure of strength, Kegan staggered to his knees. He ripped away his woolen tunic and twisted it around his mutilated sword arm, vainly trying to stay the gushing blood. He was only half a man. Where once hope for power filled his heart, now only hatred for Lugh remained. Kegan glared at the king in rage. "I curse you and all your people. From now until the end of time!"

Bare-chested, Kegan tottered up the hill to the smoldering altar and frantically shoved the throbbing wound in hot ashes. He screamed his fury to the merciless Goddess.

"I'll make that bastard pay. All of his people. I'll never rest until I get revenge." He shook his good hand at the leaden sky. "Grant me as many lifetimes as I need. You owe me that, after today. I should have been king," he sobbed as his consciousness ebbed.

Thunder rolled. Huge raindrops sizzled and hissed on the pyre. Rank smoke billowed out. A torrent of cleansing rain poured down.

Kendall fought his way back to consciousness. His body ached from lying in the cold on the fire escape. The glare of the sun hurt his eyes. He felt sick to his stomach and dragged himself inside his apartment.

In the bathroom, he vomited into the sink then splashed water on his face and gazed at his gaunt reflection in the mirror. This hatred could kill him if he didn't resolve it. Much as he dreaded admitting it, his grandmother might have been right. He had no choice except to fulfill his destiny.

Twenty-Five

This Mortal Coil

When Luke entered Euphoria's hospital room, the empty bed with fresh sheets pulled taut startled him. Why had they taken her away? Then he remembered the tests Dr. Sears ordered.

Luke set a bouquet of red roses on the bureau, positioned in Euphoria's sightline. He sat in the easy chair and took a book from the stack on astral projection. He tried to keep his mind on reading.

It wouldn't help Euphoria to worry about her, but he seemed unable to stop. Praying and sending good thoughts to her he willingly did. He'd been such a lucky man to have her in his life these past twelve years. He wanted many more years with her to learn and grow and love.

Euphoria understood how the universe worked better than anyone he'd ever known, and she selflessly helped him learn. It sounded so dramatic that he hadn't said it in words, but Euphoria had opened up his soul.

Because of her he had grown into a far better man than he would ever have been without her. He never doubted that Euphoria understood his feelings, psychically attuned as she always was to him, but he might just tell her, anyway.

Luke forced himself to attend to the reading. He had to arm himself with the knowledge to stop Kendall's attacks. The habit from practicing law served well—to know the adversary, do the research.

The wealth of books on the subject of astral projection, spanning more than a century and available at Barnes and Noble, had surprised Luke. He'd bought a dozen handbooks and anecdotal collections then supplemented those resources with several websites accessed on his laptop. As a result, he'd completed a crash course in the space of the three days since they'd returned from Oregon.

Last night's encounter with Kendall Roberts had not gone as well as Luke had hoped. He felt convinced that Kendall didn't know he'd been astral traveling to Euphoria and threatening her.

Operating out of unconscious hostility made the young man as dangerous as if he intended to harm her. He was easy to loathe, and Luke intended to protect Euphoria from him, no matter the cost.

Up till now, he'd relied on Euphoria's reports of having seen his astral body when she awakened each morning. He wondered what tomorrow would bring. The best that could happen would be for Kendall to give up his outrageous hatred and go on with his life.

If Luke's attempt to make a satisfactorily end to the problem in the physical failed, the next step had to be going into the astral to try to solve it. Euphoria's ability extended to an occasional lucid dream, but she'd not investigated astral projection in any depth before.

Luke had an intellectual grasp on what it meant to astral travel. The consciousness of an individual projected out of the physical body and entered the astral body, a portion of the bio-magnetic field that surrounded all living things. Then the consciousness could travel in the astral world, which overlaid the physical world.

The books told of individuals' slipping out of physical bodies either accidentally or purposefully and going to visit friends or to see the monuments in Washington, DC. He had read stories of travels to the South Pole, Mars, or other spots more far-flung.

The most exotic adventures involved traveling in time, to the past or to the future. One author cautioned that only those with a compelling need or drive could witness certain events outside their own time.

Some proponents of the magical philosophy insisted that they could change the physical future by working with astral substance. Once the astral had been shaped in a certain way, it manifested in the physical, sometimes as healings. Manipulation of astral substance might explain Euphoria's gift for healing

The labels witchcraft or sorcery tended to provoke unease or even fear in Luke as they did in most everyone. On the other hand, all humans constantly strove to change the future by simple declarations, such as to buy a new car or to go on a diet. What was prayer if not an attempt to change the future?

If all events were preordained, life would become a mechanistic nightmare.

At least a few of the authorities attributed psychokinesis and poltergeist phenomena to the technique of sending out a bit of astral substance and willing it to behave in certain ways, much like wadding up a piece of paper and throwing it at a dog.

Luke didn't fool himself at all. He had amateur status at this business of astral projection while Kendall might be accomplished. The young man had knocked over his book bag by the power of his mind. He might be capable of much more.

The question remained whether Luke could learn this new skill in time. When he met Euphoria and first tried to remember a past life, he had succeeded. The same with attempts to predict future events or talk to the departed. His meditation skills had developed to the extent that he could drop into an alpha or theta wave state at will. All his skills had grown with his belief in them.

Much more depended on his ability to learn astral projection. There might be no other way to save Euphoria. He intended to give the endeavor his whole attention He trusted that he could learn but feared he didn't have enough time, if Euphoria's strength failed.

Luke leaned back in the chair, settled his arms on the sides of it, began to breathe diaphragmatically, and dropped into an alpha state. He visualized a shadow image of his body floating about a foot above him. When he saw the image clearly, he imagined his conscious mind rolling up out of his physical body and into the image. He held the thought and waited, full of calm anticipation.

After a period of time difficult to calculate, he heard a whirring sound followed by the clanging of the room door as it banged against the brass stop on the wall. He opened his eyes to see two orderlies push a gurney into the room. Euphoria lay on it.

But Luke didn't see the view from the chair, he saw the view from the ceiling.

Woo hoo! I'm out of my body!

Instantly Luke plunged back into his body, eyes wide open. He hadn't expected astral projection to be fun.

The orderlies picked Euphoria up and placed her on the bed as if she were a porcelain doll. The drawn look of suffering on her face tempered Luke's exhilaration.

After the orderlies left, she awoke, pale and frail, but smiling at him. "Hi, darling. What's the word?"

"I don't know. The doctor hasn't come in yet." Luke kissed her lightly on the forehead.

"Oh, you brought me flowers. Thank you." Euphoria labored for breaths.

"I wanted you to have something beautiful to look at, just like I do." Luke gazed at her haggard face and recalled it as it had been before this illness struck. She looked as if she would break so he didn't sit on the bed. He took her blue-veined hand and caressed it, intending to delay describing his experience with astral projection until she felt stronger. "Can I get anything for you?"

"Luke," Euphoria whispered. "You did it? You got out of your body?"

"On the first try." Luke rubbed his fingernails across his heart with an exaggerated brag. Of course she would read his mind about something so important. He described every detail of the event, finishing with a flourish for a headline: PSYCHIC'S HUBBY A NATURAL AT ASTRAL PROJECTION.

"I'm proud of you, even if you had the briefest out of body experience of all time." Euphoria must have felt better because her voice carried a teasing tone.

Luke wanted to tease back, but the urgency of what they were trying to do weighed him down. He kissed her hand. "I'll be able to protect you, no matter what. No one will ever hurt you again."

Before she could respond Dr. Sears, a spare man with a protruding lower lip, arrived with the dreaded news that she needed surgery, the sooner the better. "I've scheduled you for a heart valve replacement tomorrow morning at seven."

Euphoria waved a hand as if to protest, but Luke shook his head, warding her off from voicing any objections.

"All right," Euphoria sighed. "I'll do it."

"You won't regret the decision, Mrs. Brock." Dr. Sears made a point of closing the door as he left the room.

"Good girl." Luke meant it. He felt more hopeful with the plans made and wanted Euphoria to share his optimism.

Her eyes misted with tears. "I wish Psyche could be here."

"I'll send the pilot for her if you want me to."

"No. It's sweet of you to offer, but she shouldn't take chances with the little girl inside her womb." Euphoria pressed a hand to her breast, and her eyelids fluttered. "I'm very tired. Will you stay even if I go to sleep?"

"Can't get rid of me. Period." Luke climbed into bed and wrapped his arms around her. "I'll just lie here quietly and practice my astral projection."

Euphoria felt too warm when she nestled against him. "I love you."

"I love you too." Luke felt an urgency for her to understand the depth of his devotion. "Also I'm grateful to you for being on my karmic path and...for opening up my soul." His voice cracked, but he didn't care.

"It's good to hear you say so." Euphoria sounded weary.

"Everything will be all right, darling." Luke wanted to reassure her and hoped his voice carried more conviction than he felt. He feared Euphoria wasn't strong enough to withstand either the physical assault of surgery or the psychical assault by Kendall.

As she slept Luke made several unsuccessful attempts to duplicate what he had done earlier before he gave up. Disappointed, he fell into an exhausted catnap.

In a dream, Luke flew out of the top of his head and sailed around the ceiling. Everything in the room looked vague and grayish blue, including Euphoria, who continued to sleep.

Kendall, shadowy and white, hovered beside the bed. Luke raised an arm as if to attack. Sparks flew from his fingertips, and Kendall took off flying through the ceiling.

A nurse called out, "Mrs. Brock, you need to wake up now."

Luke awoke, hungry and disoriented. He eased Euphoria out of his arms and crawled from the bed.

With a disapproving glance at Luke, the nurse offered a clipboard to Euphoria. "Here's the release form for the surgery. You'll need to sign it."

Listlessly, Euphoria scrawled her signature across the paper then dutifully took the pills the nurse offered.

"Mr. Brock, why don't you get some dinner." The nurse clucked her tongue. "There's nothing you can do here. I've got to prep her for surgery."

Although he had promised Euphoria he would stay, Luke kissed her cheek and walked out the door. "I'll be right back, love."

The nurse moved around the bed and fussed over Euphoria so Luke couldn't tell whether she heard him or not.

Striding down the hall, he took the elevator to the empty cafeteria. He bought a pastrami sandwich, a banana, and a coke from a machine and sat at a corner table. He ate fast because he couldn't relax while away from his wife. The food tasted like cardboard.

Someone had left a newspaper on the table. The headlines read: HURRICANE LEVELS PALM BEACH and SCOTS OCCUPY BUCKINGHAM PALACE, BRITS SURRENDER PARLIAMENT.

Photos of survivors picking through rubble all over the world would depress an angel. What next? That supposed Plan by the Divine to create a more loving humankind? What a flop!

Luke tossed the newspaper aside. He had to remain as optimistic as possible and stay strong for Euphoria. After he stashed his leavings, he rode up on the elevator.

As soon as he stepped off at the seventh floor, the Code Blue alarm rang.

"No!" Luke ran down the hall. He knew what he would find.

Med techs, doctors, and nurses swarmed over Euphoria with machinery everywhere.

Feeling defeated, Luke watched as the line on the heart monitor surged, leveled out, then surged again. With his back pressed against the wall, he prayed for Euphoria to survive.

But she died anyway.

Twenty-Six

A Covenant to Keep

The sound of the flat line still rang in his ears when Luke barged into the doctor's office without knocking. "What the hell happened?"

Rising from his desk chair, Dr. Sears offered a handshake. He looked crestfallen.

Luke felt livid with himself for leaving Euphoria for one moment and livid with the hospital personnel for incompetence. He could slap a lawsuit on them in no time. He cared nothing for courtesies. "Tell me, damn it."

"I don't know." Dr. Sears gave a rueful frown. Yes, Euphoria needed the operation, but she wasn't critical. If she had been, I'd have done the surgery right away."

"Is it possible the nurse did something wrong?" Luke had to understand what killed Euphoria and where to direct his rage.

"No, of course not. We have the finest staff here. Your wife had a massive heart attack." Dr. Sears chewed on his lip as he came around the desk and clapped Luke's shoulder. "Unfortunately we don't have all the answers. I wish we knew what happened."

Luke could make a good guess at what happened and who to blame. He would set this to rights himself and have his revenge.

Hustling out of the hospital, he climbed into the Jaguar and drove through the midnight traffic to ASU. The Bio-Design building stood dark. No ambitious student worked late tonight. Luke fished in his pocket for Kendall's address, the one Aaron had given him earlier. Luke ran the few blocks to the third story apartment and knocked on the door.

Receiving no answer enraged him. Luke banged on the door. "Get out here and face me, you coward."

A pajama-clad woman pulled back the curtains of the apartment next door.

"I'm looking for Kendall Roberts. Do you know where he is?"

She shrugged for answer.

"Look, I'm his father and I need to talk to him." Luke disliked lying to the poor girl, but he could think of no other way. "If he keeps on avoiding me I'm going to stop sending his checks, and he'll have to drop out of school."

The young woman creased her brow, as if considering whether or not to believe Luke. At least he looked old enough to be Kendall's father, if not his grandfather.

Losing patience with her indecision, Luke started down the hallway. "All right, I'll go get the super."

The girl opened her door and leaned out. "Try the mosque over on Sixth Street. He's a fox. I pay attention to where he goes." She blushed, evidently thinking Luke cared how she knew.

"Thanks for the tip."

"Tip? Hey, you aren't police, are you?"

With a sarcastic shrug, Luke dashed down the stairs and out the front door of the building. If he decided to make a citizen's arrest, he would have to drive the murderer to jail, so he ran to his car and drove the several blocks to the mosque. Its arches softly lit from the inside lent an eerie glow to the golden dome of the circular building.

At Luke's knock, a middle-aged Arab in a white robe and headdress opened the door. "May Allah bless you. How may I help you?" He spoke in accented English.

Behind him several young men in T-shirts and jeans, mingled around the sanctuary. Some sat on the blue and white tile floor, among them Kendall.

"I need to speak with one of your...uh...guests. Kendall Roberts."

"We have no one here by that name."

Luke pointed toward the villain. Kendall glared back. "There he is."

With a wry smile the Arab turned toward the group. "Ah, you speak of Karim. He has taken that name to signify his new life in Allah." He didn't play dumb at all convincingly.

"I need to speak with him." Luke controlled his voice, deeming it counterproductive to reveal his rage at this point. "It's a very important matter."

The way the Arab holy man stood squarely in the doorway gave little doubt of his intention to prevent Luke from entering. When the Arab glanced back toward the young men, his headdress disguised whatever signal he made, but two young men ushered Kendall out of the room.

The Arab turned to Luke and smiled in a beatific way. "Mohammed, peace be upon him, has sent Karim as a sign to our people. His life is blessed."

"Maybe you should say cursed." Luke spat out the words.

"No, Karim was born as a sign to our people. Sent by Mohammed, peace be upon him." As he closed the door, the Arab said, "Peace be upon you. Come again any time."

Furious, Luke knew he couldn't get a court order. What would he tell the judge? *I think this guy killed my wife from the astral world?*

There didn't seem to be any point in confronting Kendall with these self-appointed Muslim guards as audience. He would just lie, like he'd done last night. Luke had no recourse in the law. If he were to have vengeance, it had to come elsewhere.

Luke drove back across the Valley to the Hilton near the Mayo Clinic. He had rented the room the day Euphoria checked into Mayo's but used it only to shower and change.

He strove to keep his rage at the forefront. The time would soon come when the wall around his heart would cave in, but for now it held the despair at bay.

Dropping onto the bed in his hotel room, Luke opened his arms and prayed, "Divine spirit, help me understand what binds Kendall and me together. Show me what I must do to stop him." He believed with every ounce of his being that help would come to him. He would wait for it.

An imagined body made of light, his astral body, materialized above Luke. His conscious mind entered the astral body and adjusted focus to the faintly bluish air. Turning he noticed his sleeping physical form with its slack jaw. He looked a hundred years old and tired as hell.

Luke flew out through the roof of the hotel, above the city, and into the night sky, vivid with stars. He thought only of returning to his source, the reason for the vendetta, the first cause, vowing to understand.

Years, then centuries, passed like the pages of a book fluttering in the wind.

Luke saw himself on a battle field, a warrior king, who ruthlessly subdued Kendall, then cut off his hand to prevent him from taking up arms against the throne. Luke hated the barbarity within himself and remembered with a pang the difficulty of keeping order among his people. He'd had a profound vision of what earthly life could be—to unite the clans in integrity, independence, and freedom. Luke had failed in all of them. Kendall and many others wanted Luke's blood. Only violence prevented Luke's falling into disgrace and being murdered.

The pictures changed as if a great hand turned the pages of a family album.

Filled with hatred, in the 1700s Kendall shackled Luke, a child now, to a bed and held him for ransom. Kendall murdered Luke's foster mother by tying her hand to toe and killing her for a witch. Grief for the good woman flowed through Luke. A fascination with the romance of war, with the romance of vengeance, obsessed him.

Luke saw himself fighting in the colonial army and watching men die. He hated war yet it magnetized him. He felt the longing of the warrior. He used his skills as a doctor to help further the cause of the Revolution.

During the Civil War he fought gladly and died gladly for the same principles.

Both lifetimes helped him toward reclaiming his soul. Such a long way back to honor. Would it never end? He longed for peace but knew no way to claim it.

The page turned again.

Luke sat in a great gathering of souls and listened to an old one request volunteers to help end violence on Earth, a great experiment to poise humanity for a paradigm leap into grace. He volunteered. So did Melinda. So did Kendall.

Another page.

A great fire exploded from an airplane that plowed into the World Trade Center. Karim piloted. No wonder Kendall had taken the name of Karim. He had murdered thousands of people, one of them Melinda. Luke remembered the agony of searching for her and not finding her. But for Divine intervention through his mother, he would have died that day too.

He understood why the Divine had set the Plan into action, with the forlorn hope that all mankind could one day thrive in peace.

Those who died on Nine Eleven sacrificed themselves to bring a new order to mankind. Their loss could never be vindicated.

Many on Earth had pledged to forgive and go on in peace, but their voices drowned in the cries for vengeance.

Angie's spirit had cautioned him that he must grow into spiritual maturity the slow and tedious way. It took a long time to temper the steel of a warrior and turn him toward peace. Perhaps the change could not happen in earthly incarnation.

Once again the blood lust bore through Luke. He would make Kendall pay for all the pain he had caused. Luke turned his heart and desire toward 2018.

Instantly he arrived at the mosque. He could see Kendall asleep on the floor and held out a beckoning astral hand to him.

Kendall flew out of his body like an adept. His astral sheath murky, his face set in anger, he circled Luke. Kendall aimed one hand toward Luke and sparks jetted out of it.

The sparks shot through the air. Luke imagined they would kill him, but he desired to deflect them instead. The sparks dissolved before reaching him.

Luke started to return fire, but what would that do? Continue the standoff through how many lifetimes? In or out of the body?

Kendall trained the sheath of his astral body on Luke. He flew at Luke like a bullet. Sparks burst all around them.

Kendall's hatred surged through the space. *Give it up, old man. You're no match for me.*

Backing away Luke realized he hadn't been hurt by the attack.

When Kendall raised both arms for another volley, Luke held up his astral hands to ward off the blows and thought, *You give up.*

I swore to kill you and I won't stop until I do.

Don't you see how pointless this all is? If you kill me, I'll just come back in another body.

Oh, but the satisfaction of knowing I interrupted your life. I intend to have that.

Kendall flew at Luke.

Luke imagined that a great white light surrounded him. He was safe and protected inside.

Immediately Kendall stopped as if he'd hit a glass wall. Kendall looked confused then irate.

Go back to your churchmen, Luke commanded. *Maybe they can teach you to love. I forgive you.*

I don't want your forgiveness. Kendall's astral sheath grew dense and dark. *Someday I'll grow stronger than you. Then you watch out!*

Turning, Kendall flew away into the darkness.

Willing himself to return to his physical body, Luke awakened in the hotel room bed, certain that he had done the right thing. Kendall had allowed himself to be controlled by the past, as if he didn't have a choice, but Luke did have a choice.

The future, always fluid, held space for new ways of being. That was the foundation of spiritual growth.

Luke sighed, relieved to be back in his worn-down body even though it meant giving himself over to grief for his wife. Tomorrow he would have the melancholy task of making the arrangements for Euphoria's funeral, just as he had for Angie and for Melinda. He resigned himself to coping with grief as a part of his soul development.

All his life he had wanted to protect his family from harm. He had not been able to protect his mother from cancer, or Melinda from her destiny on Nine Eleven, or Euphoria from either her illness or Kendall's harassment.

No one could have succeeded, but they didn't need his protection. They were all as indestructible as Luke. All immortal!

Astral projection had shown him the existence of his soul. Never could he doubt the Afterlife again.

Luke understood why he had incarnated—to grow spiritually. That's why he volunteered for Nine Eleven. The Divine forces had prevented his death that day for only one reason, to parent Aaron.

Out of gratitude, Luke intended to spend the rest of his life practicing the gifts he had received and teaching others. That would honor Euphoria's spirit in a way she would treasure. He hoped his mother felt proud of him for choosing this path. He considered it a path with honor.

Life on Earth was sacred. Humans incarnated in physical bodies to learn and to overcome obstacles. The death of a loved one seemed the biggest of those obstacles. Luke attuned himself to the grief he had caused down through the centuries and to the grief he now felt.

Although mourning for his mother and his first wife had mellowed, he remembered the anger that spiked through him and prevented him from feeling the brunt of sorrow. With Melinda he had even managed to forget her infidelity. He would allow himself no psychological hiding holes in this time.

How poignant to open his heart. Luke's chest ached with the thought of living on without his precious Euphoria. He allowed himself to feel the sadness.

Euphoria was the epitome of love and joy. He would miss her every day that he remained alive without her. Tears rolled down his cheeks.

The scent of peppermint, fresh and light, filled the dark hotel room with Euphoria's presence.

I'm not dead, darling. I'm right here with you.

Acknowledgments

Over the years while I have imagined and written the *Alma Chronicles*, many people have influenced my life and thought. Some have given me support, encouragement, and love. I would like to thank these people here and tell them how grateful I am for their presence in my life. Even though a few have died, I trust they know I appreciate them.

Aaron Heathcotte, Annette Lewis, Barby Heathcotte, Betty Joy, Beulah Fesler, Brandon Heathcotte, Brock Heathcotte, Bruce Heathcotte, Bryan Heathcotte, Carol Gibson, Chip Myers, David Perez, Dean Gordon

Emily Heathcotte, Greg Williams, Howard Fesler, Jacque Beatty, Jim Green, Joe Perez, John Bergman, Josh Heathcotte, Judith Lynn-Perez, Larry Crosley

Maggie Perry, Martha Davis, Mary Livingston, Mike MacCarthy, Mike Murphy, Nancy Brehm, Noonie Crosley, Pat Kennedy, Phil Shirley, Rick Aynes, Rick Williams

Rita Heathcotte, Robert Meya, Sharon Atkins, Sonny Crosley, Stephanie Heathcotte, Tearle Dwiggins, Ted Moore, Tom Brehm, Tom Franklin, Tom Larkin, Trena Aynes, Vijaya Schartz

I thank these authors for their books:

Deepak Chopra, Dick Sutphen, Ernest Holmes, Jane Roberts, John Edward, Judith Orloff, Ralph Waldo Emerson, Richard Bach, Walt Whitman

Toby Fesler Heathcotte is both mother and grandmother. A former teacher, she now serves as president of Arizona Authors Association and lives in Glendale, Arizona.

tobyheathcotte.com and outofthepsychiccloset.com

Write to her at toby@tobyheathcotte.com

Books by Toby Fesler Heathcotte

The Alma Chronicles

- *I Alison's Legacy*
- *II Lainn's Destiny*
- *III Angie's Promise*
- *IV Luke's Covenant*
- *V The Comet's Return*

Out of the Psychic Closet: The Quest to Trust My True Nature published by Twilight Times Books

Program Building: A Practical Handbook for High School Speech and Drama Teachers

Seeds for Fertile Minds: Eight Curriculum Integration Tools with Betty Joy

279